Running from the Puppet Master

Running from the Puppet Master

D-L Nelson

FIVE STAR
A part of Gale, Cengage Learning

GALE
CENGAGE Learning™

Detroit • New York • San Francisco • New Haven, Conn • Waterville, Maine • London

GALE
CENGAGE Learning

Set in 11 pt. Plantin.
Printed on permanent paper.

LIBRARY OF CONGRESS CATALOGING-IN-PUBLICATION DATA

Nelson, D. L., 1942–
   Running from the puppet master / D. L. Nelson. — 1st ed.
    p. cm.
   ISBN-13: 978-1-59414-708-1 (hardcover : alk. paper)
   ISBN-10: 1-59414-708-6 (hardcover : alk. paper)
    1. Runaway wives—Fiction. 2. Bankers—Switzerland—Fiction.
3. Secret societies—Fiction. 4. War—Economic aspects—Fiction.
5. Social conflict—Economic aspects—Fiction. 6. Profiteering—
Fiction. 7. Business and politics—Fiction. 8. Switzerland—Fiction. I. Title.
PS3614.E4455R86 2008
813'.6—dc22   2008031603

First Edition. First Printing: November 2008.
Published in 2008 in conjunction with Tekno Books.

Printed in the United States of America
1 2 3 4 5 6 7 12 11 10 09 08

Dedicated to anyone and everyone who actively works for peace and planet preservation.

Chapter One:
Escape
GENEVA, SWITZERLAND
AUGUST 1990

Holding her breath, Leah inched past the two double beds and a spindly writing desk with gold leaf drawn in a thin line along its curvy stick legs. Her elbow hit the tent card listing the hotel's television channels and knocked it over.

She sucked in her breath and watched it tumble silently to the thick carpet. With each step she paused and listened, afraid a creak would give her away.

At the door she held her eye level with the peep hole. A man, his arms folded, stood in the hall opposite her room. She swayed but caught herself before her body touched the door. Moving back at the same creeping pace, she lowered herself to the bed. Despite the drawn drape hiding Lake Geneva and the mountains, her eyes had adjusted to the gloom.

The hotel room was old-fashioned with high moulded ceilings. The oak armoire was from another century. There was a second door leading to the next room. Typically of old Swiss hotels, it was bolted on her side and she was sure, on the other side as well.

She inched her way to the window and peeked through a crack in the drapes, barely moving the material.

The balcony, unconnected to others, was five floors above a terrace leading to the lake. If no one could enter that way, neither could she leave by it.

Leah suspected the man hovering outside didn't know she was in the room. If he had he would have burst in. But how had he known she was registered? She'd paid cash and used a fake name, praying the clerk would think she was an unfaithful housewife.

Could Jean-Luc have sent her picture to every hotel in Switzerland this fast? The thought made her shiver. Calm, I have to be calm. Breathe deeply, keep oxygen going to the brain, she told herself.

Suddenly she was overcome with thirst. Damn, damn, damn, she thought. A hot flash was sure to follow. Being forty-five was a bitch. She pinched the skin on the back of her hand, knowing it would go down slowly, then felt stupid that in the middle of running for her life, she'd stopped to think of age. Sweat drenched her body and for a moment she felt as if she'd smother.

Waiting for her body to cool she thought how she should be getting her daughter ready for the lycée and her son packed for university. What would they think of her desertion? If only she'd minded her own business or maybe she should have been nosy earlier.

Two plastic bags from Placette, the Bloomingdale's of Geneva, lay on the bed. Changing into her new clothes wouldn't be enough of a disguise. Coloring and cutting her hair, white for the last ten years, prematurely she liked to think, and now a dead give-away, would take too much time.

Her temperature dropped to normal, leaving her linen suit clammy against her skin. The double door into the next suite was her only chance. Walking to it with her fingers gripping the rope handle of the shopping bag, she put her free hand on the handle. It creaked, a whispered creak, but a definite sound nonetheless.

She froze.

Her Mont Blanc watch ticked, reminding her of Michael.

She hadn't thought of him for years. His watch had ticked next to her ear the first night they'd slept together, the day

Kennedy was killed.

Placing her ear against the door, she heard a television. She could make out a discussion about Saddam Hussein. Must be CNN because the announcer spoke English not French.

What if her neighbor was one of them? Leah had no choice. She turned the lock.

In kinder times, Tribble, her cat, had scratched to be let into her bedroom. Leah scratched then listened. When there was no response, she scratched a second time. The television voices ceased, and footsteps came to the door. The latch turned.

"What the hell?" a man said before Leah covered his mouth. His beard's stubble felt scratchy against her palm. He wore underwear and one sock.

"Shh." She pushed passed him, closed the door behind her without even making a click and locked it.

He looked at her. They were the same height, five foot six, but he was fifty pounds overweight.

Putting her finger against her lips she tiptoed to his television. The remote control lay on top. She hit the on button, hoping to muffle their conversation.

A commentator filled the screen and spoke of embargoes.

"I know you'll think I'm crazy, but there's someone in the hall. He wants to kill me," she said.

The man stepped back. "You're right. I think you're crazy." He started to unlock the connecting door.

Leah's hand shot out and stopped his. "You've got to believe me." She certainly wouldn't have believed him had their positions been reversed. Convincing him was a matter of survival. "Look in the hall. You'll see him."

The man backed toward the door, keeping his eyes on her. She caught her reflection in his mirror and hoped he'd think her too well dressed to be an escaped lunatic. Lately whenever she saw herself it was her mother's face staring back. At least it wasn't her grandmother's. Yet. If she didn't get out of here, she'd never live to see herself as an old lady.

He glanced at the peep hole. "I can't see anyone. Now, please go back to your own room, lady."

Leah's eyes darted around the room and settled on his tray with the remains of a sandwich and a half drunk cup of coffee.

"Put your tray out for room service to pick up. You'll see him."

"Then will you leave?"

"Please."

He shrugged. When he picked up the tray, the cup rattled against the saucer. As he opened the door, Leah ducked behind the bed. He put the tray down on the floor to the left outside the door. "There is a man, but he left when I came out. Doesn't prove he wants to kill you."

Tears ran down Leah's face. She brushed them away with the back of her hand. "Just let me use the bathroom. I need time to change. A disguise." She held up her Placette bag.

He looked at his watch then at her. "I've a dinner appointment in an hour."

"I'll be ready."

"Oh hell. Why not?" He sat on the bed and put on his second sock. Shaking his head he said, "My wife will never believe this."

Disappearing into the bathroom, she thought him an unlikely hero. In the movies the heroine finds Tom Cruise or at least Kevin Costner. But this wasn't the movies, and she wasn't a heroine. Heroines looked like Julia Roberts or Bridget Fonda and went toward the danger when the scary music started. Leah ran away.

When Leah came out of the bathroom a half hour later, she had short brown hair curling around her face. She wore a man's suit and dark glasses.

"You certainly look different. Younger."

She took a deep breath and went for the door.

"Wait," the man said. He was now dressed in slacks. A shirt, tie and sports coat lay on the bed. She turned.

He took a water glass from his bed stand, opened the door and put it onto the tray resting in the hall.

Shutting the door, he said, "Same guy there. He's around the corner."

Leah leaned against the wall and closed her eyes. Somewhere she needed to find strength. The man put his hand on her shoulder. "We'll leave together. I'll talk about the meeting we are going to. Just let me shave."

Leah faced the Gare du Cornavin as she waited for the Ferney-Voltaire bus. There was a long line, mostly *frontaliers*, French workers who cross the border daily, more than usual for August, a heavy holiday month. The humidity had given way to a summer breeze. Leah felt warm in her shirt and jacket. She held a copy of the *Tribune de Genève* in her hand, just another commuter heading home. Heading to safety was more like it, if there were a God in heaven, which she doubted.

She still didn't believe how easy her escape from the hotel had been. As her good Samaritan had jabbered about contracts and strategy, the man in the hall hadn't given them a second glance.

Businessmen and women in suits waiting for the bus checked and rechecked their watches. One man glanced at the posted schedule frequently. Geneva buses were normally on the minute. Those numbered 5, 8, 14, 9, 6, 3 and 10 came and went several times.

"There it is," a woman behind Leah said as the orange Ferney-Voltaire bus pulled up. "Finally." Like salmon at mating season the crowd surged up the three stairs. Leah found a place to stand behind the driver.

An inspector got on. He stood behind the line where passengers were forbidden. There'd be no way for him to check tickets. "I'm just going to the next stop," he said to the driver. "How's it going?"

The driver said, "What a day. They search every damned bus leaving Switzerland. I've never seen it like this. Any idea who they want?"

The inspector shrugged. "Maybe it's got something to do with the Iraq-Kuwait thing. A terrorist?"

"Who knows?"

Leah rode one stop, fought her way off through the crowd to dismount, then retraced the route to the train station. Commuters rushed back and forth.

Soldiers paced with their rifles cocked. These weren't normal Swiss military going by train to their annual training. Those men wore their rifles over their shoulders, talked, jostled and joked with each other, not like these men who kept looking to the right and left, not cracking a smile. Five soldiers stood at gate eight where the TGV was about to leave for Paris. They held their guns in front of them and spoke to every person heading towards the customs desk. Two looked at a photo. Their faces were grim as their eyes passed by her without a hesitation.

France was out. It wasn't safe to cross the border. Should she run for Italy? Germany? Leah went to platform six where a train was leaving for Basel. She got on. As it pulled out she watched ten soldiers jump off the French TGV. Swiss soldiers searching a train on the French side of the border sent shivers down her body. She wondered if all borders would be sealed.

"Ticket?"

She jumped. The conductor spoke French with a Swiss German accent. Pulling her wallet from her pocket, she searched for a green fifty and red ten.

Her fingers felt the Braille bumps on the bill. I'll get off in Neuchâtel, she thought, as he took his little book and wrote a receipt.

As the train chugged into the countryside, she wondered what to do next. She couldn't rent a car. Using her credit card would leave a trail. The train's first stop was Yverdon. No one got on. Leah sighed. How had she, a little girl from Stonefield, Massachusetts, a former artist and current wife of a powerful Swiss banker, gotten herself into this mess? Get ahold of yourself, girl. Think, she told herself.

The Alps rose in the distance. The vineyards, late summer lush with grapes, gave way to fields. "I wish I were back in New England," she thought.

Her thoughts transported her to the place of her birth. She imagined her mother telling her bedtime stories about the day Leah was born. How protected I was: I didn't even know it, she thought. She shook her head as if to make the realization bouncing around her brain settle in its proper slot. As an adult when she felt protected by her marriage, she had really been in danger. Everything that had happened in the last few days was so unreal, so out of anything she might have conjured up, that she felt as if she were living in a made-for-television adventure.

Her mind, with a will of its own, drifted back: back to a time when life was simple and good, bringing her the calm she needed. She hoped in some way, some how by examining what brought her to this point that she could find the strength to survive what loomed ahead.

CHAPTER TWO:
PLANTING THE SEEDS
STONEFIELD, MA
1945–1952

Baby Stockbridge snuggled in her mother's arms and sucked on her mother's little finger. An empty bottle was on the night stand next to the bed. A bracelet, one bead for each letter of the family name, circled the infant's wrist. Mother and child cuddled in a private room. Grace Stockbridge shifted the infant to hide the milk stain on her yellow silk bed jacket.

The overpowering smell of too many flowers reminded Grace of funerals. Cards, covered with storks dropping babies down chimneys, hung on a cork board. Her free hand adjusted her brown hair tied with a ribbon the same color as the jacket. Her lips were fresh with Max Factor's Dewey Pink lipstick.

She glanced at her Waltham wristwatch, a gift from Alexander the day after she'd told him she was expecting a little bundle from heaven. She'd let him wander in on her as she crocheted booties. For months Grace had imagined how she would look the moment that she presented their son to him. Contrary to her plans, this baby was wrapped in a pink flannel blanket.

Looking up, she saw her husband limp into the room. He wielded his cane as an extension of his body. He'd regained most of the weight he'd lost in the Veteran's Hospital before being shipped home. He made it to his wife's side and looked down at the infant. When he touched the baby's palm, her fingers curled around his. A tear ran down his face as a bubble escaped the baby's lips.

Grace touched the tear. She'd thought him strong when she'd retired into marriage. Her vision of waving him off to work, fixing a home and being a leading hostess disappeared eight days later when the Japanese attacked Pearl Harbor.

Another man had returned inside Alexander's body. This man, racked by nightmares, was no longer light-hearted.

"What shall we name her? Alexander Charles Stockbridge III won't work," she said.

"Leah," he said. "After my mother."

Grace thought of her late mother-in-law's lectures on how a tea bag should make three cups of tea and how one should make do with a maximum of two squares of toilet tissue. "Leah Abigail Stockbridge. After both our mothers."

"If she takes after both, I hope Leah Abigail never wants the moon. The rest of the world would miss it." He took the infant from his wife.

The young Stockbridges brought the baby to Grace's childhood home. It made sense for the young bride to stay with her mother when Alexander had been away fighting the Japanese. When he returned, it made equal sense that the widow Abigail Holt shouldn't rattle around in a five-bedroom house which cried out for children to run through the rooms and to play in the gardens or pine grove in front.

Everyone was happy to let Grace's mother run the house with the help of Mrs. Stickler. For years Leah would think her father's oft-quoted phrase, "stickler for details," came from the personality of the housekeeper.

Abigail and Mrs. Stickler were staring out the window as Alexander drove up with his young family in his 1935 Ford. The car, seldom used, had almost not started that morning. Although the Japanese surrendered the week before, gas rationing continued. Even Abigail, once known as the woman with the Ford by all of Stonefield, went by bicycle wherever possible.

Still no one expected a new mother to bike home from the hospital with a baby stashed in a basket.

As soon as the car turned into the long drive, the women rushed out. Abigail opened the car door almost before the Ford stopped. She plucked the baby from Grace's arms. Alexander helped his wife, who winced as she maneuvered out of the car. She started to lean on him, but was afraid her weight would upset his balance.

They took Leah to the bedroom where her great grandmother had died the year before. The walls had been painted blue. Grace had made blue checked curtains and tied them with blue ribbons. The infant was placed in the bassinet that had held Grace and her brother, who'd disappeared over Germany three years before.

Grace looked around the room. "If I paint some fluffy clouds and birds it will be more feminine."

Leah would look at those clouds until the room was redecorated when she became a teenager. Her father would blame her dreaminess on them.

Leah couldn't quite order her early memories.

One involved her grandmother bustling around her bedroom saying, "Everything in its place, and a place for everything." Leah translated it as, "Better put these toys away now."

Another was being frightened by the moon staring in her window. When she cried, her parents came in. They were dressed for a party.

Alexander swept the sobbing child into his lap. "Everyone is scared sometimes. I've been scared lots of time, especially during the war, and it helps to talk about it."

Grace, standing nearby, glanced at her watch.

"The moon is looking at me," the child sobbed.

He rocked his daughter, wiping the dark curls off the sweaty

16

brow. "We'll draw the shade." Blackout curtains still hung at the windows.

Sniffling, Leah put her thumb in her mouth and rubbed her cheek with the corner of her blanket that had gone from bassinet to crib and now to her big girl's bed.

"I've another idea." He shifted his daughter to his hip and stood up. He had not needed his cane for over a year, although his leg still bothered him on damp days. "We'll ask Mr. Moon to bring you happy dreams. That's his job, you know."

Leah started listing dreams about dolls, ice cream, pine cones, and wading in the surf at Crane's beach where they'd gone the past summer.

Her father put her into bed, pulled the covers to her chin and dropped a kiss on her forehead. As Leah fought sleep trying to think of all dreams possible she heard her father say to her mother, "She's your daughter." It would be a phrase repeated frequently by both parents. Leah did not understand for she thought she belonged to both.

The next time she heard the phrase was from her mother, when Leah used a complicated argument to explain why she didn't need a nap. Alexander said it next, after Leah redecorated the refrigerator with finger paints.

Leah splashed in her bubble bath. She could hardly wait for the next morning when she'd go to first grade all day like a big girl instead of going only half. That was for little kids, new first graders and kindergarteners. She was now a full-fledged student on her way to being adult.

She loved school. She loved her teacher. She loved drinking the miniature bottles of milk at mid morning along with cookies that had swirls and chocolate chips. Each day her mother tied two pennies into her handkerchief to pay for the milk and cookies. Best of all Leah loved the crayons and paints and rushed her other work so she could draw.

The bath water was warm. She'd piled bubbles into a suds castle and was pretending her rubber duck was a horse galloping up to the gate.

"Time's up, Leah." Grace reached through the bubbles to pull the plug. Angry at being disturbed, Leah kicked hard, hitting her mother's stomach.

Grace pulled her daughter from the tub and wrapped her in a towel. She sat down on the toilet lid, holding Leah in her arms. "Honey, you can't kick Mommy in the stomach."

"Why not?"

"Because Daddy planted a little baby brother or sister seed there."

"I hope it's a sister seed." Leah thought of her father when he went to the garden whistling either "Old MacDonald" or "Mares Eat Oats." The garden was down an embankment that was covered in violets during spring and made a great toboggan run in winter. She pictured him wearing his straw hat and carrying a miniature shovel and hoe. As Grace shoved Leah's arm into her pajamas the child asked, "Where did he dig the hole?"

Grace had been lost in plans for a dinner she'd give for the selectmen and their wives. She'd make her ice bowl with cocktail sauce in the middle and shrimp draped over the edge so everyone would comment on what a wonderful, creative cook the young Mrs. Stockbridge was. "What?"

"Where did Daddy dig the hole to plant the baby seed?"

"My belly button."

Five years would pass before Leah would read an article, "How to Tell Your Child the Facts of Life" in *Ladies Home Journal*. Scientific fact would replace the image of her father's miniature implements.

Alexander Charles Stockbridge III, Chucky, was presented to

Leah in May 1952. Her grandmother put a pillow on Leah's lap. Grace placed the baby on the pillow. "His head is delicate. The bones haven't knit together," Grace said. Leah imagined long leg bone knitting needles.

"It's just too bad Chucky wasn't born first," Mrs. Stickler said.

"Why?" Leah asked.

"Little pitchers."

Abigail frowned at the housekeeper. She adjusted the pillow where the baby slept, bubbles and a sweet smell of milk coming from his mouth, and said to Leah, "Then you would have a big brother to protect you."

"But Chucky has a big sister to protect him. That's as good."

"Your daughter." Grace rested her head on Alexander's shoulder.

Grace believed in Dr. Spock and went out of her way to keep Leah from being jealous. "Look Chucky, there's your big sister," she'd say while Leah watched her feed the baby.

Grace believed in Dr. Freud and worried about penis envy. Leah couldn't figure out why she'd want a penis. Peter Pronk had one and went to the bathroom standing up, which meant he couldn't keep a book on his lap. She did admire Chucky's ability to tinkle in the air like a fountain. If she were a boy, she might be able to draw with her tinkle. She tried it on a newspaper but it didn't come out right. She threw it away before anyone saw, so her parents wouldn't accuse each other of being responsible.

When Leah was dragged to Ye Olde Children Shoppe next to the hardware store the week before second grade started, she figured out why she hated being a child. Others controlled what she wanted to do for herself. Her mother selected five dresses, one for each school day and a sixth for church and parties.

"I don't like ruffles, and I don't like yellow." Leah looked at the front, left and right sides of the Sunday-best dress in the three-way mirror.

"It looks really cute," Grace said.

"I look like a baby. A prissy baby." She stuck out her tongue at the reflection. She liked seeing three sides of herself.

Grace held a pair of socks the same shade of yellow with ruffles on the edge. "Be good about that dress, and you can buy that set of pastels you want."

"And the how-to-draw book?" Leah asked.

"Just the pastels."

Pastel were worth Prissy. Prissy was a word Mrs. Stickler used as in, "Don't be a prissy missy" when Leah "put on airs."

Alexander joined them for a sundae at *Toree's* below his office. As soon as the door opened, they smelled ice cream. They seated themselves at one of the dark booths worn smooth by fifty years of ice cream eaters sliding across the wood.

Mr. Toree stood behind the dark oak soda fountain and piled ice cream in three silver dishes then poured hot fudge until it spilled onto the silver saucer. To Alexander's and Grace's he added whipped cream and a cherry. Leah opened the wooden box that held the forty-four different colored sticks. They were worth the stupid yellow dress that she'd only wear to church. She began a design on her napkin. "I'll bring home used paper tonight," Alexander said as he watched.

Because the house sat on forty acres of land outside the main part of town, Leah's friends had to be driven to play with her or vice versa. She often found herself alone after school. Abigail had said it was good that Leah could entertain herself with make-believe games. Queen was Leah's favorite.

Her mother bought her a Landmark book each time she was good at the dentist. Her first had been *Queen Elizabeth I* and the second *Marie Antoinette.*

Mrs. Stickler came out the front door. "Leah, honey, it's getting cold. Better put this on." She held out the red sweater Grace had knitted with a kitten on the left side and heart-shaped white buttons. Queens were never told how to dress.

"How clever my dear lady-in-waiting to slip me a secret message in the sleeve," she said, pointing with Alexander's old cane that she used as a scepter.

Alexander, who was just coming onto the porch with Grace, said, "That's your daughter."

Chapter Three:
The Border Crossing
SWITZERLAND
AUGUST 1990

It seems as if I have always been someone's daughter, wife, mother, Leah thought as the train pulled into Neuchâtel. Only for a short time was I myself.

She saw the castle and lake shimmering in the early evening sun. The Alps hovered above the water, so faint they seemed imaginary. After two decades in Switzerland, she was still amazed at the beauty of the mountains with their many faces.

She crossed the platform in the proper place, not where the sign warned of dire consequences if she set foot on the tracks, and went into the station.

She had always been tempted to disobey and put her foot on the track and stick out her tongue at the station master who would come running out. As a proper Swiss housewife, even an American-born one, she never gave into it. Now was not the time to call attention to herself, as she entered the station.

The departure board above the snack bar showed a train leaving for the Val de Travers in nine minutes. She got on. Inside the car the windows had been pulled down in hopes of catching a breeze. Although she was alone, she smelled the sweat of commuters lingering from earlier in the day.

She'd always loved the valley with its eight picture-postcard villages. When Claire-Lise and Yves-Pierre were young she'd brought them here on summer days to play with Kathy's kids. Her friend had renovated an old barn, turning it into a studio and home. They'd picnicked by the waterfall or in the meadow and talked and painted while the kids ran wild.

Kathy believed in Leah's art even after Leah had stopped. Poor Kathy. An American like herself. An artist. A wooden beam in her living room had fallen on her along with the debris from the second story. Kathy swore someone had loosened it—not that it mattered. She was just as crippled regardless of the cause. Didn't stop her from painting. Nothing stopped her—unlike Leah.

Leah wondered what Kathy would do if she showed up on her door step asking to be hidden. Hide her, probably. More than probably. She was that kind of friend. Leah was the kind of person not to put a friend in danger. When the train passed through the tunnel, leaving her in darkness, Leah shuddered.

The train stopped at Couvet, the village where absinthe had been invented, and continued to be made, albeit in well-hidden stills. There was no law against buying or drinking it, just against producing, selling or transporting it. Leah glanced at her watch. It was 8 p.m. If she had her tent, she could camp in the mountains. Better to go to the border town and find a restaurant.

The waitress wore a black tube skirt that lumped over her thighs. Her white blouse hung short, leaving a half inch of midriff exposed. She looked down at Leah seated on the terrace of the *Restaurant de la Gare*.

"All we have left is *rösti*," she said.

"Fine."

"To drink?"

"Fendant, two deciliters." Leah looked beyond the girl to the main road. She could also see the railway tracks. She half expected to see soldiers storming the restaurant.

"It comes with salad," the girl said.

"And salad." Leah wondered how she'd choke down a meal.

The waitress brought the salad, a basket of bread and stuck individual receipts for each item into a white wine glass.

Leah picked up her fork and looked at the rapier-cut carrots next to the cubed beets and corn on lettuce. She pushed a cube around the plate. After swallowing, she realized she hadn't eaten since the dinner party last night where she had pretended life was normal.

She demolished the salad then used her fork to swish the bread through the remains of the dressing. The waitress thumped down the plate with her rösti then picked up the empty salad dish. A poached egg rested on top of the browned stringed potatoes. Leah thought of cholesterol. Hell, if Jean-Luc succeeded in killing her, she'd have sacrificed eating an egg for nothing. Using her bread, she wiped up every bit of yolk until the plate looked just washed.

She wondered if the French border guards still quit at 8:00 p.m. and the Swiss at midnight. People crossing the border after that were supposed to go to the local police if they owed duty. Smugglers were on the honor system. Leah imagined a bearded man walking into the gendarmerie in the village and saying, "I want to pay duty on six kilos of cocaine, please."

Real crooks aren't gangsters, she thought. They're like my husband: surface respectable corrupt underneath. Corrupt wasn't the right word. Crimes against humanity? No that phrase was used at the World Court. Nowhere, including The Hague, was anyone powerful enough to try him. And this was the man she had to evade if she were to live.

It was almost dark. The church clock struck ten. A cow mooed in a field. The waitress cleared the tables on the terrace and looked at her watch.

"*La note, s'il vous plaît.*" Leah wished she'd asked for *l'addition*. Jean-Luc had taught her asking for *l'addition* was not proper for their class. In a farm town, like this one, the affectation would stand out at a time when the last thing she wanted was to be noticed.

Leah, as she waited for the bill, wondered if Jean-Luc's insistence on certain wording was that different from her mother who'd made Leah say "children" not "kids" and refer to "urine" not "peepee." Yes, she decided.

My husband, although as aristocratic as it was possible for a Swiss to be, never learned decency. My mother, who aspired to a class that didn't exist in small New England towns, was decent, and that is class that has nothing to do with society. And not being aware of that difference was what had led Leah to the mess she was in. When the waitress arrived with her pencil and black change purse, Leah gave up on linguistic insights.

After crossing to the main road, she headed into the forest. A dog in one of the nearby farm houses barked, then quieted. She walked until she could see the border. Finding a rock, she sat. The light in the shack lit two customs officers playing cards, Red Beard and Baldy.

A car drove through from France. Red beard put his cards down and went out to say something to the driver. Leah was sure it was, *"Vous-avez de la marchandise à declarer?"* The only thing they ever asked about was products that might necessitate payment of duty. He waved the car on and went inside the shack. She saw Baldy open a Coca-Cola.

Another car came from the Swiss side, and Red Beard waved it through without a glance.

Ah bon, she thought, they aren't looking for anyone here. No one guessed I might come this way. Years of keeping secrets, starting in her teenage years, had worked again. She could get away with the unexpected. She had an hour and a half to wait until midnight.

The rock was hard; the evening chilly at that altitude. The moon came out full. Except for one cloud that passed over its face, it brightened the night. She could make out that the grass

25

was green, the rocks gray. The smell of pines reminded her of childhood, not that she smelled them then because she was too accustomed to their odor. Visitors would comment. It was only after being away that she discovered how clean, rich pine scent tickled her nostrils.

I can't go home this time. Can I trust Chuck, she wondered. Even if her brother wouldn't betray her, his phone might be tapped. Would Jean-Luc's arm reach across the ocean and overcome the American laws?

It already had.

"Can I trust anyone? Maybe I'll have to always rely on the kindness of strangers in hotel rooms," she whispered to the moon. She remembered her childhood fears and wished her only concern now was an imaginary monster and childhood annoyances.

She wished she could start her life over. "I can't. I have to go ahead," she said to the moon, "but at least when I think of the past I can forget how hard this rock is."

The guards closed the hut and got into their cars. Still Leah waited another hour. As she did she felt angry, wanted to get revenge on her husband for lying to her for years, for turning their son into the, the . . . she couldn't find the right word.

There were no lights in the two farm houses, the gas station or the five buildings leading to the border. One Volkswagen bus with Dutch plates went into France. A German caravan with two bicycles attached to the back entered Switzerland. The sudden traffic solved Leah's debate about crossing on the road or staying in the woods until she was on the other side. Only the woods were safe.

Pontarlier, France—she wasn't out of danger, but her chances had gone up. *What next?* The train station was ten kilometers away. She certainly wouldn't be late for the first morning train.

There were hotels along the route, but arriving with no luggage at this hour would make her unforgettable.

The lights, shining on the outside of the château high on the hill above, went out. Leah, Kathy and the kids had toured it before Kathy's accident. The resident count in the Middle Ages, returning from a crusade, had found his wife with a lover. He imprisoned her in a five-by-five cell and hung the lover on a tree. The poor wife could see the body through her window. After many years the count sent her to a convent. Angry husbands still have power, she thought. Not much has changed in six hundred years.

Her plan, albeit one derived out of desperation with little forethought, had worked so far. She didn't dare head for Paris. If they were searching the TGV in Geneva, they'd probably check stateside flights from DeGaulle and Orly. Even if Jean-Luc didn't know she'd kept her American passport in her maiden name, it was too risky to try to use it. Head south, woman, head south, she thought, that would probably be the least expected.

CHAPTER FOUR:
FEARS AND FLUTOPHONES
STONEFIELD, MA
WINTER 1954

Leah, lay face down under her desk, waiting for the all-clear. Mrs. Graham, her fourth grade teacher, signaled the end of A-Bomb drills with her kickball referee whistle. This wasn't an all-town or even an all-school drill. The last had been a year ago when the town sirens wailed. Cars stopped and occupants took cover against buildings or trees.

Peeking, Leah watched her teacher take a long drag on a cigarette. Leah didn't like her. Because she'd been her parents' teacher, she was forever saying, "You're artistic like your mother," or "You're smart as a whip like your father."

Leah resisted saying, "No, I'm like me." She vowed never to say things like Mrs. Graham did to children when she grew up, if she grew up. No one knew for sure when the Communists were going to drop The Big One.

She'd heard her parents arguing. Grace wanted to build a bomb shelter. Alexander insisted on a swimming pool. Leah had been sitting outside the living room drawing a picture of the hall table legs when that conversation had happened.

Getting the twists and turns of the wood captured on paper wasn't working.

"Grace, I'd rather melt than be cooped up in a little room." Her father had rattled his *Boston Globe* in a way that meant the conversation was over.

"You're dooming us to certain death," Grace had said.

"We'd kill each other in an hour anyway. Leah, stop eaves-

28

dropping," he'd added, spying his daughter.

Although they enjoyed the pool, Grace bought emergency rations to last six months. She'd buried them in a special lead chest in the backyard while Alexander was at work.

Besides death by A-bomb, Leah had a second fear: King Kong. Each night Leah was sure that the monkey waited outside her bedroom window to carry her to the Empire State Building. Although she wanted to see New York, hand-of-monkey wasn't her preferred transportation.

In bed panic niggled at her. "Take care of me, Mr. Moon," she'd whisper. Shadows from the trees looked like giant apes. When the fear became too big to hold, she'd creep out of bed until she came to the window. Reaching up, she'd yank the shade down. More than once Grace had found her asleep at the head of the stairs far from any window that would allow a giant gorilla hand to enter.

On a Saturday morning when only Alexander and she were up, he'd asked, "Why, just why, can't you stay in bed?"

"You'll think I'm stupid." She poured milk on her Rice Krispies, listening for the snap, crackle and pop. Despite the ads she only heard crackles, never snaps nor pops. After several months of cereal listening, she suspected the ads were another twisted grownup perception.

She didn't want a long conversation, because her cereal would be soggy. She hated soggy cereal.

Her father added milk to his coffee. "I promise not to think you're stupid." He crossed his heart, but when she told him, he laughed.

"You promised not to think I was stupid."

"I don't think you're stupid. I think you've your mother's imagination. Nightmares seem so real. I'd terrible ones after the war. Even hit your mother once as I woke up. Thought she was an enemy."

29

"Really?"

He got up and put his hands on her shoulders then dropped a kiss on her hair still mussed from bed. "It's okay to be afraid. It's not okay to give in. Fight back."

Despite his explanation how Hollywood had made the movie, Leah had her doubts about King Kong. She also doubted that grownups were afraid of anything. They had the power to control their lives and do what they wanted. Still Leah promised herself that whenever she was afraid, she'd try to beat it rather then let it beat her.

After he left for his golf game, Leah poured her soggy cereal into the garbage and replaced it with fresh that crackled but still didn't snap or pop.

During the daytime King Kong posed no problem, but at night doubts tiptoed through her mind. She'd imagine framework and machinery manipulating the monkey. Although the fear didn't disappear she managed to stay in bed all night long.

Each morning she woke with a feeling of gratitude that King Kong had sought another maiden to take to New York.

Mrs. Graham's all-clear whistle brought Leah's attention back to the classroom. The children scrambled to their seats.

Mr. Ames, the music teacher, entered, his arms crammed with narrow boxes about fourteen inches long. He held the stack in place with his chin. More were in two giant shopping bags.

He combed his remaining strands of hair over his bald spot. Once when he left the school during a windy day, Leah noticed how they stood straight up from the part level with his ear.

She preferred the art teacher who came weekly to teach about color wheels and paints. She never said shush when they laughed.

Mr. Ames thought laughing broke the eleventh commandment: "Thou shalt not have a good time."

Leah watched him open a box and pull out a red and white recorder.

"This, children, is a Flutophone." He put it to his mouth and squeaked out "Frère Jacques."

Listening to the instrument destroy the song, Leah wondered that if the teacher couldn't make it sound good, how could she? She hated doing things badly. Her grades were all ones except for arithmetic. That was a two. And she got ones for effort in all her subjects except fractions. She never understood why anyone cared about flipping a fraction.

Opening the box he'd handed her, she took out her Flutophone with its cherry red mouthpiece. A matching red line ran down the instrument. The air holes were circled in red.

Mr. Ames said, "Hold it like this. Your thumbs cover the hole on the bottom. Now blow slowly into the mouthpiece."

Twenty-two mouths produced a painful wail. Peter Pronk blew as hard as he could into Leah's ear.

Leah grimaced.

"Let's try a few scales." Mr. Ames produced something that sounded between do, re, me, fa, sol, la, te, do and chalk scraping down a blackboard.

Leah put the instrument in her mouth. The Flutophone did have a nice peppermint taste.

Leah hoped the sound would get better. It didn't.

Each week Mr. Ames taught a new song. "Long, Long Ago," gave way to "Silent Night" and "Little Star of Bethlehem," but the melodies were marred with squeaks.

"Cut it out," Leah whispered as Peter Pronk tangled his instrument in her hair while they worked on "Hark the Herald Angels Sing" for the Christmas Pageant. On Flutophone day she normally wore braids to prevent his attacks, but that morning she couldn't find elastics. She hated braids. Babies wore braids. She hated Peter. She hated Friday music class.

"Leah Stockbridge. Be quiet," Mr. Ames said. "This is our last rehearsal before the performance tonight."

Leah moved out of Peter's reach. "Sorry, Sir."

As she tootled on her Flutophone, she planned revenge.

After Mr. Ames left, Mrs. Graham stared out the window. A few snow flakes drifted to the ground, but they were the kind that wouldn't stick which meant no snowballs, no snowforts during the weekend.

An argument started in the reading corner. Someone dropped a book. The teacher glanced at her watch. She looked out the window. "Children, get dressed. Late recess, today."

The dark coat room had one hook-covered wall. A jut hid a sink and mirror. The girls slipped slacks on under their skirts to protect their legs. The boys pushed each other.

Leah ducked under the sink's cloth skirt made in a fabric so ancient the original pattern had long since disappeared leaving only something that might be called beige or dirty.

After everyone left, Leah returned to the classroom. The large jar of white paste on the art supply shelf caught her eye. During projects each child was doled out on a small piece of paper. The dob was large enough for the chore but not enough to eat. The paste tasted like peppermint mixed with banana. Mrs. Graham always yelled when she saw a pupil lick the paste from their fingers or worse, put some in their mouths in a glob.

Leah saw the pear shape bottle of glue on Mrs. Graham's desk. Its rubber top was like the nipple on her doll's baby bottle. Although hard to get out, it worked better than paste, but tasted awful.

Opening Peter's desk, she unscrewed his Flutophone's mouthpiece. She soaked two Kleenex with glue then stuffed the mess in the instrument.

Hearing footsteps, she dived under Mrs. Graham's desk.

From where she scrunched herself up against the wooden front she could see her teacher's feet.

"Where's my whistle?" Mrs. Graham asked herself, since the room would have appeared to be empty from her point of view.

A drawer opened. If she'd sat, she'd have kicked Leah, who heard a rustle followed by a match striking. The smell of smoke drifted under the desk. "Thank God," said the teacher. "Only two weeks till Christmas break." The drawer closed.

Footsteps left the room.

Twenty-two angels took their place on stage. The murmur of parents could be heard through the curtain.

The art teacher had helped them design masks, but the angels couldn't blow through them because paper covered their mouths. Mrs. Graham had suggested removing them when it came time to play, but that disturbed the wire hangar halos. Finally they cut the masks in half leaving mouths free to toot "Hark the Herald Angels Sing."

The curtains parted revealing Mr. Ames at a lectern in the middle aisle. After a third grader with adenoids thickening his speech, told of Christ's birth, the music teacher tapped his baton.

No sooner had the first notes heralded when Peter Pronk hollered, "Hey, something is wrong with my Flutophone." He tore off his mask. His halo clattered to the floor.

Mr. Ames, who'd been conducting with the great sweeping movements of Eugene Ormandy in front of the Philadelphia Philharmonic, stopped with one arm hanging in the air. He glared at Peter.

"Play!" he mouthed then mumbled, "Nothing can go wrong with a Flutophone."

"There's stuff in it," Peter said.

Mr. Ames mounted the three steps to the stage. He stood in

front of Peter, his hand out. Peter plunked the Flutophone on the open palm. The teacher turned red as he tried to blow into it.

"Everyone will sit at their desk with their heads down until the guilty person confesses," Mrs. Graham said Monday morning as soon as the class was seated.

Leah weighed the advantages of confessing. Naahh, she thought. At 5:00 p.m. several mothers arrived because they didn't want their children walking home in the dark.

Mrs. Graham dismissed the rest.

The children had no recess and were given extra homework each day until Christmas. For the holiday break they were assigned an essay on accepting responsibility plus five pages of fractions. Leah never confessed.

In January, when school resumed, Mrs. Graham collected the homework. No one mentioned the incident again.

CHAPTER FIVE:
TRAIN RIDE
FRANCE
AUGUST 1990

As Leah validated her ticket to Barcelona in the orange machine next to the door leading to the platform, she heard its thick click.

The ticket seller had called her Monsieur, although she wasn't sure if that was because she was dressed like a man or because she'd lowered her voice. More likely it was his thick-lens glasses. It didn't matter. He wouldn't be able to identify her.

She pushed the station door open. For a second she was tempted to throw her Swiss passport with her married name in the trash, but then thought if someone found it, they might trace her to Pontarlier. She slipped it in her jacket pocket next to her American passport and mounted the train. It was half-filled. She took the first free seat across from a pleasant-looking woman in her late forties.

Most of the other passengers seemed to be retirees except for two nuns and two teen-agers sprawled across the seats asleep with earphones and Walkmen.

Leah looked out the window at the cows munching grass. She remembered talking with a man who worked at an environmental agency. He'd lectured her on what useless beasts they were, taking up more resources than they ever could put back. Jean-Luc had labeled him a nut—resources were for making money.

She tried to decide where to get off, not wanting to do another border crossing, nor wanting to take a chance that they'd trace destinations of tickets purchased in border towns.

"Going far?" the woman across from her asked, cutting through Leah's planning.

Leah let an American accent come through her words. "Barcelona." She knew the woman would never believe she was a man, but she might think she was a lesbian.

"Holiday?"

"Work. Filming a documentary. Bull fighting."

"What were you doing in Pontarlier?"

"Just finished a documentary on absinthe. The crew took my cameras ahead. I wanted to poke around." She used the wrong French gender for cameras and the wrong verb deliberately.

"Interesting. Americans don't usually speak French. May I ask where you learned?"

"I spent a year in Paris after college."

"Were you with your parents?"

"No, I was looking for work. Wait a minute. I mean university. I remember your college is like our junior high." Leah rumbled a laugh, and crossed her legs so her ankle rested on her knee.

The train pulled into Dijon where most of the retirees, nuns and teenagers descended. No one got on, leaving the car empty. Leah shut her eyes. She was so tired. She heard the woman get up and rustle in her bag. "I'm going to get coffee, do you want something?"

"*Non, merci,*" Leah said, her eyes closed, her body curled on the seat. As soon as she felt the woman leave, her eyes flew open. Only one old couple dozed at the other end of the car.

Her seatmate had left her purse, having taken her wallet. Leah saw a passport sticking out of the side pocket. Reaching across, she plucked it out then slipped it in her suit jacket inside pocket. A surge of guilt then a wave of panic that she'd be caught swept through her. Her need to have another passport was greater than both.

A few minutes later she heard footsteps and smelled coffee. She forced herself to stay motionless breathing regularly and letting out a snore from time to time. She imagined the passport burning her chest not from guilt, but fear. What if the woman accused her and had her searched?

Stretching, she opened her eyes, pretending to focus. "Maybe I'll get some coffee, now."

She strolled through the train. She passed through the kiddie car where parents took children to play. Miniature tables were anchored in place and Fisher Price—type toys fastened to the walls. The room was carpeted. More than once she had found these cars a relief when she and her children had trained to Paris. Now her relief was that there were no children in the car. She pulled up a corner of the rug and slipped the woman's passport underneath.

She returned to the seat with coffee and a stale baguette with a dried piece of cheese. She bit into it, having to twist the bread to break it off. "I don't understand how any country who has such wonderful food can sell such miserable sandwiches," she said to the woman.

"I visited your country and was amazed at what a variety of really good sandwiches there were. I ate at a Jewish delicatessen in New York. Wonderful." She kissed the tips of her fingers.

"People who haven't traveled to the US think every American eats only at McDonald's. Six people here have asked me if I eat there every day."

"And Americans ask me if I go topless on the beach?"

They laughed.

Leah threw sandwich paper, napkin and Styrofoam cup in the pullout metal trash container under the window. "I really dread that bull fight. I hate seeing animals hurt." She closed her eyes while staying alert for looking-for-passport sounds. She wondered if she'd have been smarter to keep the woman talking, but she was so tired. Despite herself, she dropped off.

As the train slowed entering the Narbonne station, Leah awoke. The woman stood on the seat as she struggled with her suitcase.

"Let me help." Leah pulled the case off the overhead rack. It had attached wheels allowing the woman to pull the suitcase behind her like an obedient puppy dog.

As soon as the train left Narbonne, Leah headed for the kiddie car. A woman sat in the middle rolling a small ball to her twin sons. Each sat with their legs apart. Their chubby thighs made Leah think of the cherubs on Mama DelAngelo's lamps.

Double shit, she thought. Shit for another memory from a time long gone and shit because she couldn't retrieve the passport.

She went for another cup of coffee. Sitting on the dining car stool she watched the landscape swish by. Green pastures gave way to sandy mountains and scrub pines. They passed an old château, its yellow stone walls a fortress impregnable from attack but not tourists. She twirled the empty cup in her hands. A man in his sixties and a woman slightly younger occupied the other two stools as they drank coffee and talked about their son's new wife. An older man, a glass of wine in his hand, waited for a place to sit.

Leah returned to the kiddie car. The same woman watched her boys careen off the walls. As Leah returned to her seat, she prayed, "Dear God, I know I don't talk to you often, but please, please, don't let them kick up the corner of the rug."

They pulled into Perpignan. Leah glanced at the platform. The woman with the twins was being hugged by a man in jeans and a T-shirt as the two little boys hung on his legs. As soon as the train started she headed for the kiddie car and scooped the passport. "Thank you, thank you, thank you."

She stopped at the first water closet. The sink was dirty. There was a chocolate crust in the toilet. Leah wasn't worried about sanitation. I can never contact anyone I know ever again, she thought. Not my brother, not my mother.

Again guilt flushed through her. Her mother wouldn't recognize her if she did show up at the nursing home, but she felt Claire-Lise's absence like she'd touched fire. She opened the passport. The face had a straight haircut. Anne-Marie Jacquemart took a bad photo, bless her. Leah looked in the mirror. If she did her hair the same way she just might get away with a new identity, for a time. There was even a visa for the States stamped inside, but where would she go once she got there?

The train pulled into a village. The sign on the platform said Argelès-sur-Mer. Anne-Marie/Leah Stockbridge Perroset got off the train, only to be slapped by heat. The station was next to a cemetery. The Pyrenees poked up behind.

"I guess the first thing I need to do is get some sleep and metamorphosize into Anne-Marie. Or maybe I'm better off as a dyke."

As she walked down the narrow street into the village, she passed white and pastel-colored stucco houses with sun-bleached blue shutters and red-tiled roofs.

A stream of cars filled the street leaving the air full of stinking gasoline fumes. Sunburned men and women in shorts mulled around. Others lined up outside a charcuterie buying chickens turning on a rotisserie.

A girl, no more than five, said in a heavy English accent, "I want chips, Mother. Not chicken."

"Be quiet, Justine," the mother snapped.

Leah wanted her daughter at her side whining for *pommes frites,* French fries, chips. Just as long as she was there. But she would never be there, not as a little girl, not as a teenager. She would never see Claire-Lise graduate, never hold her future grandchildren.

Leah wanted to run back in time to her own mother, her father, her grandmother, Michael. Those good people who'd each loved her in their own way. She wanted the simplicity when she believed that the world was good and not controlled by puppet masters.

Despite herself she kept thinking of how much difficulty she'd caused her mother and wished she could erase it just like she wanted to erase the trouble she was in now. However, she had too much to do to feel sorry for herself. She continued into the village.

CHAPTER SIX:
DANCE LESSONS
FRANCE
AUGUST 1990

"Stand still." Grace spun her daughter around to tie the sash of the floor-length dress that she'd made for this occasion.

"I don't want to go," Leah said.

"Of course you do. Your left sock is inside out."

"Who cares?"

"Le-a-ah. I am at the end of my rope." Grace forced each syllable through her teeth. "It is a social honor to be able to attend the D.A.R. dancing classes. Most children would be thrilled."

Leah rejected asking to see the rope. She held back from saying she was neither honored nor thrilled. Instead she took off her shoe and turned her sock before jamming her hands into lace gloves. Tears ran down her face. She snuffled several times. "I can't go. I can't button my gloves."

Grandmother Abigail, who had witnessed the performance, said, "Let me show you something." She led her granddaughter into her bedroom. Reaching to the top of the bureau, she held a tissue to Leah's nose. "Blow."

As Leah stopped sniffling, her grandmother opened her dresser. In between two piles of corsets were two Whitman's candy boxes with their yellow-beige background and pictures of plants within a blue ricrac type border. Leah knew them well. She could play with them as a reward for extra good behavior, although often when she was sick in bed, the boxes would come out to entertain her.

One was filled with all shapes and sizes of buttons snipped

41

from clothes being retired into dust cloths or cut down to make other garments. Leah made designs with the buttons or used them as people, trees, buildings or whatever her imagination desired.

The second box contained colorful envelope linings her grandmother had peeled from envelopes. Abigail had shown her how to paste them onto bottles to make candle holders or to design mosaics. After today, Leah doubted she'd ever see either again.

Abigail rustled under the corsets to bring out a black velvet box, which held her silver bracelet with the lock heart and key and the hat pin she used when she went to town and church. Its pearl contrasted with her black hat. Leah thought it looked as if a bird had dropped something nasty.

"Here it is." Abigail held up a hook less than half the width of a pencil. "When I was a young girl going to dances, we always wore gloves." She put the hook in the loop of the glove and pulled the button through it. "This belonged to your great-great grandmother before the Civil War."

Abigail led Leah to the bathroom and ran a cloth under the cold water. She dabbed at Leah's face.

Grace beeped the horn of the station wagon.

"Now be a good girl." Abigail helped Leah into her Sunday School coat. It stopped at the knees.

"The coat looks stupid with my dress hanging below."

Abigail pushed an escaped black curl under her grand-daughter's head band. "Go. It won't be as bad as you imagine."

"I don't see why you side with the D.A.R. You told me you quit when they wouldn't let that Negro woman sing."

"No one who was part of that has anything to do with this dancing class. Go. Your mother is waiting."

Leah stomped to the car. Slamming the door she said, "If this is so special why can't we take the good car?" Most of her friends' families had two automobiles—the station wagon for the wife and children for everyday, where no one had to be careful about feet and dripping ice cream cones. In the daddies' good cars ice cream was forbidden. Leah felt sorry for all the men who not only had "to go out and bring home the bacon," but couldn't enjoy a chocolate cone with jimmies on a summer afternoon.

"The station wagon is perfectly fine." Grace turned on the windshield wipers as a few drops plashed the windshield. The wipers squeaked against the glass.

"Do you have to have a station wagon when you get married?" Leah traced a rain drop as it ran down the side window.

"The questions you ask. Of course not, but it makes driving children and lugging groceries easier. Careful, you'll get your gloves dirty."

Grace turned onto Lowell Street. Everyone in town called it the Street of Churches; all Stonefield's churches were on this one street. There was a hierarchy with the least prestigious church, that of the Seventh Day Adventists, first. Then came St. Joseph's Roman Catholic Church with the statue of the Virgin Mary on the front lawn. "Democrats go there," Grace once said. As President of the Young Woman's Republican Club, and wife of the man who chaired the Stonefield Re-elect Eisenhower Committee, she didn't know what could be more damning unless she said someone was a Communist.

Grace believed in Joseph McCarthy and was glued to the television set during his hearings. Chucky and Leah hated McCarthy, not for being anti-Communist, but because the hearings kept Howdy Doody and Princess Summerfallwinterspring off the air. When Grace waxed on about McCarthy's patriotism, Alexander would say, "Now Grace, he's a bit extreme."

The churches continued, one after another until the Stockbridges' church, St. Anne's Episcopal. It rivaled the Unitarian, across the common, in prestige. St. Anne's, made of fieldstone, was a copy of an English Church. The First Unitarian was a New England caricature with white wooden clapboards and a steeple.

Although the ballroom dancing classes were not sponsored by the First Unitarian Church, the D.A.R. felt it had the best hall. Only children from families whose parents were doctors, bankers, businessmen or lawyers, like Alexander, were asked. Grace pulled into the parking lot. "Just remember that being invited is an honor."

"Next you'll tell me that when I grow up I'll be glad I did this." Leah ran into the building, not waiting for her mother to get the umbrella.

Monsieur LeRoyer, the man who taught the course, had traveled from Boston. He greeted each arrival, bowing to the boys and kissing the girls' hands. He wore a tuxedo like Leah's father did when he went to Masons, only Alexander didn't have a moustache that looked drawn on with an eyebrow pencil.

Usually Grace disliked foreigners. They went to the Catholic church and had Irish, French and Italian names. They worked as clerks and for the sewer department. However, Monsieur LeRoyer was rumored to be an impoverished count, forced to earn a living after the Germans destroyed his château. He supported himself and his mother by teaching ballroom dancing and decorum to children.

Daisy Fairclough, Abigail's best friend, considered it a real coup that she'd convinced him to teach in Stonefield. He was heavily booked by Boston Brahmins and by groups in wealthy towns like Magnolia and Hamilton.

Leah wished Mrs. Fairclough hadn't been successful. She remembered the first time that she saw Monsieur LeRoyer standing, tall and imposing, by the closed door leading into the main hall.

"Enfants, enfants," he'd said. "You will parade in. My young gentlemen, find yourselves a young lady." No one moved.

Whack.

Everyone jumped.

Whack.

Leah hadn't noticed the walking stick at Monsieur LeRoyer's side until the second time he brought it down hard on a metal chair.

Suddenly each boy had a girl at his side.

"Present your arm in this fashion," he said.

They did.

"Mesdemoiselles, put your hands lightly on their arms like this."

The young girls did, their eyes open wide.

I really hate this, Leah had thought.

"Now we will file in. The first couple, walk around the room once." He stared at John Anderson and Sally Bates, the first couple. Leah wouldn't have been surprised if they'd melted.

"Follow me." He opened the door. *"Maman, vous pouvez commencer."*

A gray-haired woman dressed in a blue evening gown began playing the piano. A huge German Shepherd sat in front of the instrument. Leah was shocked that a dog was in a church, even one as liberal as the Unitarian.

When everyone was seated Monsieur LeRoyer said, *"Mesdemoiselles,* stand. First you will learn to curtsey. If Queen Elizabeth comes to Stonefield, you will, how you say it, be prepared like your boy scouts." He grabbed at Vanessa Hughes and made her do it, tapping his cane across the inside of her knees. Someone giggled.

Whack.

The metal tip of the cane hit the floor.

When the girls had curtsied to his satisfaction they sat waiting for the boys to learn to bow.

Leah had crossed her legs. She doubted if Queen Elizabeth would ever come to Stonefield. The only foreign dignitary that ever had visited was the fire chief of Stonefield, England. Who curtsied to fire chiefs?

Whack.

The cane hit her chair next to her knee. "Well mannered *jeunes filles* sit with their ankles not their legs crossed."

Leah had almost said, "I do not want to be a well-mannered 'June fee.'" A look at the cane made her rethink saying anything.

"Enfants, we will learn the waltz. *Maman, la musique s'il vous plaît."*

Whack, two, three. *Whack,* two, three. *Whack,* two, three. The cane beat the rhythm as *les garçons* pushed *les mesdemoiselles* around the room.

The lesson lasted an hour in real time, an eternity in each youngster's mind. Week after week, Grace dropped a sullen Leah in front of the door.

The last part of each session involved food. Some Tuesdays it was a tea, where Madame LeRoyer poured and asked, *"Sucre ou citron?"* Leah handled the tiny cucumber sandwiches without soiling her gloves; Monsieur LeRoyer checked to make sure they were clean.

This December day three months into the lessons, when Leah left the car she was no happier than any other lesson, even if it were a party, Christmas formal dinner with grape juice in place of red wine and ginger ale for white.

As *les garçons* pulled the chairs out for *les jeunes filles,* Monsieur LeRoyer said, "The first half of the meal we will use French manners, for when you attend formal dinners in Europe. The second half we will use American manners, such as they are. Take your left hands out of your laps and place the wrist on the table."

"My mother would kill me, if she saw me doing this," Bobby Tennant, Leah's dinner partner, said. Leah nodded. She was supposed to talk five minutes to the boy on the left and five to the boy on the right. Talking to Bobby was okay. Talking to Jonathan Sheldon, the class cootie, would be hard. His front teeth stood out and all he cared about was science.

"I brought my pet snake," Jonathan whispered to her as she turned to him.

She choked, spitting her "wine" on the table cloth.

Whack.

"Mademoiselle Stockbridge."

"Excusez-moi, Monsieur LeRoyer," she said.

The teacher beamed at hearing the perfect French accent then turned away.

Jonathan reached into his pocket and pulled out a snake not much bigger than a worm with a thyroid condition. Leah had no fear of snakes, toads, spiders or mice.

"Put it on the table. See where he goes," Leah said.

The reptile headed toward Becky Durrell.

"SNAKE!!!!!" Becky jumped, upsetting the table.

Dishes crashed to the floor as thirty youngsters either ran to or from the snake. Leah was the only girl who didn't run from it.

Whack, whack, whack, whack, whack, whack.

Jonathan searched frantically for his snake. "If he dies, Leah Stockbridge, it's all your fault."

Unfortunately, Monsieur LeRoyer heard. He grabbed Jonathan by the collar of his jacket and Leah by the arm. They were expelled.

"What possessed you?" her father asked that night.

Leah sat in a chair, her hated long gown stained with grape juice. She shrugged.

"Maybe it's for the best," Grace said. "He spent a lot of time speaking French and showing them foreign things."

Chapter Seven:
Breaking and Entering
ARGELÈS-SUR-MER, FRANCE
AUGUST–NOVEMBER 1990

The beach had soft white sand, not like the Riveria with its hard black rocks that pitted a body that laid there too long. Behind the beach was a pine grove and then a walkway of criss-crossed pinkish bricks. The path was flanked by boutiques and restaurants, not the least honky tonk. Shops sold beach gear, souvenirs, Indian clothing, jewelry, books, magazines, crepes and ice cream. Huge orange lamps brightened the path of sunburned tourists strolling along. A street musician sang "D'Habitude." An Englishwoman said, "That's not a French song. That's 'My Way.' "

Chairs and tables spilled onto the sidewalk from cafés with doors almost as wide as the building. People stopped to read posted menus that boasted of fish which had swum in the Mediterranean a few hours earlier. Leah succumbed when she passed a restaurant which had a rowboat filled with oysters, clams, shrimp, crabs, halibut and tuna steaks on crushed ice. Although she knew that she needed to conserve her cash, hunger won. As she wolfed down her halibut Catalan, she'd rationalized needing to keep up her strength.

Stuffed, she wandered around rather than return to her stifling room in the main village. At the end of the boulevard was a newspaper stand marked by the traditional sign, a red plume pen on a yellow background. As Leah stood next to the holders stocked with newspapers from major European cities, she could see the sea with its waves lolling onto the beach. The newspapers often arrived one or two days late. The *Tribune de Genève* hadn't appeared for the last three days. That night she found all the missing issues hidden behind the *Stuttgarter Zeitung.*

Leah took the papers to *La Reserve,* a café with a terrace facing the sea, where she found one small white table vacant. When the waiter arrived, she ordered mint tisane to soothe her stomach. For the past two weeks bile had risen in her throat each time she read the paper. Inhaling, she turned the first page.

The lack of news frightened her. Could a reporter disappear with no news? Could a banker's wife?

Apparently. Then she saw something that made her understand the phrase "made my blood run cold" as she came to the back of the paper.

Monsieur Jean-Luc Perroset
Mademoiselle Claire-Lise Perroset
Monsieur Yves-Pierre Perroset
Anne-Joëlle et Pierre Laurens et ses enfants
Antoinette et Franz Huber et ses enfants
Charles et Amanda Stockbridge
Paige Stockbridge
Madame Leah PERROSET née Stockbridge
Leur bien-aimée épouse, maman, soeur,
belle-soeur, tante enlevée à leur tendre
affection,
le 15 août dans sa 45ème année.
La cérémonie religieuse aura lieu en la
chapelle de L'Eglise St. Pierre, où la
défuncte repose, le 18 août à 11 heures.

Underneath was a second notice.

IN MEMORIAM
Leah PERROSET
1945–1990
nos pensées
Kathy Sullivan
Dorothy Sullivan
Sophie Perrin
Florence Corboud

Leah had heard jokes about the news of someone's death being announced prematurely and about people who didn't start their day until they checked the obituaries to see if their name were listed. They weren't that funny then: they weren't funny now.

For a second her muscles relaxed as she thought, if I'm dead, I'm safe. Then she realized that the person she feared most was the one who knew she was alive. Jean-Luc officially killing her off removed that last doubt, however minuscule, that she'd overreacted when she bolted.

She didn't know for sure if Raphaël was really dead. She'd only heard a shot and a thud followed by Jean-Luc running. But the man outside her hotel room had been real, as had the soldiers in the Geneva train station.

Could she verify Raphaël's whereabouts? Was it too dangerous to call the television station? His house? If the PTT couldn't provide bills with phone numbers called, did they have the equipment to trace a call from France?

The tisane had cooled. A breeze fluttered the palms lining the terrace. On a stand at the edge of the sand three gypsies strummed guitars. After finishing the tisane, she began the mile walk back to the village.

She had time to think about options. Contacting Kathy was

too dangerous for everyone.

Telephone Chuck? His phone might be tapped. And what a shock. She could just imagine an operator saying, "Will you accept a long-distance call from your sister?" Would he ask if they had phones in heaven?

Fly to the US using Anne-Marie's passport? What if she went to Canada and crossed the border by bus using her own passport? Either way she still had no place to go. Her thoughts twisted and turned, repeating themselves, in a way that threatened to paralyze her.

Here she had a temporary identity, bless trusting Anne-Marie for leaving her pocketbook unattended. However, if she registered at the town hall or got a legal job, she would risk exposure.

"I have to make a plan and stick to it," she said to herself.

She heard the drone of Catalan music as she entered the village. Rather than enter her room, she watched tourists dance the simple three steps right, three steps left.

When the train stopped in Perpignan, Leah got off and entered the station. The ceiling, a swirl of pastel circles within circles, caught her attention.

Ugly, she thought. A man behind her noticed her looking up and said, "Dali painted it. Proclaimed this station the centre of the universe."

"Thank you," she said.

"Have you time to have a glass of wine with me?"

Leah appraised the tall, thin, white-haired man. Probably he could be trusted, but what if he had been sent by Jean-Luc? I'm becoming paranoid, she thought. Next I'll look under my bed each night. A better reason for her to say no was the list of things she needed to do before going back to Argelès.

In a phone booth, she inserted the phone card she'd bought

from the tabac and dialed 19. When the international line buzzed, she called Television Suisse Romand. Maybe they'd trace the call, and maybe they wouldn't. Lots of people called television stations from lots of places.

"May I speak with Raphaël St. Jacques?" she asked.

"He no longer works here," the operator said.

"Do you know where he went?"

"No. He mailed us his resignation and disappeared. Can anyone else help?"

Leah hung up. The phone spat the card out of its slot. Should she risk calling his apartment? No, too dangerous. Since forty units remained, she tucked the card in a compartment in her wallet.

Leah's next chore was to buy a gun for self protection. The tourist office told her where she could find rue Jean Jaurès where the hunting store was located.

Back in Argelès, Leah looked at the price of peaches, the last of the season. The green grocer's red-checked gingham-lined basket made the fruit look so tempting. She debated if she should spend the money. It had been years since she'd counted centimes or even francs.

"My day sucked," she said, "I've earned peaches." Taking a plastic bag she chose three pink/orange globes. As soon as she paid, she put one in her mouth, let it warm then pressed it with her tongue. The juice exploded, tasting even sweeter than expected.

Climbing the stairs to her room, she chewed over her problems.

She couldn't buy a gun without police approval. She couldn't get approval without real identification.

Opening her door, a curtain of heat engulfed her. Stripping to her panties, she lay on the faded bedspread. Sweat ran between her breasts leaving them glistening. Sadness pressed her body, a weight as real as if the ceiling descended crushing her. Instead of falling asleep she heard the clock strike each hour. The last that she remembered was it donging four times.

Each morning Leah allowed herself a treat; a croissant and café crème at the tea room next to a chestnut tree. Walking by the boulangerie she sniffed the hot yeast smell of baking bread mixed with the slightly sour one of wine from the local cellar where people brought their old bottles to be refilled from casks.

The tourists had dribbled to a few, usually older, childless couples. No longer did Leah have to wait for a place to sit. The chestnut tree was gray with hundreds of migrating birds. People sat as far from the tree as possible, not just because of droppings, but because of twittering from hundreds of tiny throats.

She chose a table not far from the halfbrick wall separating the terrace and street. The waiter brought her coffee and moved a basket with three croissants from another table without them exchanging a word.

Conversations were louder as people raised their voices to be heard above the birds. A couple in their mid-thirties dressed in jeans and sweatshirts, sat at the next table.

"*Et puis*, smart man, what do we do now?" the woman asked. She brushed her bangs back from her forehead. They fell back as if she hadn't touched them.

"I can't believe mother," the man said. His black hair curled in ringlets around his face.

"Five caretakers in five months. And don't even think about thinking of taking her back to Paris with us. Unless you want a divorce that is," the woman said.

Leah turned to them. "Excuse me, perhaps I can help?"

The couple to whom Leah had introduced herself were Claudine and Louis Perez. The three of them went to his mother's large house, hidden in the woods behind the village. The front of the house was a vegetable garden. Late season tomatoes grew next to teepee pole beans. Ten rows of zucchini would have defied even the most imaginative cook.

"Maman sells the surplus. Monsieur Polli picks up on Mondays," Louis said as if reading Leah's mind.

To one side a mother goat and her almost grown kid poked their head through an opening in the fence that separated them from the garden. Together they were finishing off everything in nibbling range.

Louis pulled a cord attached to a bell that bonged. Opening the door into a ancient-green tiled hall without waiting for an answer, he led the two women down a corridor to a parlor.

An old woman sat in a horsehair-stuffed chair that once may have been red or perhaps apricot, it was impossible to know. Her feet rested on a stool.

A book was on her lap. She wore glasses and had a magnifying glass in her hand. The man ducked as Madame Perez aimed her cane at his left ear. Leah caught it. "I'm not putting up with any more of your bitchy maids," the old crone said. Her face was lined, and she bore a dowager's hump. "So just turn around and go back to Paris." Her accent had a heavy Catalan lilt.

Leah held the cane in her hand. Before Louis Perez could answer, she said, "First, I'm not a bitch. Second, I'm not a maid. I'm a companion. I'm here to do some of the chores that you find difficult. Those beans outside need picking and preserving. Your goat needs milking. And I can walk to the village easier than you can."

"Give me my cane."

"Not if you're going to use it as a weapon."

The couple watched, their heads turning from Leah to Madame Perez as if at a tennis match.

"I don't need anyone. Especially not anyone paid by my

ungrateful son." The old woman pretended to spit on the floor.

"Doesn't matter," Leah said. "I'm here to stay whether you like it or not. We can be miserable, or we can try and get along. How hard you make it is up to you."

The old woman said nothing.

Leah handed her the cane. "I'm Anne-Marie Jacquemart. You can call me Madame Jacquemart."

"I hope you can cook better than the last bitch they left me with," Madame Perez said.

"Probably not," Leah said.

The woman started to smile, but caught herself.

"Well at least you don't lie." Turning toward her son she said, "She can't sleep here. She has to stay in the caravan." She punctuated her order by tapping the cane on the floor.

Leah followed the couple out the back door.

The house was the only one down a long dirt road and totally hidden from the main route. They entered a copse of cork trees with portions of bark regrowing for future cuttings and emerged on the other side into a sloping meadow.

At the far end was a wood filled with pines so dense no sun could penetrate. To the left a small stream had been reduced to a trickle. To the right stood a caravan.

"It's not much," Claudine Perez said, turning the key. A musty odor greeted them as they entered.

Leah ran her fingers across the table. Her fingertips turned gray. "It needs more than airing. It needs to be demildewed." Spying an oil lantern on the table straight out of a Victorian painting, she asked, "No electricity?"

Claudine and Louis exchanged looks. Leah turned as if to leave.

"We can run a wire, Madame Jacquemart," he said.

"When?"

"As soon as we can arrange it," Claudine said.

"I'll start right after it's done."

The caravan when aired, disinfected and well lit was still ugly. At the Saturday marché Leah bought a violet-patterned sleeping bag and material for curtains, stuffed pillows and covers for the torn chair. In the woods she found wildflowers for the vase. She nicknamed the place "Cocoon."

Her duties were simple: do a quick cleaning, feed Madame Perez and the goats, run errands and take care of the garden. She also had to make sure that Madame Perez took her medicine. They developed a ritual.

"Why should I take my medicine? No one cares if I live or die. In fact, my son would be happier if I were dead," the old lady would say, holding the pill in her hand.

"Make him mad. Stay alive," Leah would reply and hand her a glass of water. The woman would look at her, then swallow the tablet.

"I don't know how you stand her," Monsieur Polli said, when he picked up the last batch of zucchini.

"She's not so bad," Leah said. She meant it. Having solved her immediate problems; a place to stay and money, her only worry was Jean-Luc finding her. Her husband's power had taken on mythic strength as if he could bounce mirrors off the moon and see her in bed each night.

Leah remembered her father having her wish on the moon. "I wish I had a gun," she said to the moon. "And while you're at it, keep both my husband and King Kong away from me. In fact, if you have to send one or the other, make it King Kong." The full moon just hung in the sky. Leah reached up and pulled the curtain across the window, batted her pillow until it was comfortable, and closed her eyes. She fell asleep faster than she had expected.

The weather had changed. Nights were chilly.

In November it began raining. The river bed that split the old village from the new one filled, hiding the rocks that had been dry all summer. The creek near the caravan could be heard gurgling all night. Leah would rest in bed and listen, thinking of it as music.

The old lady sent Leah to the village for more rennet to make goat's cheese. Leah put on her yellow slicker with its hood and boots for the twenty minute walk. Passing an art supply store, the familiar Rembrandt oils caught her eye. They were glued in a mosaic to a backdrop. Brushes and other supplies were arranged on clear plastic shelves.

The owner stood inside the door which opened as a customer left. He caught Leah's eye. *"Bonjour."* He spoke with an accent, Australian or South African, Leah wasn't sure. "Can I help you?"

"I used to be an artist," Leah said.

"Once an artist, always an artist," he said.

Madame Perez had filled Leah in on all the merchants. She'd described this man as the decadent foreigner, a lover of men, desecrator of God's will. It was kinder than some of her other descriptions.

"Come in. Look around."

Leah did. The first thing she saw were miniature canvases. Her fingers itched to get around a brush, but she wanted to do something different from anything she'd done before. She couldn't go backwards. Then she spied a sign, "Cloth painting supplies." The store owner showed her the squat bottles marked Dupont paint.

"Can I smell them?" she asked.

He undid the bottle of salmon pink and held it under her nose. It had a soft smell, slightly metallic.

When she left the store she had everything she needed: a roll of silk, brace, paints, brushes, fixative. For a moment she felt like she'd bought salad fixings because the paint bottles were named artichoke green, grapefruit yellow, grape, cherry. Carrying the plastic bag, she passed up the temptation to dance on the wet sidewalk as she belted out "I'm Singing in the Rain." If she had, she wouldn't have been surprised if an orchestra picked up the melody and accompanied her. Instead she restrained herself.

Not due back for another hour, she decided to look at magazines: maybe get some ideas for her first silk painting. It had been a while since she had last been there because the store no longer carried foreign newspapers. Tourists were sparse, a couple here or there getting away for a long weekend, but they were almost always French with no interest in international papers. Leah hadn't wanted to call attention to herself by ordering one.

Usually she approached the store on the same side of the sidewalk, but today coming from the art store, she was across the street. She looked up and saw a second sign next to the red plume: a fishing pole and gun against a yellow background. She knew half the floor space was devoted to fishing gear because she had to march by poles and a table of lures to get to the magazines.

"The store is for hunting and fishing. They must sell guns, too. Fantastic," she said. The reminder that she lived in danger dampened her spirits more than her leaky boots had dampened her feet.

For two weeks Leah cased the store daily by buying a magazine, a notebook or envelopes. She checked for detection devices, alarms, other exits.

She visited a private detective in Perpignan and bought a lock pick from him. When he looked at her strangely she explained how she had an old locked trunk in her attic. He looked as if he didn't believe her. Leah didn't care. After Madame Perez was in bed nights, she practiced picking her bicycle lock.

On the fourth Thursday in November she was ready. At two in the morning, dressed in her black jogging outfit, she let herself out of the caravan and walked into town. The smell of smoke from fireplaces hung heavily in the air. The rain had stopped, but the wind, *La Tramantane*, was picking up. No one was around. The *gendarmerie* was closed at night, another fact she'd checked.

Going to the alley behind the store, Leah ran her credit card between the jamb and door. She'd noticed earlier the lock was the same as Madame Perez's, and she'd doubled-checked on her employer's door to make sure the credit card would work as well as it did in the detective stories she'd read. She moved as fast as she could to the front of the store and up the stairs where she knew the guns were kept. She had been there when a new *gendarme* had come in to buy his weapon.

Her bag, containing her tools, hung heavily on her shoulder.

At the back of the upper story was a locked case. She pulled the pick from her bag. Although she had a flashlight she felt safer not to use it in case someone going by looked up and saw a light.

The wind howled outside. Had she known it would be blowing so loudly, she could have used an electric saw. She stabbed and twisted, twisted and stabbed with her pick. The lock wouldn't give.

"Shit, it works in books," she said to herself.

The several shotguns and hand-guns rested in the case so close to her and yet so out of her reach.

The clock struck three. Soon the baker would come in to his bakery next door to start making his bread. She crept out the back locking the door behind her. Walking home she felt vulnerable. Maybe I'll just have to stay vulnerable, she thought. I give up. I'll stay unarmed.

"You look like hell," Madame Perez said the next morning.

Leah agreed with her. She was exhausted from lack of sleep. When she returned to the caravan she trembled thinking of the risks she'd taken for nothing. *Nothing!*

"Today is the day," Madame Perez said. "I'm finally going to throw out my husband's things. Or rather you are." She snorted. "He won't be coming back. Must be dead by now, I hope."

Monsieur Polli had whispered to Leah that Monsieur Perez had been a *gendarme*. After years of his wife's nagging, instead of reporting for his afternoon shift, he got on a train and never was seen again. It was the day the May 1968 riots started in Paris.

Leah had seen the dusty masculine clothes, some in tatters from years of moths' snacking on them hanging in the closet of the back bedroom.

"What do you want me to do with everything?" she asked the old lady.

"Whatever you want. I am going to watch television."

The woman hobbled through the hall, her cane thudding on the tiles.

Working will at least keep me awake, Leah thought and began emptying the armoire. Her hands were coated with the dust. She choked.

Getting a chair she climbed to get a metal file off the top shelf. Probably papers, she thought and debated whether to interrupt Madame Perez or not. If the woman hadn't needed the things in twenty-two years, she probably wouldn't need them now.

It took the better part of the morning to get everything into a big pile.

After Madame Perez called frequent complaints about hunger

from the living room, Leah stopped. As she cracked eggs into a bowl, she imagined her employer's face on each one.

"Omelettes? Again?" Madame Perez asked stabbing at her plate and pushing bits of yellow around with her fork. "You're trying to choke my arteries."

Leah said nothing. Finishing her own lunch, she removed the dishes and helped the elderly woman to her room for her nap. As much as she'd have loved a nap herself she went back into the unused bedroom to finish. She put the clothes into sky blue trash bags, fastening each with a yellow tie.

"I can use the file box for paint supplies," Leah said. Opening it, her face broke into a smile. Inside was Monsieur Perez's gun, holster and hundreds of bullets.

She hummed as she carried it to the caravan, amazed at fate bringing her what she needed, when she needed it. All her plotting and planning to acquire a gun to protect herself and one had been within grabbing distance.

Once inside her cocoon, she examined the weapon, loaded it and slipped it under her pillow.

That night in bed she imagined if Jean-Luc were to walk in, how she would grab the lump under her pillow and protect herself. "Could I shoot the father of my children?" she asked, her voice sounding hollow in the empty caravan. A real gun, one that kills, was different than the imagined one she had been looking for. Yet, there was a level of relaxation that she had not felt since before she left Switzerland.

However, one thing bothered her. Could the gun go off on its own? She tried putting it in a drawer and timed herself on how fast she could pull it out. Too slow. Her solution was to put the gun as far away from her head as possible.

The wind outside howled, twisting and thrusting the branches of the trees outside her window. Their shadows cast on the wall opposite her bunk resembled a man throwing his arms open. It reminded her of how she'd run into Michael's bear hug greetings. Although she might have expected regrets or sadness at the thought, what she felt at that moment was very, very different.

"Damn you for leaving me." The intensity of her anger left her shaking, shocking her. No matter how she punched her pillow and tossed in her sleeping bag it took her a long, long time to fall asleep. Every time she almost dropped off, the past intruded, jerking her awake.

Chapter Eight:
The Whole Truth
Stonefield, MA
1961–1962

Leah slammed her locker door. It hadn't closed right since Steven had kicked it. The corridor was dark. The neon light bulb had blown. Hugging her books to her chest she turned and saw Steven.

He hugged her. "Hi. You thought more about trying out?"

"We've been over and over it. I haven't time."

"You're probably the only high school girl in America that doesn't want to be a cheerleader."

"Probably." She glanced at her watch. "I'm late."

"So am I. Stop by for me after practice?"

Steve pecked her on the nose.

Leah rushed of in the direction of the art room. It smelled of oil paint. Michael DelAngelo dipped brushes into turpentine. Seeing her, he smiled. Most Stonefield High girls would have sold their souls for that smile. Enrollments in his art classes were over-subscribed with teenage girls.

"Hi, Indian Girl. How's it going?" he asked.

He gave nicknames to most students. Hers was easy since she often wore a beaded headband around her forehead holding her long black hair in place.

She dropped her books on a table, put on her smock and went to the easel that he'd left set up for her. She shrugged.

"Steve?" he asked.

She nodded.

"You don't have to enter *The Globe* Art Contest. There's still time to try out for cheerleader."

She squeezed yellow, white, blue and red paint onto her palette, smushing them around until they matched the colors on her canvas. Instead of working, she placed the palette on the stool.

"Sometimes I think I'm abnormal."

He capped the turpentine jar then pulled a chair next to her. "You look normal. For an Indian."

"No, I mean I don't like doing the things my friends do," she said.

"Like?" He threw his leg over the chair and rested his head on the back.

"You know. Shopping. Talking about boys."

Thank goodness, her skin was too dark to blush. "I don't even have a subscription to *Seventeen*, for God's sake."

She thought about the amount of time her friends spent trying to find out where the art teacher lived or if he had a girlfriend. Picking up her brush, she stabbed at the canvas. The color looked wrong.

He plucked the brush from her hand. "Work is a good escape, but don't take your problems out on this." Going to the supply closet, he took out a fresh canvas. "Slash at that."

The smell of leaves burning tickled Leah's nose as she walked into the football stadium. She could see her breath. She wore a heavy coat over her obligatory going-to-football-games costume of knee socks, black Bermudas, and blazer and red sweater, the school colors.

Gail and Janet, waiting at the gate, were dressed the same way. "I'll die if they lose today. The last game of the season and all," Gail said. "Peter will be so depressed." Since Gail started dating Peter Pronk, her speech was peppered with the gospel according to him. "How do you handle it when Steve is upset about a game?"

"I don't. It's his problem," Leah said. They handed in their tickets.

Janet slapped her forehead. "But he's the junior football captain." Her tone would have been no less reverent if she were talking about President Kennedy. Probably Kennedy would produce less reverence for Janet's family was even more Republican than Leah's.

"Sometimes I think you're nuts. Next year you could be a cheerleader, he'll be captain, you'll be Rainbow Worthy Advisor. He'll head DeMolay. You'd be the class couple to end all class couples."

The crowd pushed them through the gate. The stands of both Stonefield and the visitors' side were almost filled. The girls scrambled up the bleachers and wormed their way to a free spot. Waving their pennants, they watched as Stonefield High School's band led in the team, cheerleaders and baton squad. Then Woburn's team entered. Everyone stood for the "Star Spangled Banner" before the two sides lined up for the kickoff.

"Look," Janet said. Her voice was a squeal.

"There's Mr. DelAngelo. He's with a girl." Leah looked. The woman had dark hair, teased and fastened with a headband, reminding her of Priscilla Presley.

"He's so beautiful. Just like Sal Mineo," Gail said. She'd mentioned that at least twenty times since she and Peter had seen *Exodus*.

"I wonder if it's his wife," Janet said. "She looks a little trampy with that white lipstick, don't you think?" Before they could rule on a tramp quotient or Leah could answer, the crowd screamed as Stonefield scored its first touchdown.

"Steve's going to kick the point. Aren't you proud, Leah? I'd just die if Peter was doing it," Gail said.

The cheerleaders yelled, "Give me another one just like the

other one." The crowd picked up the chant. "Give me another one just like the other one."

A few snowflakes fell. Leah wrapped her black and red scarf around her neck an extra time.

"Leah, you're his pet. Go ask him who he's with?" Gail said.

"I'm going for a hot chocolate. If I run into him, fine. If not, fine, too," Leah said.

Everyone standing on seats, holding arms and swaying back and forth as they sang the school song, made Leah feel seasick as she pushed her way to the stairs.

The line at the refreshment stand was nonexistent. The cop on duty drank a cup of coffee and stamped his feet.

"Can I buy you something, Indian Girl?"

Leah jumped as Mr. DelAngelo stepped in front of her. The woman by his side smiled.

"Rosalie, meet my best pupil."

"You must be Leah Stockbridge. My brother's told me so much about you."

When Leah got back into the stands she said to Janet and Gail, "It's his girlfriend." She had no idea why she lied.

The car windows fogged up. Snow and leaves blew around the car. Steve and Leah had left the victory dance early. He had unbuttoned her blouse.

She rebuttoned it. "Please," he said.

"We'd better go. My parents will be worried."

"Your curfew isn't for another hour."

"Think of the brownie points I'll get for getting home early."

He put his tongue in her mouth. She liked that, and let him dry hump her until he collapsed. He straightened up and slid under the wheel. The car choked and started. He backed out of the cluster of trees onto the road.

When they drove into Leah's yard, the porch light was on.

"How long do we have before it starts to flash?"

"Five minutes," she said.

"Three," he said.

"Bet ya a soda at Torre's."

"You're on," he said.

Leah picked up his wrist and sat it on her knee. They both stared at the watch. Four minutes later the light flashed on and off.

"Draw," Steve said. He walked Leah to the porch.

"Want some hot chocolate?" Grace asked as the couple entered the living room. Snow melted in their hair, leaving little sparkles as the light caught the droplets.

Alexander sat next to the fireplace, *The New England Lawyer's Journal* in his lap. A few embers glowed among the ashes. Two empty cups sat on the coffee table between *Boston Globe*s and *Time* magazines. Although he was still dressed in a fisherman knit sweater and cords, Grace wore a blue quilted bathrobe and matching booties. Her makeup was still on.

"I better get home. My parents will worry what with the snow." Steve said. "Talk to you tomorrow." He chucked Leah on the chin.

"Nice time?" Alexander asked.

Leah kissed the top of his head. Taking off her coat she was about to drop it on the chair until she saw her mother shake her head. She hung it in the closet. "Good night, folks."

Grace followed Leah to her room. As Leah picked up a hair brush, Grace said, "Steve is a nice boy, but don't let him go too far. Remember, a man doesn't buy a cow if he gets the milk for free."

Leah wanted to say as she did each time her mother said that, "Men don't buy cars without a test drive," but edited herself. Instead she said, "I'm not a cow, Mummy."

"You know what I mean." Grace glanced at the pile of clothes hiding the chair. "Tomorrow pick up your room. For all I know I've another child buried under that pile. Then Monday we'll go shopping for a dress for the Christmas Assembly Ball."

Leah groaned. "You go. I promise to wear whatever you buy."

Had it not been required that all girls wear red, green or white, she'd have worn her blue formal from the Rainbow Cotillion. Usually she choose the first one she saw. Grace wanted her to try on everything in the store.

Digging through the clothes, she found her flannel pajamas. The only reason she was going to the ball for graduates of the D.A.R. dance class was that Steve had invited her. She worried Monsieur LeRoyer would remember the snake.

"I need every afternoon to finish that painting."

"You should spend as much time on your other subjects."

"I want to go to art school, not a university," Leah said. The idea had just popped into her head.

Or perhaps Mr. DelAngelo had planted it when he talked about his training at Mass College of Art.

"Take a look at Pissaro's use of color dots."

Mr. DelAngelo pointed to the photograph. "Of course, the real painting shows it better." Because the art room was in the basement, a snow drift cut the light coming in. He held the book under a lamp on his desk. Leah stood almost in touching distance, but when her sleeve brushed his he stepped away.

"Too bad I'll never see it," Leah said. The world floated just out of her reach. She pictured herself married with a station wagon, white washer and dryer, short hair. She saw Steve or a Steve look-alike coming in at night saying, "What's for dinner, honey?"

She imagined the older Steve or look-alike lose his temper, pick up a dish and throw it like Steve's father had done the week before. She felt for his class ring that she wore in a chain around her neck; the noose, she called it.

"It's at the Boston Museum of Fine Arts. Go in. See for yourself."

"I've never been to Boston by myself." Her mother felt with the country club, the new Peabody Mall, their own pool and tennis court—everything the family needed was right near Stonefield. "No need to visit a dirty city," she'd say.

Alexander, who went into the Boston and Cambridge Courts as necessary, was content to stay home nights and weekends. A swim, his garden, a game of tennis or golf was enough.

"Come next Saturday," Mr. DelAngelo said. "I'll show you."

"Tell me which train. I'll meet you."

Leah got off the train after her first train ride. She thought of the French impressionists paintings of Parisian stations. Although North Station was smaller and more wooden than the prints she'd seen, she shivered with excitement, as she pretended she was in Paris for a moment. Then she looked around but saw no one. Her next shiver was of fear. She had no idea how to find anything in the city.

"Going my way, Indian Girl?" a voice said. She turned. Mr. DelAngelo in khakis and a Mass College of Art campus jacket and baseball hat took her by the elbow. He directed her toward the street.

They passed a store selling Boston Celtic and Bruins memorabilia. "Ever been to a basketball or hockey game here?"

Leah shook her head. Her father went to a Celtics playoff once, but there was never any suggestion of anyone else going. He'd brought a Bill Russell poster home for Chucky.

They caught a Greenline E car to the Museum. At the entrance she was given a little blue button with a number three to pin on her shirt. At the foot of a marble staircase he asked, "What's your desire? Impressionist, Egyptian mummies, medieval . . ."

"Pissaro, Van Gogh, Renoir, Manet, Monet, and every other painting in the Museum." For the next three hours, Leah followed her art teacher from gallery to gallery. She veered off as they passed a Paul Revere silver bowl.

"After learning that stupid poem, I never thought I'd see something he touched," she said.

"Listen my children and you shall hear of the midnight ride of Paul Revere . . ." he quoted.

"You had to learn it too?"

"Learn it? I live across the street from his house," Mr. Del-Angelo said. He pointed at a painting of a mother hugging her child. "That's a Mary Cassatt, an American who moved to Paris. Her subjects were women, babies, home, etc."

Leah stopped in front of a second painting of women sipping tea. The wallpaper behind them was stripped. She wanted to sit down and talk with them as she drank tea with them. How much more interesting these paintings were than those of Madonnas and Christs. This was real life of another time.

"Are you going to get it?" Chucky asked when Leah walked in the door.

She had made her way home directly from the station. She wished she could have a cup of tea from Mary Cassatt's tea party. A piece of lemon cake would go down well too.

"Get in here, Leah," Alexander said from the doorway of his den. "Where were you?"

In front of the book-lined walls Grace, her face blotched, sat on the couch. Her grandmother was in the easy chair, her arms folded.

"I said I'd be back by five. It's only four thirty. What's wrong?"

"Where were you?" Grace stood up and shut the door in Chucky's face.

A series of lies flashed through Leah's mind. "I'd never been on a train, so I thought I'd take one."

"Train? Are you crazy?" Grace asked. "They're so dirty."

Leah was tempted to point out her mother hadn't been on a train within her memory, but didn't.

"Where did you go, honey?" her grandmother asked.

"Boston? Boston? Alone? You could have been kidnapped," Grace said.

"That's a bit of an exaggeration," Alexander said. "What possessed you to sneak off?"

Leah couldn't figure out what the big deal was. In two years she'd be a student in the city, although her parents didn't know that yet. She didn't understand her mother's attitude either. When Janet's mother went in last week to meet an old college friend for lunch, Grace had said that there were plenty of good restaurants on the North Shore.

"I just wanted to," was the only thing she could think of to say.

"And you knew if you asked, we'd say no," Grace said. "We'd never have known if Mrs. Stickler hadn't seen you get on the train."

Leah thought of all her choices. Admitting she was wrong seemed the best. "I'm sorry."

"You'll be sorrier. You're grounded until February," Alexander said.

"I've been grounded, Steve," Leah said, when he met her outside home room.

"Does that include the Christmas Ball?" When Leah nodded he said, "But I already bought the tickets. They cost $15."

Janet walked by and waved. Leah had an idea. "Take Janet."

"I'd like my ring back," Steve said. He caught Leah as she headed into the art room.

"Sure." She reached into her bag. "I've been meaning to give it to you."

Steve hadn't given her a Christmas present and had taken Janet not only to the Christmas Ball but Peter Pronk's New Year's Eve party. He'd stopped telephoning Leah.

Gail, five minutes before, had told her that both she and Janet had been made cheerleaders.

When Leah dropped the ring in Steve's hand, he pocketed it, and nodded. "See ya around."

Leah went into the art room.

"Sorry, I couldn't help hearing. Are you feeling hurt?" Mr. DelAngelo asked.

"I feel free," she said.

When she'd been painting about fifteen minutes, she put down her brush. "You know what bothers me?"

Her art teacher shook his head.

"My so called friends. I spent hours tutoring Janet so she'd pass French. And Gail and I don't hang out any more now that we aren't both football wives."

Mr. DelAngelo patted her shoulder.

CHAPTER NINE:
POWER POLITICS
STONEFIELD, MA
SPRING 1962–SPRING 1963

"As long as you live under my roof, you'll do as I say." Alexander slammed his hand on his desk. Leah sat in a leather chair, her arms folded. "Choose any college you want: Pembroke, Tufts, Bradford Junior if you don't want to do a full four years."

"I want the Museum School or RISDI." Although not given to pouting, Leah tried it to prove her point.

"Stick that lip in. Art school is no place to meet a good husband. And don't roll your eyes either." He sighed. "I only want what is best for you."

Leah said nothing. She knew he wanted the best for her, but what he thought was best and what she thought bore no relation to one another.

"I've lived a lot longer than you have, seen more things; the depression, the war."

Leah rolled her eyes.

"Don't give me that look, young lady. I know more than you do."

The sounds of "The Lion Sleeps Tonight" crashed down the stairs from Chucky's room. Hot in his first crush he played it incessantly, because his girlfriend liked it.

Leah fantasized the record in shards. Chucky slammed the door between the second round of owahs.

"If I were at art school, I wouldn't be under your roof," Leah said raising her voice several decibels.

Her father sat at his desk slapping a pencil against his hand as if he wished it were a ruler to be used for a spanking. "But I'm paying for it. Therefore, I make the decision. Give me credit for . . ."

She didn't wait to hear what she should give him credit for. Storming out, she headed for her rock that had been dropped by a departing glacier. It was the size of an elephant. A pine tree left it half shaded. She climbed to its flat back and lay on her stomach, as she did whenever she needed escape.

She let the hot May sun bake the anger into her pores. The smell of damp earth from last night's rain filled her nostrils. As she turned over and to look over the edge, she saw a snake, its green skin contrasting with the brown pine needles.

"It's a fact of life: the person with the money has the power," Mr. DelAngelo said after Leah asked his advice. He sat on his desk, one foot anchored to the floor, the other dangling as he watched her pace.

She knocked over an easel, catching it before it fell. "This is family."

"Families have power structures, too," he said. "Same rules as bigger society only with more emotion."

"Are you a Communist?"

The teacher looked at the open door. The corridor outside was empty. "Are you trying to get me fired?"

"I'm sorry." She perched on a stool and moved her hands as if she wanted to say something. Tears ran down her face. He got up and took her his handkerchief. For a moment he paused as if he were going to wipe her tears, but handed her the cloth instead.

"I get so frustrated," she said.

He nodded. "If you paid for school yourself and were willing to live in poverty for four years, you could put yourself through Mass College of Art. I did it with the G.I. Bill. But I lived with my mother."

Leah jumped off her stool, hugged him. "What a wonderful idea."

He pulled her away, but held her shoulders.

"Leah, you've no idea about poverty. You've your own car, for God's sake."

"It's four years old."

"Mine's six. You've never worked a day in your life."

"Watch me," she said.

Fred's Dry Cleaning didn't need any clerks. Taylor's hardware store only hired boys because they knew about tools, but Mr. Torre was tired of working alone. Dipping into the tubs of ice cream didn't help his fingers gnarled by arthritis.

"Well, I've known you since you were a little girl. Why not start Saturday?" His thick moustache, which he waxed until the ends curled, quivered.

He smelled of cigars, although he only smoked in the alley, saying, "Cigar odor doesn't marry well with ice cream."

"It won't hurt her, Grace," Alexander said. "Lots of kids work."

"But a soda jerk," Grace said. "She should be swimming and playing tennis. This is the time of life when she's free. What will our friends think?" In the next breath she told him. "They'll think we're having money problems."

At first Leah loved the smell of the ice cream, especially vanilla, when she handed cones over the counter. But each day before they closed the shop, as she scrubbed the freezer, the smell became less pleasant and more like sour milk. After the first week, she gave up eating ice cream.

"Thanks Mr. Johnson," Leah said to her customer as he stood by the cash register with his check for a cup of coffee. "By the way when your wife was in here the other day, she was really tempted by the fudge. Bet you'd make real brownie points, by buying her some. I can fix it up so it looks like a special gift."

The man nodded. "How about half a dozen pieces?"

Leah took a little red box with fluted edges and nestled the pieces then covered them with a piece of waxed paper. She fastened the box with a seal that had the name of the store on it.

After the bell on the door dinged and they were alone, Mr. Torre shook his head. "You're incredible. You got him to buy something else."

"I try and see how high I can get the order," Leah said. "It's a game to make the day pass."

"Well my sales are up from last year." He nodded his head a couple of times.

"How about a commission?"

"I'll think about it."

When Leah's father stopped in a few minutes later to see if she wanted a ride home, Mr. Torre said, "You've got a good kid, Mr. Stockbridge. Good worker."

Leah folded the cloth she used to wipe the counter into a gray wet square and took off her apron. "Hi Daddy. Mr. Torre is thinking of paying me a five percent commission."

The old man twirled his moustache. "One percent had crossed my mind."

"Tell you what. I'll say four, you'll say two so let's settle at three," Leah said, stacking the last of the silver ice cream dishes in front of the mirror that covered the wall behind the counter.

"Deal," Mr. Torre said.

Leah opened a bank account. Except for art supplies every penny she earned went into it. To save money she bought miniature canvases. Sitting on the big rock in the late afternoon light, she'd paint a leaf, a tree, a group of pebbles, moss. If Chucky wasn't home, she'd be accompanied by birds. When he was home, and the wind was wrong, "A Lion Sleeps Tonight" drowned out the birds.

"I'll miss you when school starts," Mr. Torre said the last week in August.

"Can't I work part time, Saturdays and stuff?"

"If your grades slip, your father will hang me out to dry."

"They won't."

"Friday afternoons and Saturdays. I get to see your report card, too."

"This is ridiculous, Leah. You should be at football games, not making sodas and sandwiches," Grace said as she got out the family's fall clothes. She held a skirt up to Leah. "I think you've stopped growing. Everything still fits."

Instead of arguing, Leah picked up an Irish knit sweater her grandmother had given her for Christmas. "Well, I probably won't be working every Saturday, Mummy. I just feel so sorry for Mr. Torre with his arthritis. Have you seen his hands?"

"You can't take on other people's cares," Grace said. She noticed a moth hole in Leah's red cashmere. She counted the moth balls in the trunk that was almost empty now that last year's woolens were piled on Leah's bed. "Should have been enough to kill an army of moths," she said. Searching in her sewing box she found a sample of yarn that had come with the sweater. Within minutes the hole was invisible.

"Thanks Mummy, I love that sweater." Leah kissed her mother's cheek.

The kids gathered at Torre's after the football game. Janet was there with Steve's arm draped around her shoulder. He got up from the bench.

"Hi Leah, two strawberry sodas. Going to the victory dance tonight?"

Looking over Steve's shoulder, she saw Janet watching. "I don't know."

"I'll dance with you. You haven't had a date since we broke up."

"Gee thanks. That will be seventy cents." She didn't say, "No extra charge for your nerve." Leah didn't go to the dance. She painted a miniature of a candle, its wax dripping down a pewter candlestick holder. Before she went to bed, she checked her bank account. It had $350. It would cover her tuition, but not much more. She had eleven more months to work.

"In the jungle the . . ." was interrupted by the phone. Chucky was closest. "Leah, it's for you." She put down the essay on *Candide* she was writing for French VI and went to the hall. The music started again as she said hello.

"Hi, Leah, it's me. Can I come over?"

"My parents are at the country club, Steve. Grammy has gone to bed with a headache. Not a good idea."

"I wish you'd talk to me."

"Talk to Janet."

"Janet is boring."

"I've a lot of homework. See you in class." The phone clicked.

"Leave my boyfriend alone," Janet said. She'd cornered Leah as they hung up their coats in their gray metal lockers. Although it was Saturday morning, the senior class had descended on the school to take their SATs and Achievements.

"Janet, he's yours. I don't want him." Leah turned to leave but Janet blocked her way. She grabbed Leah's pocketbook and shook its contents out and threw the bag on the floor and walked away.

Leah banged her hand against her locker door, picturing Janet's nose, melting under her fist.

Breathing deeply, she bent down and picked up her wallet, her hair brush, sketch pad, pencil sharpener and the three No.2 lead pencils she'd need to fill in lots of little boxes over the next few hours.

Concentrate on what's important, not that bitch, she told herself. She had done fine on the practice tests last spring. This is a right of passage, like menstruation, she thought as she filed into the auditorium with the other college-bound seniors.

They sat, some drumming with their pencils, others rustling around trying to get comfortable. Each chair had a board that could be pulled out from the arm making a half desk to write on.

Leah chose one with a left board to accommodate her left-handedness. There weren't too many, but after four years of study halls in this place, she knew every one.

"I still want to deck her," she said to herself.

Steve pushed by to the empty seat next to her. The row was almost filled. Shit, I don't need this, Leah thought.

Janet was in the section in front of them. She hadn't turned around. I could flirt with him to make her jealous, but then I'd be stuck with him, she thought. She sharpened her pencils, giving a few quick turns, then testing the point.

The proctor, a student teacher, walked onto the stage. He wore thick glasses and was already beginning to lose his hair and he always acted like students would attack at any moment. "Leave a seat in between each of you," he said. No one moved. He repeated it with only a slight less of a quaver in his voice.

Leah got and walked to the front row where no one else wanted to sit and where was another left hand desk. She didn't check out if Steve moved. Later she saw him eating lunch with

Janet before the afternoon Achievements. She'd signed up for three: French, History and English. Mass Art only required the SATs. The places her father wanted her to go asked for both.

Leah knocked on her parents' door. Alexander was reading *Advise and Consent,* propped up with pillows against the massive head board. "Can I talk to you, Daddy? Before Mommy comes up to bed."

He patted the quilt that Abigail had made. Because she was in socks Leah stepped from braided rug to braided rug avoiding the cold floor boards.

"What is it, Kitten?"

"I still really want to go to art school."

Alexander sat up a little straighter and ran his hand through his hair. He still had a full head with graying temples that would make him a perfect Gregory Peck or Clark Gable stand-in. "We've been through all that."

"I could take commercial art."

"Leah, a woman goes to college to find a husband. Who will you meet in art school? I'll tell you who. Someone who'll expect you to live in a loft, that's who. Poverty kills love."

A tear rolled down Leah's cheek. She brushed it away.

"It's not a terrible thing to get a liberal arts education," he said. "Trust me."

Leah kissed her father on the forehead. "Night, Daddy."

Leah found a parking place in front of the Reading post office. She passed the fountain as she ran up the stairs on the left side. Inside she rented a post office box. While she was there she mailed her application to Massachusetts College of Art, listing her new P.O. box as her return address. Her father's forged signature was below her own. She would have loved to apply to the Rhode Island School of Design, but there was no way she could have afforded that on her own.

"They've got to accept me," Leah said to Mr. DelAngelo on Valentine's day. "Every other college has. Why are they taking so long?"

"How should I know? I did my part. I wrote a great recommendation and mentioned how you were a finalist in the '62 *Boston Globe* Art Contest."

Leah shuddered thinking about the next half hour. Every time she drove to Reading she was afraid she'd find a rejection in the box. "Come with me when I check the box."

"I can't," he said.

"You're my guide."

"I'm your teacher and it isn't a good idea for teachers to be alone with students."

"We are alone in the art room."

"With the door open. Always. Sometimes, Leah, I can understand your father's frustration." However, he smiled as he said it. "Go check your mail."

Leah turned the key to her post office box. She pulled out an announcement of specials at the Atlantic Supermarket announcing low prices on lamb chops and Green Giant canned corn. Underneath was an envelope with the state seal. She carried it to her car, a 1958 gold and white Chevy. She sat behind the wheel holding the envelope. Twice she started to open it, but stopped. Finally she tore it open. "Yahoo!" she yelled.

She went to Winslow's, a food store and coffee shop across from the train station.

"Phone?" she asked the guy behind the counter.

He pointed to the back of the store next to the soft drink case filled with Coca-Cola, Pepsi and Dr Pepper. Several phone books from different regions with dog-eared pages were tied with string to a metal bar bolted to the binding then fastened by a chain to the side of the booth.

Leah thumbed through the Boston City one until she found the D's. Shaking, she put in her dime and dialed. A woman with a heavy accent answered.

"Can I speak to Michael DelAngelo, please?"

"He isn't here. He's still at school."

"Could I leave a message?"

"Of course."

"Tell him Leah Stockbridge was accepted. He'll understand."

Instead of going into the house, Leah, dressed in shorts and ice cream–stained blouse, dove into the pool. Chlorine stung her eyes, as the water sucked heat and fatigue from her body. She swam a lap before splaying out on the rubber raft. Shutting her eyes, she let her hand trail in the water.

"You're home," Abigail called from the bay window in the dining room overlooking the pool. Although Leah couldn't see her, she pictured her grandmother standing among the plants that filled the bay.

"Just got here." She hoped she wouldn't get a lecture about not changing into her bathing suit.

"If it weren't your birthday, I'd talk about bathing suits," Abigail said. "Supper is in fifteen minutes. Corn on the cob. Fresh from the garden."

Leah paddled to the edge of the pool and went into the house.

"Happy birthday to you," the family sang as Mrs. Stickler carried a confetti angel cake to the table. Eighteen candles burned on top. Leah blew. The candles flickered and went out. Six came back. She blew again, they went out and flared up. On the fifth try, she plucked them from the cake and tipped them into her water glass. "Whose idea was the joke candles?"

Chucky waved.

"Guess I don't get my wish, thanks to you, baby brother."

"What was it, Honey?" Abigail asked.

"I'm not going to say, just in case." Leah turned to open her presents stacked on the buffet behind Alexander. Each was wrapped a different designed paper with ribbon.

Grace's was done with up with that special fold where she didn't need to use scotch tape to fasten the wrapping. Leah held up the blue watch plaid slacks with a matching blue sweater set and looked in the mirror over the buffet. "They're lovely, Mummy. I'll try them on later."

Her father had given her *The Group*. "Last chance for a good lazy read before you start classes with all that required reading," he said.

Abigail handed her a tiny box wrapped in violet-covered paper. Leah pulled the purple ribbon. Inside was a circle pin, her initial L in the middle and a pearl. "Thank you, Grammy," she said.

Chucky gave her a Snoopy poster. The matching Snoopy greeting card read, "For your dorm."

"Thank-you everyone," she said. She thought of asking why no one listened when she had told them all she wanted for her birthday was art supplies. Manners overruled desire.

After dinner the family sat on the porch reading and listening to the sounds of insects and birds. As it grew dark, fireflies flashed. Leah thought of all the hot summer nights she and Chucky ran around catching and putting them in jars to keep as night lights by their beds. They had always awoken to dead fireflies.

First Abigail said, "Think I'll turn in and pretend to read." The family knew within minutes, a book would be flat on her chest, her glasses and light would still be on and Abigail would be giving her regular little putt-putts that eventually would become rip roaring snores.

Chucky and Grace followed after. Only Alexander and Leah remained. "Daddy, we need to talk."

"Go ahead, Kitten."

"I still want to go to art school." Alexander picked up his pipe and stuffed it with tobacco, tamping it down with the tool that he kept in his pants' pocket. Leah remembered how she'd overheard him telling a new secretary in his law office that he used it as a buying-time technique while she waited for him to finish work. He lit it and drew in his breath until the tobacco in the bowl glowed bright then subsided. "But you've told Pembroke you're coming."

"Only because you made me."

"It's too late." He started folding *The Boston Globe* that he'd been reading before it grew dark.

Her mother had asked him to not throw it out. She wanted to cut out an article marking the anniversary of Marilyn Monroe's death as well as a blueberry cake recipe from "Confidential Chat" the only part of the newspaper that Grace read word for word. Her mother had many scrapbooks full of eclectic clippings including each time Leah's name had appeared in the *Stonefield Chronicle* as being on the honor roll.

"I've been accepted at Mass Art."

"I don't want to hear another word." He gathered his tobacco pouch, lighter and tucked the newspaper under his arm.

"I'm going to go. I have the money," she said as he started to leave.

"Don't be ridiculous." He went inside.

When Leah arrived home from work the next afternoon, Grace asked. "Have you energy to go to North Shore for school clothes? I also need to get a wedding present for Steve and Janet, stupid kids."

No one could say Steve and Janet these days without adding "stupid kids." Stupid kids couldn't control themselves. Stupid kids ruined their lives.

Leah swallowed her comments about Steve buying the cow even if he got the milk for free. Considering how mad her parents would be when she moved out in three weeks, she didn't want to add the expense of a new wardrobe to her guilt. "Mummy, I don't want you buying me clothes."

"Don't be ridiculous. You can't start college with high school clothes."

"Why don't I wait to see what others have. My first weekend home we can go shopping." If you let me come home, she thought. "Besides, the shopping mall will be mobbed, and prices will be lower after school starts."

Leah slipped into Boston, praying all the way she wouldn't have an accident with the family car. She had spent days studying maps, hoping she wouldn't get lost in the city.

Within four hours she found an apartment in a three-story brownstone within walking distance of the art school. She loved the name of the street. Wigglesworth. Silly name. The apartment, on the top floor, had a bay window in the living room—good light for painting—a small kitchen, bedroom, and the best part was the cost—$75 a month. An old lady, the owner, lived underneath. A couple lived on the first floor. He was at Harvard Medical, her new landlady said. An A student. The wife worked as a secretary somewhere. The landlady didn't know for sure because she'd just changed jobs.

"They're nice. You'll like them," the old woman added.

Then Leah found a job making sodas at Sparr's, the neighborhood drugstore. It was between her apartment and the school and everything was within minutes of each other. She wouldn't waste time commuting and she would even have to pay for a T. She hummed the Kingston Trio's song about Charlie on the MTA. She wouldn't get stuck because she lacked a nickel to get off. What she did lack was her parents' okay and on her checklist of things she needed to do was to convince her parents.

August 28th—two days before moving. Leah tried repeatedly to talk with Alexander. "Don't start," were the words most often heard.

August 29th—when Grace shopped with Chucky for his school clothes and supplies and Abigail visited a friend, Leah carried most of her personal possessions to the car, the station wagon. Her mother had borrowed Leah's Ford sedan because she was trying to decide to keep it in place of the station wagon since Leah couldn't take it with her to Pembroke. Freshmen weren't allowed cars. Leah hadn't expected to be lucky enough to have Abigail's friend pick her up leaving the station wagon free. She left a note saying she was running some last minute errands, since she had failed to ask permission to use the car in advance. That breach of the rules would be minor in comparison to what was coming.

Mrs. O'Brien, her landlady, had said she could move her things in, even if her rent didn't start until the first.

At the Salvation Army she bought a table, chair and all the dishes, pots, pans, knives and forks she would need. At Zayre's she found a sleeping bag and towels. At a factory outlet she found a flawed mattress and decided to do without a pillow. Her $922.13 bank balance had dwindled to $618.20.

September 1st—Light flooded Leah's window. From her bed she saw blue sky between green pines.

Grace knocked at the open bedroom door. "Get up lazy bones, we need to get you packed." Leah didn't want to deal with this before brushing her teeth. Her mother entered carrying the front half of a trunk by the side strap. Mrs. Stickler held onto the back.

Grace opened Leah's dresser drawers, one after another. They contained one bra, three pairs of panties, cut off jeans and a T-shirt. She opened Leah's closet. Only a sun dress hung there.

"Where are your clothes? They aren't in the laundry."

"I already moved most things into Boston, Mummy."

"You what?"

Leah explained.

Fifteen minutes later Alexander's car landed in the driveway. The car door slammed then the screen door. Leah sat in the living room, her hands in her lap, trying to stay calm.

"You're going to Pembroke. That's all there is to it," Alexander hollered as he walked in.

Leah shuddered. It was the first time she had heard her father raise his voice to that volume. Usually, he let it grow softer when angry until she had to strain to catch each word.

Leah tried the explanation she'd practiced in front of the mirror when there was no one to hear. "You said, as long as I was under your roof and you paid the bills, I'd have to do as you say. Well, I met your conditions. I won't be under your roof. I'm paying my own way."

Grace dabbed her eyes with her handkerchief. "We should never have let you work."

"Shut up, Grace," Alexander said.

"Don't tell me to shut up."

"I'll handle this," Alexander said.

"You've done a rotten job so far," Grace yelled.

Leah hoped they'd fight with each other forgetting her. No such luck. They came back at her full force, yelling, cajoling then yelling again. When she knew they'd never give in, she stood up. "I love you both, but it's my life, not yours," and walked out of the room. Taking her jacket from the coat rack next to the door, she put her keys on the table next to a photo.

Abigail sat in the middle with Grace and Alexander on each side. Leah and Chucky stood behind their grandmother. As

Leah shut the door to walk to the train, she heard Alexander say to Grace, "She'll never get a penny from me until she sees reason."

Chapter Eleven:
Promises are for Keeping
BOSTON, MA
FALL 1963

Leah couldn't decide what she loved most about her life as an art student. She went from color studio to her elements of design class then to three dimensional art in a whirl. Ideas rushed into her head, a torrent impossible to dam. She'd run from class to work and then home to paint. Many nights when she looked at the clock, she'd realize that it was well after midnight, and she'd forgotten to eat again. When she let herself, she felt sad her parents hadn't understood, but she could imagine herself doing nothing other than what she was doing.

"Sugah, Sugah," the fat man called out. "Sugah sweet cohn. Last of the season." His hair stood up in the early fall wind as he arranged the ears on his cart overloaded with fall vegetables. His breath puffed white from his mouth in the early morning air.

"How much?" Leah asked. The corn would be good eaten on the cob tonight and in chowder the rest of the week. When she tested an exposed kernel with her finger nail, it oozed milky liquid. Fresh. Not quite like from her father's garden, but as close as she would get. For a moment a wave of homesicknesses rode through her being, but only for a moment. She suspected that sometime in the future her parents would accept what she was trying to do. It was a matter of waiting them out.

"Dozen ears, seventy cents. Hey, I don't like Chinks touching my produce," he barked at a woman. She was dressed as any peasant would be if they worked in the fields near the Great Wall.

The Chinese woman dropped the ear that she'd picked up. Leah put hers down at the same time.

The small woman scuttled away with her used Stop&Shop bag clutched in her left hand.

"Guess you don't like white girls touching either?"

"That's different. How many ears you want?" he asked, one hand on a bag the other on the corn.

"None," Leah said. "I don't do business with bigots."

Haymarket was almost deserted. Some merchants were still unpacking peppers, pumpkins and the first gourds of the season. In another hour it would be next to impossible to push through the crowds between the produce-laden carts.

"How much?" she asked the lady behind another cart as she pointed to the corn.

"Sixty cents a dozen." Her gray hair was covered with a scarf that tied at the back of the neck.

"Take it, it's a good buy," a voice said behind Leah.

She turned. "Mr. DelAngelo." Her voice was almost a squeal.

"In the flesh, Indian Girl."

"What are you doing here?" they asked together.

"Shopping," they said together.

Together they bought a bushel of tomatoes for Michael's mother to make what he called gravy and Leah would have called spaghetti sauce. Then they bought bananas and cheese for Leah.

"Let me buy you an espresso?" he said.

"I've never had espresso," she said. "I've read about it."

"You're in for a treat. You can tell me about school."

He led her under the overhead expressway's army-green girders as cars and trucks rattled overhead. He turned into the North End with its narrow roads and brick three-story houses abutting the sidewalk. The smell of baking, onions, and coffee mixed with gasoline fumes.

Leah saw a grocery window with a chicken hanging dead by its neck and a rabbit skinned except for fur on its feet. Long strands of pasta hung from a broom handle suspended the full length of another window. Under the strands were porcelain bowls with blue and yellow sunflowers.

As her senses absorbed this strange new world, Mr. DelAngelo propelled her into a small café. A mural of an Amphitheater, filled with cheering Romans watching a few Christians battle lions, covered one wall dwarfed the rest of the tiny room. Michael pointed to one of five circular tables, each not more than two feet in diameter. Leah took a seat as Michael said something in Italian to the man behind the counter. He nodded and raised one bushy eyebrow as he looked carefully at Leah.

There was a shush from a machine and he gave Michael two cups that looked as if they belonged to a doll set. When Michael sat Leah's in front of her, she noticed it was only half filled with dark liquid, good for one or two sips at best.

"Do this." Mr. DelAngelo picked up a sliver of lemon rind on his saucer and rubbed it on the edge of the cup.

Leah noticed she had one too and copied him. She sipped and opened her eyes wide. "Anyone ever use sugar?"

"Only sissies. Now catch me up on the news."

He gulped the espresso and put his empty cup on its saucer.

She spoke briefly about the fight with her parents and in detail about her classes.

"So you like my alma mater?"

She nodded and then mentioned a project that had given her trouble.

"Then Professor Fenwick's still there. He's good but tough," he said.

"How did you know he was the teacher?" she asked.

D-L Nelson

"Fenwick was the only one who taught that course," he said.

Leah looked at her watch. "It's almost 8:30. I've gotta get to work by 10:00."

"I'll carry your groceries to the subway. Have we time to drop my mother's stuff off? It's on the way."

They entered a two-story red brick building, and walked up one flight of narrow steps. Michael unlocked the door. Unlike the dark hall, the room was light with white silken wallpaper. The living room furniture was upholstered with a light green brocade. Lamps were held by fat-thighed golden cherubs.

An older woman came out of a door pausing at the dining room table to wipe her hands on her apron. Her gray hair was pulled into a chignon.

"Mama, meet Leah Stockbridge, Leah this is my Mama."

"I'va heard lotta about you." She then described the painting that Leah won second prize with in *The Boston Globe* Art Festival. Leah watched red diffuse on her former teacher's dark skin. She didn't think he could blush.

"We gotta go, Leah has to work," he said.

"Coma dinner soon. You need meat on those bones," Mrs. DelAngelo said. "Nexta Saturday night."

"Do," Michael added.

Leah sniffed the air. Wonderful odors drifted from the kitchen. If that was a sample of what it would be like, she wanted to come. "Yes, thank you."

Leah had never eaten so much. "Mama makes her own raviolis," Michael's sister Rosalie said. She sat as close to the table as her protruding stomach allowed. Roberto, her husband, repeatedly patted it, calling the baby Roberto, Junior. As Roberto went to the living room to smoke a pipe, the three women did the dishes, despite Mrs. DelAngelo's protests that Leah was company.

"She won't be long if my brother has his way," Rosalie said.

Leah turned to see Michael blush as he deposited the last of the tomato-stained plates on the counter.

"We'd better catch the subway," he said, as they left after Mrs. DelAngelo had tried to force feed them another serving of rum cake and espresso.

"I can go home alone," Leah said.

"No you can't. Besides, I want to see what you're working on."

Michael looked at Leah's narrow living room, which contained only one chair. The wall on the street side was a three-panelled bay window where she had stashed her easel. An alcove was filed with book shelves but only one shelf held books, all texts. The rest had paint tubes, larger than any toothpaste, a Maxwell House coffee can with brushes sticking out of it, a palette and paint-stained rags. Stacked canvases were lined up next to a closet door.

He bent down and flipped through them, taking first one out and holding it up, then another. She watched with her hand over her mouth. "That pile is class-work. This is my own." She pointed first to the wall by the closet, then to the area under the middle window of the bay.

He carried a painting under a lamp and looked at it closely. "Your brush work is getting stronger."

"Would you like some coffee, not espresso, Mr. DelAngelo?"

"I need to go. Mama doesn't sleep well until she knows I'm in. How about a movie next Friday night?"

"I work till nine."

"We can do the second show."

"Deal," she said.

As he left he brushed his lips to hers. "Maybe, if you're going to be my girlfriend, you should call me Michael," he said.

"I waited until you finished high school." Michael picked the last snow pea pod from the white cardboard container. They had picked up the meal after seeing *The Birds*.

Leah drank her Coke. "I never knew you even noticed me except as an art student."

Michael stretched. "If the school board knew what I wanted to do to you, I not only would have been fired, I'd have been arrested." He leaned over to kiss her. Although he didn't put his tongue into her mouth, she felt it waiting behind his lips.

They fell into an easy routine without discussing it. Michael would pick up a pizza, Chinese food, fried chicken, then stop by the drug store. Without saying a word Leah would give him her keys. When she arrived home, he would have dinner waiting for her. He brought his paints and canvases and most nights, they'd paint, breaking for a conversation and a cup of tea or espresso between ten and eleven. After rinsing the cups, he would kiss her good night and head home to the North End.

Leah found that instead of Michael cutting into her work time, he enhanced it because she had instant feedback. However, he also asked her for her opinion on his work. "What's wrong with this?" he would ask.

"Shadow," she'd say, "too blue."

"You're right." He would squeeze a tube of white, grey or black into the blue spot onto his palette.

"Goodnight Rosalie, Roberto," Leah said.

Roberto had his arm around Rosalie as they stood at their door.

"Little more practice, Sis, you'll cook almost as good as Mama," Michael said. His sister stuck her tongue out at him.

Leah rested her head on Michael's shoulder as they walked

to the subway. A full moon played peek-a-boo with the clouds. "I feel so good," she said.

"You had too much wine." He put the coins in the slot and pushed her through the turnstile. Then he dropped in more change and followed her.

"Don't be shilly," she giggled as they descended the stairs where the Greenline car was just pulling into the station.

Inside Leah's apartment he unscrewed the espresso pot that he'd bought her, filled it with water and spooned in ground espresso.

Leah watched. "I think I'll lie down," she said.

By the time he brought her the coffee, she was asleep, her hair spread out making a black halo on the sheet. He took off her shoes, unzipped her sleeping bag and threw it over her before letting himself out.

Leah had no Friday afternoon classes. She painted in the morning, then reported to work replacing the lunch cook for the afternoon soda crowd as they spilled out of nearby Wentworth University, Harvard Medical, Harvard Dental and the Harvard School of Public Health. Sometimes Leah felt with all the schools and hospitals in her neighborhood, she was getting campus experience as much as if she had lived in a dorm.

The grill glistened with fat. Pieces of onion, bits of hamburger, and the brown lace of a fried egg were burned on the gray metal surface.

Tying the strings of the white apron around her she picked up the spatula. The scraping of metal on metal set her teeth on edge as she pushed the grease and bits of burned food into the trap.

A student wearing a purple Boston Latin jacket, burst through the door. The kids usually didn't get out for a couple of more hours. They made up the afterschool, not the lunchtime eaters.

Tears ran down his cheeks. He made no move to brush them away. "They shot the president," he screamed and disappeared.

"My God," Leah said.

Mr. Sparr, the druggist, turned on the radio he kept behind the counter for baseball games. He flipped from station to station.

The reports were jumbled with words like: ". . . condition not known,"

". . . Mrs. Kennedy with him,"

". . . a priest arriving,"

". . . Governor Connelly shot also."

An eyewitness told of hearing shots and then seeing the slow moving cavalcade speed up. Then the announcer said, "It is official, President Kennedy has been pronounced dead from bullet wounds at Parkland Hospital, I repeat, Presi . . ." The druggist clicked off the radio, put his head down on the cash register and cried.

Leah sat in her landlady's living room, a cup of cold tea in front of her. Larry and Patty, the couple downstairs, were there too. All of them watched the black and white television. It looked out of place in the room. The green over-stuffed furniture would have been comfortable in any Victorian home right down to the last doily under the lamps.

"He shook my hand once," Mrs. O'Brien said. "At a St. Patrick's day parade in Southie. He was still a senator and rode in a Ford convertible. Or maybe it was a Chevy. I do know I was worried he'd fall out because he was standing up when he reached out and touched me. Even then, you could see he was special."

"Poor Jackie," Patty said. She was from Georgia and drawled

the word *poor,* extending the vowels and dropping the *r.* "Poor Caroline. Poor John-John."

"Poor America," Larry said.

As they watched the judge arrive to administer the oath of office to Vice President Johnson, a knock interrupted. Mrs. O'Brien let Michael in. He asked to use the phone.

"In the kitchen, next to the fridge," Mrs. O'Brien said.

When he came back he said, "Mama is okay. She's at Rosalie's."

Hours passed before Leah and Michael went upstairs.

He folded her into his arms. They stood swaying. When they kissed, his tongue parted her lips. She led him to the mattress. Their movements were as inevitable as a tide.

Afterwards, Leah lay in his arms. "Thank you," she said.

Michael propped himself up on his elbow. His features were clear in the moonshine. "For what?"

"For being gentle. For being you," she said.

"I love you. I'd planned to wait until we were married," he said.

"We're getting married?"

"Originally, I thought we'd wait until you graduated, but I'm an old fashioned Catholic boy. I want to make an honest woman out of you."

"I'm an old-fashioned Protestant girl."

"Ah but," he said and kissed her nose. "Old fashioned WASP girls don't do what you just did."

"Maybe. Let's have a civil ceremony next week. We can sort the religion out after I graduate." She lay down, her head on his arm and listened to the ticking of his watch. She almost felt guilty at her happiness in a time of national tragedy.

"Itsa not the goverment who I care about. Itsa the pope," Mama DelAngelo said, when they told her Thanksgiving morning they were planning a quick civil marriage. The Macy's Day parade was on the television, but Michael had turned the volume down leaving a giant Mickey Mouse balloon bouncing across the screen in silence.

"Leah has some family problems, Mama," Michael said.

"She gotta us." Mama said and patted her future daughter-in-law's knee. "Just promise one day you marry in the Church."

Leah was tempted to say, "I promise we'll get married in a church," without specifying, but she couldn't play games with her mother-in-law. There was no need to protect herself from this woman. "I promise someday I will marry your son in the Catholic Church."

"And all your babies will be brought up Catholic."

The stove timer dinged as Leah nodded.

"Good, now let'sa eat." She brought out the dish of lasagna and antipasto which would prelude the turkey dinner.

Leah ran up the stairs two at a time. Her fingers itched to get back to the painting that she'd left unfinished to go to her last class before the Christmas break. She'd quit shortly after midnight the night before when her eyelids had grown so heavy and she'd known she would have to undo whatever she tried. More than once she complained to Michael that she ran out of day long before she ran out of list.

Mrs. O'Brien's door was ajar as she rushed by the landing from the second to the third floor. "Come in Leah, dear, if that's you."

Leah poked her head around the door. Her grandmother, wearing her black hat and sensible shoes black shoes that laced to her ankles, sat at the table with a cup of tea. Crochet patterns were spread out on the table.

"Grammy."

As Abigail scooped Leah into her arms, the older woman

said, "Am I glad to see you."

Mrs. O'Brien swept them upstairs as Abigail thanked the landlady.

Leah watched her grandmother look around the apartment.

The old woman smiled. "A bit sparse, your apartment, but certainly right for an artist." Abigail looked at the canvas on the easel. "Perspective is a bit off here, but that one over there, is great."

"How did you find me?" Her tone was curious not hostile.

Abigail pulled the hat pin out and took off her hat. She pushed the pin back into the hat and looked for a place to put it down. Not finding one she hung it on the door knob. "I went to the art school. They really were a bit careless in giving your home address out, but to be fair, it was a student that I bamboozled into giving it to me. Told her I stupidly left it at home and wanted to surprise you and take you out to dinner." She winked.

Leah brought her two chairs from the kitchen.

"A cup of tea?"

"I've had so much, I'm gurgling. Mrs. O'Brien and I had a lovely visit till you arrived. I was so concerned about you in the city, all alone, but now that I've met her, I won't worry any more."

"How are Mummy, Daddy, Chucky, Mrs. Stick . . ."

"Fine. Everyone's fine. Your parents are still very upset, which is why I'm here." Leah started to speak, but Abigail held up her hand. "Families shouldn't fight like this. I've told both of your parents that. I think they should be proud of you. You're a brave young woman." She nodded her head as an exclamation point.

Leah hugged her grandmother. "You're wonderful."

"Now tell me everything."

Leah did, including Michael. "Rosalie just had a baby boy." Then her grandmother's frown stopped her.

"Honey, your parents blamed Mr. DelAngelo for encouraging you in the idea of being an artist. They've convinced the superintendent that they shouldn't give him tenure next year. I don't know all the details."

"They can't."

"You know how the town works."

"Favors for friends. What can I do?" Leah asked.

"Let me think. Maybe if you made up with them. Now don't make that face. Not capitulate, but make the first move so they can save face."

Leah crossed her arms.

"Don't get stubborn with me, young lady. I'm seventy-three years old. I've limited time, and I don't want those I love fighting. Life is too short for that even when you're eighteen." She stood up and started looking around the apartment, opening kitchen cabinets and the refrigerator. "You don't have a phone. I kept calling information, but thought maybe it was just unlisted."

"Can't afford it."

Abigail opened her pocketbook and took out two fifties. "I thought my favorite granddaughter might need something. Get a phone so I can call you and chat. As for the rest . . . think about it."

Leah walked into her parents' driveway. It had taken about thirty minutes to pick her way from the train station around snowbanks and over icy patches on the street where the sidewalks hadn't been cleared, almost double the normal time.

Pines in the center of the semi-circular drive rustled in the wind. She'd forgotten the sound, or maybe she was hearing it for the first time. Only half the driveway was plowed. The house had electric candles in each window reflecting out onto the lightly falling snow. She knocked on the door.

Grace opened it.

"I brought Christmas presents," Leah said.

Grace opened her arms to hug her daughter. Leah could see her grandmother give her a thumbs up sign over her mother's shoulder. If nothing else, Leah had to give her mother credit for pretending nothing was out of the ordinary. She was not going to break the unspoken truce.

When Alexander arrived home for lunch, his office closing in the afternoon for the holiday, Leah, Abigail, Chucky and Mrs. Stickler were doing a jigsaw puzzle in front of the fireplace. The tree was decorated and blocked the living room window. Presents were stacked hiding the lower three branches and included the ones Leah brought. Stockings hung by the chimney. Hers was missing.

He walked in, his arms full of logs. He stopped. Then he put down the wood.

"Hi Daddy."

"What do you want, Leah?"

"We've had a disagreement, but that doesn't mean I don't love you. I was hoping you could come to accept what I'm doing."

Alexander stamped his feet, although all the snow was off his boots. He took off his coat. "It is Christmas," he said putting a piece into the puzzle. "Can you stay over?"

Two days after Christmas Leah and Michael signed the book at Boston City Hall. The Governor of the Commonwealth of Massachusetts had sanctioned their marriage. The pope would have to wait. Their honeymoon was a night at the Parker House. They walked through Boston Common, with all the trees lit with bulbs of many colors. There was blue tree, a white and one with a mixture of colored lights.

"Someday we'll have a real honeymoon," Michael said.

"In Paris?"

"Let's think about living there. Starving painters. Garrets and all that," he said. "After you graduate, of course. I get to see your report card, too."

Chapter Twelve:
All the King's Men
Couldn't Do It
STONEFIELD
AND BOSTON, MA
MAY 1967

"I can't believe I'm hearing this," Grace said. The rest of the family were sitting in the dining room. Abigail had made one trip to the kitchen already to clear the table from their New England boiled dinner. The plates had remnants of purple from the beets and a few pieces of fat. The serving plates held enough leftovers for red flannel hash, which the family preferred to the dinner, but the dinner was necessary to get the leftovers.

"You're marrying that foreigner. And in the Catholic Church!" She sighed, rubbing her upper arms as if the temperature were not in the high 70s. Wasn't her mother too old to pout, Leah wondered, although she had expected every line falling from Grace's lips. "What will people think? My grandchildren will bow down to bloody statues. I'll never be able to hold my head up in this town again. Why can't you be like other daughters?" She'd delivered them, one after another with barely a breath in between.

Abigail sat back down in her seat. She looked at Leah, who nodded ever so slightly.

Leah let her mother talk herself out before speaking. "First, Mother, Michael was born in the USA. Second, he fought for his country in Korea just like Daddy did in World War II." Looking into her mother's eyes she asked, "Why can't you just accept me as I am?" She looked towards her grandmother for support.

"She has a point, Grace. You might enjoy her more if you

did," Abigail said. As she'd promised her granddaughter, Abigail was riding emotional shotgun for Leah's announcement. The two of them had planned the strategy.

Alexander, whose frown showed that he was no more pleased than his wife, said, "Leah, are you sure you know what you're doing?"

One disadvantage of being secretly married was that Leah couldn't say that of course she knew what she was doing. After all, she'd been Michael's wife for three years and it kept getting better and better. She wanted to blame her parents for putting her in a position where she'd felt the necessity to lie by omission for self-protection. However, she was honest enough to admit that she'd guarded the secret because it was easier.

Likewise she wasn't about to tell them they were planning to try living in Paris for a year, a new lost generation. That could wait until after the wedding. Instead she said, "Mama D would like us all to come to dinner. She's a wonderful cook. Makes her own raviolis. And her rabbit and polenta . . ."

Grace's mouth dropped. Her hands flew to her chest. "Oh my God! You eat bunnies?"

Alexander, Leah and Abigail exchanged looks then Abigail started to giggle. Alexander followed. Grace looked confused. "I don't see what's funny."

"First you're upset that Leah is marrying a foreigner and a Catholic. Now you're worried about her diet," Abigail said.

Grace forced a smile.

"Grace, listen to me. I'm still your mother," Abigail said.

Grace fumbled in her pocket and brought out a white handkerchief with a pink-laced edge. Dabbing at her eyes, she looked at her mother.

"Leah's choices may not be ours, but she has to go her own way. I did. You did," Abigail said.

"But we did what everybody else did, not run off with, with . . ."

"Your mother's right," Alexander said. "Leah will do what she damned well pleases anyway, so it's better to support her. Fighting only alienates everyone in this family."

"I wish we had him fired when we had the chance."

"It wouldn't have changed anything," Leah said.

Grace held up her hands, palms out in front of her chest. "I give up."

"Good," Leah said. "I've got to get back into Boston, but is next Saturday night okay for the in-law meeting?"

Alexander drove his daughter to the train. As he angled the car into a parallel parking place in front of the station he said, "May I suggest that your future mother-in-law not serve bunny?"

Leah kissed her father as she got out. "Sure."

She had no way of knowing how much he wished he'd had Michael fired instead of listening to his mother-in-law.

"How did it go, Indian Girl?" Michael looked up from his painting as Leah dropped her bag in the only small empty space on the table in the bay window. The rest was covered with paint tubes, jars full of brushes and turpentine, a coffee mug with mold on the surface and rags splattered with dabs of color.

"Better than I thought. Not as good as I wished." She came up behind where he sat and put her arms around his shoulders, her belly to his back. She rested her head on his. He pulled her around and angled her into his lap. Her long hair cascaded to his chest.

"No way were they going to say, 'Isn't it wonderful,' " he said, twisting around to kiss her. Leah wrinkled her nose and got up to check out his work.

"What does it need?" Michael asked.

"More highlight, there." She moved her finger a millimeter away from the surface of the canvas. "I didn't tell them about us moving to Paris."

"Probably better to let them digest it a bit at a time." He stood up and pulled her to him and kissed her so that she felt it all the way to her toenails.

Together they exchanged that look that said—"Bedroom, Now."

The mattress Leah had bought her freshman year was on a full fledged bed. She'd salvaged the frame from the trash before the garbage men could cart it away. Together she and Michael had repaired the headboard and two missing slats then took turns sanding it.

One of their few fights had occurred at the hardware store because they couldn't decide on cherry or oak varnish. Michael suggested flipping a coin. Leah had agreed, but when he took a nickel from his pocket, it had fallen and rolled under the counter and the owner had crawled under to retrieve it as the neutral party. When they told the story six months later to Mama D, who came for dinner and to inspect their workmanship, neither could remember who wanted which finish.

Two orgasms later, still sticky with sweat and semen, Leah said, "Tell your mother not to serve bunny Saturday night."

Leah dashed upstairs with her mortarboard in one hand and her graduation gown flapping over her arm. Unlocking the door, she called, "Anybody home?"

Michael wasn't there. She glanced at her watch. He wasn't due home for another half hour. Going into the kitchen, she put two tea bags in a bottle of water and set it on the fire escape outside the bedroom window for sun tea.

The roses he had bought her for passing her senior project, her last hurdle before graduation, were in an old tomato juice bottle sitting in the middle of the kitchen table. The petals had fallen until there was a sea of red on the wood. Nude stems stuck up from the vase, their thorns a slightly darker color than the stalks.

Leah got her pastels to sketch the fallen blooms. Still lives of dying things were rare. In art history she'd fallen in love with Chardin although she preferred his women doing household chores to his dead ducks and rabbits draped on tables.

She heard a siren, nothing unusual for a neighborhood near several major hospitals. Putting her pastels away, she decided to go to Calumet Market for strawberries to add to the banana and melon fruit cup she wanted to make for dessert.

On her way to the street she stopped at the second floor landing and knocked on Mrs. O'Brien's door. The tap of the walker that the old lady had used since her stroke four months before clattered, followed by three clicks of locks being turned.

"Need anything at the store, Mrs. O'Brien?" Leah asked.

"Milk? Just a pint. For my tea." She let go of the walker to reach for her pocketbook resting against a statue of the Virgin Mary on the table next to the door.

"Pay me when I get back," Leah said.

Wigglesworth was a short street with nine brownstones on each side. An Arby's was at the end of the street where the trolley stopped. Although Leah should have turned left to go to the market she noticed a crowd, three cruisers and an ambulance to the right across from Arby's. A street car was obviously off its tracks. She could tell by the angle. She decided to look.

"What happened?" she asked a bystander. He was probably a student, if his age, jeans and Northeastern T-shirt were any indication.

"A car hit someone as they got off the street car. Then rammed the trolley. Damned hard. Knocked it right off the track," the kid said.

Normally, she would shut her eyes rather than see a dead dog or cat on the highway. Sometimes when they passed something on the road, Michael would reach over and touch her knee and say "It's OK to open your eyes. It's only an old bag someone tossed from a car." This time she pushed forward a little trying to get a better view. Leah watched two attendants lift Michael into the ambulance. "Let me through, let me through," she screamed at the policeman who tried to hold her back. "It's my husband." Suddenly she felt herself propelled into the ambulance.

One attendant was behind the wheel. The second fiddled with the sheet covering Michael. A large wet red stain enlarged behind his head. The ambulance smelled of blood and antiseptic, like a butcher shop washed with chlorine. Michael's face was untouched and looked as it had that morning on his pillow when she woke first and watched him sleeping for a few minutes before putting her hand on his shoulder to gentle him awake. Leah reached for his hand. It was cold and wet with blood. So much blood . . .

The attendant pushed aside an IV bottle with a clear liquid as the vehicle began to move. The attendant put the stethoscope he wore around his neck to his ears and held the other end to Michael's chest. He moved it several times. Shaking his head, he pulled the sheet over Michael's face.

"Don't," Leah said. Somewhere she thought she had read that only doctors could say when someone was dead. She saw his name tag said Dr. Schonberg. "He won't be able to breathe."

"I'm sorry, we've lost him," the attendant said and reached out, touching Leah on the shoulder.

She screamed and after that could never remember what happened.

CHAPTER THIRTEEN:
OF ROCKS AND TREES
STONEFIELD, MA
AUGUST–SEPTEMBER 1967

Leah sat on her rock, the rock of her childhood, unable to remember the feelings or play from another lifetime. There was no song about sleeping lions. No birds sang.

Her back rested against the stump of the pine tree that had been struck by lightning two weeks before, leaving the inside exposed in raw, ragged pinnacles of light beige wood. Sap oozed from the stump and was sticky to the touch and biting to the nose. The pine needles of the fallen branches without nourishment from the trunk were turning brown in the summer sun. Perhaps they didn't know that they'd been mortally wounded, she thought. Stupid tree. Laying on the ground. Waiting for Alexander and Chucky to chop it into firewood. Waiting to be burned and to disappear into nothingness.

Leah wished she could disappear into nothingness. Because the stump gave no shade, her forehead glistened with sweat. The underarm area of her blouse had big wet circles. Because she was imagining herself melting like wax, she didn't notice her father approaching.

He sat next to her, his back also propped against the tree. He reached for her hand which stayed limp within his firm grip. Neither spoke. Leah didn't know for how long. She had not worn a watch since the accident.

"We're really worried about you, Kitten."

"I'm fine." Her voice was monotone.

"No you're not. Your mother and I can deal with you as a

111

rebel. What we can't get used to is our daughter as a zombie."

"I can't help feeling dead."

"Kitten, losing someone you love hurts like hell." He rubbed her arm. He started to say something, and stopped, searching without finding not just magic words, but any words: a speechless lawyer. After more time passed he burst out with, "Your grandmother lost her son then her husband. Your mother lost her father and brother. I lost my parents. I lost friends in the war, and knew I could do nothing."

Leah looked at her knees then the house through the trees and finally the sky.

He took his handkerchief with its blue plaid edge, and wiped his forehead. He offered it to Leah, but she shook her head. The silence was punctuated by the buzz of a heat bug.

Then, for want of anything else, he said, "Losing is part of living."

"Please. Just leave me alone, Daddy."

He did.

In her bed, Leah's eyes snapped open. She'd been jarred awake by mid-morning sounds: dishes clattering as they were taken from the dishwasher, the lawn mower growling, voices muttering, the vacuum humming. Although all she wanted was to stop existing, she realized that she wasn't being successful at it. She still woke each morning against her will.

Sometimes, for one minute when she opened her eyes, she thought it had all been a nightmare. Michael was really still alive. He was just in the kitchen getting ready to bring her a morning cup of coffee which they'd drink while they talked about moving to Paris—how they would settle in an attic studio on Montmartre and sell their paintings on the sidewalk. This was one of those mornings.

Then she saw pine trees out her window and her high school pennant over the mirror instead of her portrait that Michael had painted and hung opposite their bed on Wigglesworth Street. The pain rushed back, engulfing her until she willed herself to sleep, to escape for just a little longer.

The house's quiet woke her an hour later. Her nose felt cold from the September breeze coming in the window. She dared the leaves to turn drab instead of red and yellow this year. What right did they have to be so cheerful? She put on her robe and went downstairs. No one was home.

She ran water into the kettle then turned on the burner. Reaching for the mustard yellow Tupperware canister, she pulled out a tea bag. The cover didn't go back on easily so she left it, knowing at some point she'd get a lecture about not burping it and stale tea. Since Grace wasn't there, she felt no need to put a saucer under her cup. Who cared about all this anyway? She heard the station wagon pull into the driveway and two doors slam.

Abigail followed by Mama DelAngelo clutching her black purse wearing a black dress with a black sweater over her shoulders walked into the kitchen where Leah sat at the table, drinking her tea.

"Mama D," she said, standing up.

"Don't Mama D me, young lady," Michael's mother said. "Iva heard terrible things about you."

"And I was the one who told her," Abigail said.

"Sit down, Leah. Coffee or tea, Maria?"

"Tea," Mama D said looking over her shoulder to where Abigail was. Then she turned back to Leah. "Now, what's this I hear? You hang round the house? Do nothing? If our Michael coulda see you, he'd be mad. Real mad." She draped her sweater over an empty chair. Abigail busied herself with a tea pot taking

113

another mustard Tupperware canister in which they kept loose tea leaves.

Leah said nothing. She wrapped her hands around her half-empty tea cup.

"What woulda he think, my Michael, if he coulda see you? I tell you. He'd hate it. Probably give you a slap. Lika they do when someone is hysterical." Mama DelAngelo reached out and put her hand on Leah's arm, jarring it. A little tea sloshed over the edge of the cup, but neither noticed the stain on the bathrobe sleeve.

The tea kettle's whistle pierced their silence. Abigail poured water over the tea leaves, and put the pot on the table with cups, saucers, spoons, sugar and creamer. She added a small silver mesh strainer with an acorn on its handle for separating the leaves from the liquid. The two older woman busied themselves with pourings and stirrings, but Leah just sat there, holding her cup and looking out the window.

Abigail and Mama DelAngelo exchanged a look.

Mama DelAngelo shifted in her seat, and leaned forward. "I remember Michael as a baby. He was the most stubborn kid in all the North End. And the most beautiful. Never forget nothing. He want to go to art school. I never hada no money after his Papa dies to send him. He went to Korea. He goes to art school when he comes back. Thanks Uncle Sam." Ignoring a tear running down her face, she swallowed several times. When she began again, her voice cracked. "I . . . I lost my angel. But he would wanta me to go on. He'd wanta you to, too."

Leah stood up. Pouring the rest of her tea down the sink, she swished water around the cup and placed it in the dishwasher.

CHAPTER FOURTEEN:
SHAPING UP
PARIS 1967

If the pilot had said, "Shape up, Leah DelAngelo," as he announced the plane's descent into Paris, Leah wouldn't have been surprised. Everyone else she knew had. Even her brother had looked her in the eye and said, "Geez, Sis, when are you going to shape up and quit moping?"

Tired of being nagged, Leah had announced the week before that she was moving to Paris, fully expecting her parents to stop her. Instead they'd said, "Wonderful. When are you leaving?"

Leah had expected Mama D to suggest that perhaps they live together, caring for each other and saying mass for Michael's soul each morning. Instead Mama DelAngelo had said, "Michael woulda really like that you do that. See Paris for him, too."

Abigail had added her "two cents worth," which after months of nagging was more like hundreds of dollars of advice. "About time you shaped up," she'd said and gone out to buy two Michelin Guides of Paris, one for Leah and one for herself. "That way when you write and tell me what you did, I can look it up."

Despite Leah's doubts, her family had shepherded her to the airport, kissed and hugged her then pushed her down the ramp with her boarding pass clutched in her hand. It had taken all her will power not to run back. But back to what? Nothing. Forward to what? Nothing.

The TWA flight had been half empty allowing Leah three seats to herself. To comfort herself, she pretended Michael was with her, only he'd gone for the longest pee in history. When she played these games, she worried if her grief might have driven over the line into insanity.

"As long as I know it's pretend," she said and looked out the window. The clouds engulfed the plane as it tipped its nose down heading for the tarmac at Charles de Gaulle.

During her first three days in the City of Light, Leah stayed at the Hotel Pacific in the 15th *arrondisement,* sleeping almost around the clock. She only went downstairs for *petit déjeuner* then climbed back to her room. There was no elevator. And there was no one to say, "shape up."

Although she found the thin cylinder pillow covered by the bottom sheet no good for punching into a comfortable position, she still stayed in bed, her lower lip jutting out, angry that no one could appreciate her misery. The pillow was hard, making her neck ache.

When she sat on the toilet, she checked her copy of the Michelin Guide that explained this was a typical French substitute for a normal pillow.

"Why can't I have a real pillow?" she said to the toilet paper. "Why can't Michael be here? Why didn't my parents stop me instead of throwing me out of my own country? What am I going to do now?"

Toilet paper, never much good for advice, served only the purpose of which it was intended. Toilet paper couldn't tell her to shape up, either.

On her fourth day she had to admit that she was even boring herself. She bathed in the half-length tub sitting on the built-in porcelain seat. The hand held nozzle spewed a weak stream of water, but she felt fresher than she had since she arrived. "If I were home, I'd have missed this strange bath/shower," she said as she ran a comb through her tangles.

A half hour later, in the dining room with its walls painted with gigantic flowers of no known species, she ate the croissants that madame something or other, the hotel owner, brought her. The croissants left the white linen cloth freckled with crumbs.

The woman bustled in and placed the stainless steel pitcher with hot, frothy milk next to that of the coffee. Leah spilled a little as she poured them both at the same time into her cup as she'd seen other guests do.

When finished she asked the owner, who Leah found sitting behind the reception desk outside the dining room entrance, for a newspaper. After the older women produced *Le Figaro,* Leah flipped through the pages but found no "apartment for rent" ads. She explained to the owner what she wanted. The woman said her brother had a studio on Montmartre near the Metro stop Abbessess. Within minutes the owner was on the telephone.

The flat was on the fifth floor, which Leah discovered meant sixth since Europeans don't count the ground floor as one. Without an elevator, Leah started up the stairs. The first two flights were fine, the third and fourth less so but she staggered up the last flight. Panting, she waited until she caught her breath before knocking.

The hotel owner's brother opened the door and fired sentences at Leah. Despite years of French in junior high and high school, Leah discovered the Gatling-gun speed of most Parisian speech bore no resemblance to that of her French teachers.

Looking beyond the man, who kept talking without waiting for Leah to respond, she saw a bed with two normal pillows, hot plate, sink, toilet and table, but nothing else. She paced the space: Ten giant steps in one direction, twelve in the other. She flushed the toilet. She tried the taps. After a few minutes a trickle of water dribbled out, lukewarm regardless of which tap she stuck her hand under.

Glancing out the window she saw the red and gray tiled rooftop with cylindrical smokestacks of the houses below. Touching the window she looked at her finger, gray with grease. The man continued talking.

"*Je le prendrai. Aujourd'hui.*" The man smiled at her agreement to take the flat.

After moving her things from the hotel and buying a duvet but not sheets, she wrapped herself up and slept, getting up only to go to the toilet or out to buy bread and cheese. When she could sleep no more, she stayed in bed looking at rooftops.

Days melted into nights and back again.

She dreamed about Michael.

"You're like a caterpillar in a cocoon," he said.

"It's a chrysalis, not a caterpillar," Leah snapped.

"I was an artist, not a scientist."

"Biologist."

"Doesn't matter. Become a butterfly. Shape up, Indian Girl."

Leah sat up in bed. The crescent moon hung over the roofs. She could almost smell his shaving lotion. "I can't believe that I was arguing with my husband in a dream." Pounding her pillow she hit her hand on the bed post. She shook it until the pain subsided.

When the sun came up she decided to see Paris, not for herself, but for Michael: for all the people who told her to shape up.

Accompanied by his presence, she fell in love with the Metro's rounded ceilings. She absorbed the eight-foot billboards and the overheated hair dryer smell mixed with that of urine from a wino who had peed near where he slept.

Cars came and went every few minutes. "The rubber tires don't squeak like the Boston Subway's metal ones," she said to him. Then her breath stopped as she pictured the auto crushing him. She felt him push her to put that thought aside.

After several explorations—and for the first time since Michael's death—she began noticing people; not just normal businessmen rushing back and forth, housewives or kids with book bags on their backs.

The metro was peopled with weirdos. She counted how many she found each trip. The first was a dwarf with a Jackie Kennedy hairdo, pillbox hat and four-inch platform shoes. The woman still didn't stand three feet.

A man sat across from her as the train pulled out of the Metro station St. Jacques heading toward Nation. He kept pulling faces and folding the corner of his coat until it formed a triangle as he talked to himself.

Although it was only two in the afternoon, a man in a tuxedo stood on the platform. As the doors opened he hollered, "I've a headache!" Holding his head in one hand, he pretended to masturbate with the other.

If the freaks intrigued Leah, couples holding hands and nuzzling each other pained her. One couple had a man with short curly white hair. His blue eyes crinkled. His lover was probably in her forties, stylish in the way of French women. Her scarf picked up the color of her coat as she carried herself with an air that said she knew she was attractive.

Leah bit the inside of her cheek to keep from crying but couldn't control her anger that she'd been robbed of the chance to grow old with Michael.

When the couple dropped hands, the man began to sign. The woman answered, a diamond ring catching the light as her fingers twisted, turned and pointed as she mouthed the words along with her actions. With no more to say, their hands intertwined again. A deaf lover is better than a dead one, Leah thought.

Despite the creeps, freaks and lovers, Leah preferred being

underground to emerging at the Louvre, Notre Dame or Sainte Chapelle. When she inevitably turned to Michael to say, "Look," a vast wave of emptiness would drown her.

Swallowing after one of the waves, she entered Notre Dame and slipped into a chair next to the aisle. A man in blue coveralls lowered a chandelier so he could change the bulbs. An English tour followed the raised umbrella of their leader, while a Japanese group toddled behind a guide holding a fan over her head. She half expected an American group would show up and be led by a guide holding a Coke bottle.

Then an organ struck a cord. This time Leah couldn't stop the tears. Her body shook with sobs. Michael put her arms around her, but when she turned it was a sister, her elderly face peeking out of a wimple. "May I help you, dear?"

Leah brushed her eyes with the back of her hand. *"Non soeur, merci."*

The nun passed a handkerchief into Leah's hand. "Keep it, dear. I'll pray for you."

Back in Montmartre, her face still blotched from crying, Leah passed a paint supply store. "Time to get to work, Indian Girl," she felt Michael say. She went in to look at oils and brushes. A young woman in a smock said, "I haven't seen you before."

"I just moved here."

"You're American."

"Did my accent give me away?"

"Oui." She stuck out her hand. "Monique Galy."

Michael whispered, "I'll leave you two alone."

More and more often when Leah went exploring, Michael's memory stayed behind. More and more time passed without Michael stomping through her thoughts as Monique dragged Leah to exhibitions and cafés, introducing her to a variety of artists, some serious, some who spent more time talking about painting than doing it.

Leah found herself buying wine and going to dinner at this or that studio. Sometimes the talk gave way to the latest strike and the political unrest spreading through the city, but mostly it came back to the favored topic of the hour, day, week, month: art and artists.

Coming home after any of these events, she felt Michael asking, "Have a good time?" She no longer felt guilty when she said, "Yes." Then he'd say, "Maybe you should start painting, again."

In early April the days alternated between rain and beautiful blue skies. The trees sent forth their leaves. Leah set up her easel, arranged her paints, then looked at her pristine palette for hours.

The middle of April, Leah came home from a café at 10:00, her head spinning from too much wine. Getting into her pajamas she crawled under the duvet and fell asleep. Michael sat next to her bed, a hand on her shoulder. "OK, Indian Girl, you're on the right route. But you've got to start painting."

"Why can't I dream about you without you lecturing me?" she asked. She felt his lips touch her forehead.

"I can't spend eternity here. Start painting. Become a butterfly."

Leah woke. The full moon staring in her window was so bright that she could see the roof tiles. "I wonder if he'd settle for a moth."

CHAPTER FIFTEEN:
PARIS PUPPETS

PARIS AND GENEVA
FALL–WINTER 1969

"He's back." Monique used the *pomme frite* at the end of her fork as a pointer. A glob of mustard dropped from it onto her steak. *"Oh la la. Il est adorable."*

"Who?" Leah dipped a frite into ketchup and looked around the Café St. Catherine. There was no one adorable around. She and Monique and an elderly couple were the only ones there.

"Outside. To the left of the door. In the suit. He's been here every day for the past week. He keeps looking at you. Haven't you noticed?" She blinked through her kohl-lined eyes as she scraped the mustard off her meat.

Leah looked out of the café to where the man sat at an outdoor table facing the Place du Tertre. Artists of all ages sat with their easels and some of their work displayed. One was doing a portrait of a woman in her forties, making her look younger than she did in real life. He was no fool.

Most of the work was what they called airport art, that people bought for souvenirs of the one time they visited Paris. Three artists displayed their more serious work, abstracts, a scene all in white with the layers of paint defining an Arab man against a stone wall.

"No."

"You get so caught up in your work that I doubt you'd notice if Jean Paul Belmondo came through riding on a dinosaur." Monique divided the last of the red wine from the gray stone pitcher between their two glasses. "It's amazing. Even when you're doing that touristy shit, you space out. And speaking of touristy shit, I better get back to my easel. Someone might want to buy something."

"Thanks for lunch," Leah said.

"It's the least I could do after you loaned me money last month. Saved my life." She rummaged in her bag, which was almost the size of the table. After giving Leah a 200 franc note and leaving coins for the waiter, Monique kissed her on each cheek before breezing out of the café.

Not quite ready to take up her work with the other artists adding their ambiance to Montmartre, Leah ordered an espresso. The waiter brought it immediately. After unwrapping the sugar cube, she put it on the spoon and dunked it. She watched the brown run up the cube until it disintegrated then drank her coffee in a single swallow.

"*Pierre, l'addition, s'il te plaît*," she called to the waiter. He ambled over to the table, his white apron almost to the floor, but he didn't take out the small black wallet. He tore the receipt almost in two. "No need to pay me, Leah. That man did." He pointed to the same person Monique had shown her.

After Leah placed her red checkered napkin on the table, she went down the metal staircase to the squat toilet. Holding her skirt up, she placed one foot on each porcelain foot print then angled her body over the opening. She held her breath against the odor of urine imbedded for decades into the spaces between the tiles. When she went back upstairs to thank the mystery man, he was gone.

Three firm knocks diverted Leah's attention from her painting, a view out her window with a surreal angel floating over the rooftops on a full length canvas, her reward to herself for doing X amount of her commercial paintings. The face was blank. She had tried to put Michael's face under the black curls, but couldn't get it right. In desperation she had painted it white.

She opened her studio door to let Monique and Yves in. They each carried a bowl, one with salad, the other with vegetables and rice.

"We've missed you," Yves said kissing Leah once on each cheek. He had to bend a little to do it. "It's been almost two weeks since you've been to Place du Tertre. So we decided to bring supper over."

Leah pointed to a pile of miniatures. "I need enough for my show. That's more important than selling to Sacre Coeur tourists."

"You're lucky. You Americans are really aggressive. I wouldn't have been able to talk that restaurant owner into displaying my stuff," he said.

"Nothing to do with being American. You're shy. I'm not. What I hope is a gallery owner will eat there and decide they can't resist this new, young artist. Monique. Open the wine. I'll get some plates. Monique?"

Her friend was staring at the large canvas. "This is incredible."

"I can't get it right," Leah said.

Leah checked her billfold. She had three more weeks before her check from Michael's life insurance was due to arrive. After glancing at her watch, she put her easel, palette, paint case and some of the Paris street scene miniatures into her canvas sack.

Outside the Café St. Catherine, Monique and Yves were already in their places. A tourist, a woman in her early sixties with tightly permed hair and an American drawl, held one of Yves' paintings of Columbine, his white clown face a contrast against the red wine he held as he sat at a table in front of the Café St. Catherine. Everyone else in the painting looked like normal French men and women. Yves sold at least five copies a week. It was his most popular work. For an extra twenty francs he would add the face of the purchaser and tell them how in medieval times, the patrons of a painter would be included praying in the corner of a painting.

Monique waved. "Can you translate, Leah?"

"Oh, thank goodness. Someone who speaks English. I do want this darling painting," the woman said. By the end of the transaction she had also bought one of Monique's and two of Leah's works.

"Thanks," Yves said. He put a blank canvas on his easel. "By the way, there was a man here yesterday asking about you."

"Who?"

"Never saw him before?"

"What did you tell him?"

"Nothing. Maybe he knows you don't have a *carte de séjour*, and they want to deport you."

"I can't let myself worry about it," Leah said.

There were fewer tourists now that August had given into September. The temperature had dropped and the pollution-laden gray sky had been replaced by blue. A few leaves from the trees fluttered around the artists' feet. No one tried to buy anything more. Leah glanced at her watch: 10:30.

"Psst," Monique said. "Don't look at St. Catherine's, but that adorable man is back."

Leah dropped her brush so that when she picked it up she could peek unnoticed. Because he sat under the red awning, it was hard to see him because his face was shadowed. She could make out he was slim and blond. Unlike tourists in casual clothes, he wore a suit and tie. He dipped a croissant into his cup. She rested her brush on the easel tray.

"What are you doing?" Monique whispered, keeping her back to the man.

"Watch." Leah sauntered to the white plastic tables on the

sidewalk outside the café. His eyes met hers. Neither looked away until Leah stood in front of him.

"Thank you for buying our meal."

"If you really want to thank me, let me buy you another." Because the chairs were all placed side by side with their beige basket weave backs to the restaurant's window there was no way he could pull one out for her. He stood and offered it with a hand gesture.

Leah sat facing the area where Yves and Monique were painting. When the man wasn't looking, Monique gave a thumbs up sign.

The waiter Pierre appeared from the doorway where he'd been leaning. "What would you like, Leah?"

"Hot chocolate."

"Your name is Leah," the man said. "I'm Jean-Luc Perroset."

Leah reached across the table to shake his hand. Pierre brought the hot chocolate in an oversized cup and changed the empty basket for one filled with croissants. When Jean-Luc reached for his wallet, Leah noticed French and Swiss money.

She broke off a piece of her croissant. "Do you always buy people you don't know meals and hot chocolate?"

"When they're as pretty as you."

"Then you must spend a lot of money because so many women are prettier."

"I'm sorry," he said. "I'm having a terrible time placing your accent. I know it's not Parisian, but . . ."

"Guess . . ."

"Brittany?"

"Further west."

"You can't be English?"

"Further west."

"Montreal? Quebec? No that's definitely not the way the Quebecois speak."

"South."

"Not American? Americans don't usually speak French at all, and if they do they sound like this." He held his nose as he talked.

Leah rolled her eyes. "I love it. When Americans want to imitate French they hold their noses too."

His eyes narrowed. Then he laughed with her, but his eyes didn't catch up.

Leah finished her hot chocolate. "Thank you."

"I repeat myself, but if you really want to thank me for the hot chocolate, let me buy you dinner tonight. There's a Thai restaurant where I eat each time I'm in Paris."

"As long as I don't have to dress up. I don't have any good clothes. Meet you here at 19:30?"

Leah glanced at her watch to see she was three minutes late.

He was seated directly inside the door staring at his watch. The wind was just a bit too brisk to sit outside. He stood up when she approached the table. He kissed her hand. "I ordered kir royales for our apero. Then we can catch a taxi, Mademoiselle Stockbridge."

"I love kir royales," she said. She didn't remember telling him her last name. "I'm not sure which makes it taste best, the champagne or the cassis."

"Our reservations are for 21:00. And it's a dressy restaurant." Before Leah could say anything, he produced a bag. Reaching in she found a black sheath, shoes and stockings. A shawl with various colored roses on a black background had long tassels.

"I can't accept this," she said.

"So consider it a loan. Like Cinderella you can give it back to me at midnight. But I did want to show you this particular restaurant. It's called Les Marionettes de Thailande."

How charming he is, she thought.

"*Bonjour,* Monsieur Perroset, Mademoiselle."

The oriental maitre d' swept them to a table up three stairs and in an alcove.

It was covered in a pink linen tablecloth. Matching napkins stood fanned on the plates. When Leah put hers in her lap it felt hard from the starch.

The waiter flourished his lighter and the pink candle in the middle of the table flamed. "And everything is well in Geneva, Monsieur Perroset?"

"Fine, thank you."

Leah looked around the room. The walls were covered with puppets, silhouettes with sticks attached to their bodies and hands. Although they were almost works of art, something was offputting, giving her an unexplainable shiver.

"I come half for the food, half for the puppets. I'm a collector," he said.

"Do you perform?" Leah asked.

He put back his head and laughed. "Heavens no, I'm a very proper Swiss banker. Makes me a collector of money, too. Good Calvinist, except for this aberration with marionettes." He leaned forward and whispered, "But when no one is looking I still play with them. Anyone can make a marionette move, but it takes a delicate hand to manipulate it gently."

"What got you interested?" She pictured him sneaking a puppet out of his desk and have it sit on a stack of money. In her imagination, his secretary knocked, and he hid the puppet.

"When I was little, maybe four or five, my governess took me to a puppet show at Plainpalais every Wednesday; that's a field in the center of Geneva for flea markets, the circus, etc. It was stupid. Puppets kept hitting each other. I thought of how much more could have been done." He took her hand.

"Enough about me. Tell me what you're doing here."

"Painting. Paris is the art capital of the world."

"Actually New York is becoming more so."

The waiter put two flutes in front of them. The pale liquid sparkled and bubbled in the candlelight.

"To our happiness," Jean-Luc said. "And to our beginning."

Their glasses tinkled as they touched.

"I like it hanging there better," Monique said to Leah, who was standing on a chair. Leah wore jeans and a sweat shirt, but Monique was dressed in a black jump suit with a black shawl thrown over one shoulder. The restaurant where the women were hanging Leah's paintings was deserted, except for a waiter who was setting up the evening table service.

"Maybe I should give up miniatures. It takes too many to cover a wall." Leah adjusted the painting. She had given up on her life-sized Angel over Paris work for the time being. "Is it straight?"

"Left corner, down three degrees," Monique said.

Leah jumped from the chair and picked up her café au lait. She took a drink of the liquid now cold as she turned in a slow circle, taking in every detail. "Looking good?"

Monique nodded. "Will Jean-Luc be coming?"

"He's on business in the Middle East somewhere. This is the first weekend I haven't seen him in three months." Leah began pasting little numbers in the lower left hand corner of each frame. "Monique, check the price list for the title 'Fried egg on blue dish.' What number is it?"

Monique picked up the price list on the black-lacquered table. It had been slipped into a plastic cover. "Nineteen. So is he good in bed?" Then she let out a rumbling laugh and adjusted her shawl. "Look, at the New England puritan. She's blushing. How many men have you slept with?"

Leah watched Monique put the price list down on the table next to the empty coffee cups. "Only two. Jean-Luc and Michael." She stuck a white circle with nineteen on the corner of the frame containing the fried egg.

"Finally, I learn something about you. Who was Michael?"

"Someone I loved a lot. He left me," Leah said, her voice a whisper.

"That was stupid of him. Leah, getting personal information out of you is next to impossible. Do you still love him?" Monique asked.

Leah's finger had a white paper circle with a printed twenty balanced on its tip. She stopped before placing it on the work called, "Sleeping cat by a dirty window." Getting the glass streaked right had taken her several weeks. At one point she'd thrown the canvas across the room.

At that second she wasn't thinking about price coding the painting. Michael's presence was with her again for the first time in over a year. He stood next to the table, his thumbs in the air, saying, "Go get 'em Indian Girl."

She'd almost stopped dreaming about him. Except every now and then there was a nightmare with ambulances and blood, following a good memory: a picnic on the bank of the Charles, making brownies at three in the morning, watching fireworks from their Wigglesworth Street roof. Even those had not happened for three months, about the same time Jean-Luc had first taken her to the Thai restaurant.

"Leah. You okay? Why are you just standing there? Leah?"

"I'm sorry, Monique. I spaced out. Pretending I'm the next Picasso." She put the twenty on the frame. "In reality, I'd be happy to sell a couple."

Leah opened her studio door. Jean-Luc, dressed in suit and tie, pushed twelve red roses at her. "I wanted to get you eleven and say you were the twelfth, but that's such an old line."

"When did you get back?" She pushed the tendrils of hair from her face.

"To Geneva on Monday. I hated waiting until the weekend to come." He put his arm around her and led her to the bed where he pulled her down and kissed her.

She straddled him and undid his tie. "Part of being a stuffy banker is working hard."

"Well this stuffy banker wants to know how your showing went."

"Strange." She unbuttoned his shirt.

"Strange?" He slipped his hands under her sweatshirt. Leah wore no bra.

"Everything sold. Three people came in and bought all of them. The owner said that had never happened before."

"Maybe interior decorators who were doing a wall of miniatures." He was rubbing his thumb and forefinger around her nipple.

"Three of them? Unlikely. However, it was great for my pocketbook, but I had hoped one of the gallery owners would have . . ." She didn't finish because his tongue covered hers.

Leah wrapped a blanket around herself and went to her hot plate to boil tea water. Jean-Luc stayed in bed watching her. The December morning sun arrived late in Paris, and although it was almost eight, only a few pink streaks alleviated the black through the skylight. So many times when they lay in bed like this, birds tiptoed across the glass showing their undersides.

"I wonder what the birds think of us making love?" Jean-Luc asked as he gazed up at the skylight.

"I worry more about helicopters." Leah poured tea from the cast iron pot into two bowls, added milk and sugar and carried them to the bed. Jean-Luc drank half of his, then pulled her to him. By the time they finished making love, the tea was cold with a slight scum on the top.

Jean-Luc inhaled deeply on his Davidoff cigarette. The brown package lay on the floor next to the mattress. "What are you doing Christmas?"

Leah nestled into him, her head on his bare chest. There was a relaxed contentment in the way she threw one leg over his. A year ago she would have thought it impossible to be this pain-free.

An early December rain that had started at their moment of orgasm, beat on the skylight washing the Paris dirt into new patterns. "Probably I'll go to Monique's and Yves'," she said, twiddling his chest hair between her thumb and forefinger.

He turned, and raised his head on his elbow. "Spend the holiday with me in Geneva?"

The Swiss border guard at Cornavin handed Leah her passport. She stuffed it in her bag as she walked through the door into the main train station.

Across the corridor from Quai Eight, Jean-Luc sat at a closed café. Although the tables and chairs remained outside, they were fastened with chains. An unopened newspaper was folded next to his arm.

She saw him search each face, yet he missed hers. She walked to him. "Waiting for someone?"

He jumped up, hugged her and took her case, throwing the strap over his shoulder. Holding her hand, he led her through the almost deserted station with its shuttered shops. They walked down the escalator which had been turned off for the night. The steps were just the wrong height for comfort.

At an orange machine he clicked the parking receipt. It read two francs. Seconds after he dropped change in the slot, the canceled ticket spit out.

132

A clock struck midnight somewhere and the bells echoed through the cavernous parking garage.

"Which car do you prefer? The BMW or the Porsche?" he asked about the only two cars left.

"Both are nice," she said. "I really don't pay much attention to cars."

He deposited her suitcase in the Porsche's trunk then kissed her before unlocking the passenger door. "I'm thrilled you came," he said as he arranged her coat so it wouldn't get stuck when he closed the door.

"That's the UN," he said, after they'd been driving about five minutes through the ghostly streets. "We have so many international organizations that Geneva is half foreigners. Our price for being neutral, I guess." He turned and pointed to a building high on a hill. "Before you go back, I want to show you the Red Cross Museum and the old city and . . ." He took his hand off her knee to down shift as he turned into a driveway marked by two stone columns.

A two-story house with large square stones stood at the entrance, its shape and color clear in the moonlight.

"The house is beautiful," Leah started to say, but Jean-Luc continued down the drive. "That's where the Schleppis live. They're the couple that oversee the house for Maman." He pulled up in front of a small château. "This is the main house."

A lamp shone on each side of a massive door. Most of the windows including those on the two turrets that flanked each side of the building were shuttered for the night.

Jean-Luc went around the car to open Leah's door. "Welcome to my home, *Chérie.*"

Leah woke the next morning and dressed for breakfast. Madame Perroset sat at the head of the dining room table. Her white hair was pulled into a chignon, and her dress was the same sky blue as her eyes.

Jean-Luc kissed his mother on the cheek. "Maman, I would like to present Leah Stockbridge to you." Leah was a little taken back, that he addressed his mother with *vous* and not *tu*. She had heard of that being done, but only in the upper echelons of society. It made her want to curtsey to the woman ruling the table.

Madame Perroset shook Leah's hand with a firm single pump. "You will forgive me for not waiting up last night?"

Leah thought of Monique sneering. The Swiss go to bed with the sun. "You'll be bored to tears."

Leah smiled and said, "Of course I understand. We got in well after midnight."

"My son has told me so much about you. I am delighted you will spend Christmas with us. What will you have—tea, coffee, or hot chocolate?"

"Hot chocolate, *s'il vous plaît*."

Jean-Luc pulled out Leah's chair. The table was set with a white linen cloth, napkins, and china. In the center was a silver basket filled with pine boughs and two red candles. A large basket held sliced bread and croissants. There was another loaf of bread with raisins. "That's tailuaille, a sweet bread, we eat Sundays," he said. "Try some."

Leah accepted the piece he cut for her then helped herself to some butter and marmalade. The latter was in a little dish with a miniature silver spoon. What a nice painting that would make, she thought. Especially with the orange jelly and the slightly darker orange pieces.

"I know Americans like butter and marmalade with their bread," Madame Perroset said. "I like to indulge from time to time myself. Breaks the monotony of plain."

She explained the program of the day: church, lunch, a brief tour of Geneva, a light dinner and an early bed. Again Leah thought of Monique.

On Christmas morning when Leah opened the shutters to look at the fields, she saw the stables muted by a white veil of sifting snow. There was only one horse. Jean-Luc had shown her yesterday. He'd said there were once five: one for himself, one for this mother and father and one for each of his sisters. His mother no longer rode and his sisters had taken their animals with them when they married.

The sisters had arrived last night, Antoinette with her husband, Franz, who ran the Zürich branch of the family bank and Anne-Joëlle with Pierre, who worked under Jean-Luc. There were four children, two boys, two girls. Leah hadn't sorted them out since they were all about the same age and seemed to interrelate the same with all four adults.

Before she came downstairs Christmas morning she looked in the armoire trying to decide what to wear. Never had she wasted so much time worrying about clothes. If Grace could see her now, she would be thrilled that her daughter was using social conventions. Jean-Luc had warned her about the formal dress. "Didn't you and your sisters ever tumble out of bed Christmas morning to see what Santa had brought?" she asked.

"Never," he'd said. "And it's Père Noël." If he hadn't tweaked her cheek she would have thought his words were a reprimand.

After church and after a dinner that started with smoked salmon and ended with a chocolate *buche de noël,* complete with minature ceramic squirrels and birds, perched on the bark-like frosting of the cake, the family traipsed into the library. The fire had been started earlier. The large real log had arrived at the stage where it glowed red from inside, creating silhouettes of gray ashy wood squares. Snaps of dry kindling had long passed into quiet.

An eight-foot tree decorated with antique ornaments and real candles was set near the floor-to-ceiling windows. Matthieu, somebody's ten-year old, lit each candle.

"I've never seen real candles on a tree," Leah said.

"Probably because of your wooden houses," Franz said. He had worked for a year in New York and insisted in speaking English to Leah because as he said, "I don't get much chance to practice. It makes me rusty." Leah had discovered everyone including the children were fluent in English, French and German, and the adults spoke Italian as well.

Jean-Luc arranged a petit-pointed pillow with woodhens and peacocks between Maman and the straight back of her chair. All the family members seated themselves.

"Maud, you may begin distributing the packages," Maman announced.

Maud was eight, dressed in a long dark green dress that came almost to her ankles hiding her white stockings. She did as told. No one opened anything but sat with their hands folded.

"How does this compare with your Christmas, *Chérie?*" Jean-Luc asked.

"We hang stockings on the fireplace, and leave a snack for Santa Claus. That's Père Noël," she said to Maud who handed Leah a small box and then two larger ones.

"I don't believe in Père Noël," Maud said.

"I do," Leah said.

"It's Maman and Papa," Maud said. The other children nodded.

"He doesn't exist as a man in a red suit, but he is that spirit of sharing in us, don't you think?" Leah asked.

"No," Maud said.

Maman opened the first present, a book of poetry. She folded the paper and put it on the table. She laid the ribbon next to it. "Thank-you Anne-Joëlle." Anne-Joëlle went to her mother who kissed her three times, alternating cheeks.

It was Anne-Joëlle's turn. She slit the tape holding the gift wrap in place using her fingernail. The room was so quiet, that each rustle of paper, each release of tape could be heard.

This was Leah's present to her, a miniature of a bowl of eggs with a whisk and a pitcher of milk. She had done miniatures for everyone when Jean-Luc had told her that the tradition was one present for everyone. He had given her a list including the ages of each of the children. "How clever," Anne-Joëlle said, folded the wrapping and gave Leah the ritualistic three kisses.

And so it went, quiet, paper rustle, thank-you, kiss-kiss-kiss, fold, quiet, paper rustle, thank-you, kiss-kiss-kiss, fold. This was certainly not the chaos of Leah's childhood Christmases with everyone in pajamas, robes and slippers, oohing and ahhing, trying things on, beginning to play with them. Even the children waited their turn.

There was only one present left, and that was for Leah. "It's from me," Jean-Luc said. Leah knew. Every time she had gone to open it, he had said, "Wait." She pulled the paper from the velvet box as slowly and as carefully as any Perroset. The lid stuck.

Jean-Luc took it from her and maneuvered a small catch. Then he turned it to her. A diamond ring caught the light from the fireplace. "Marry me?"

Looking around the room, Leah swallowed the desire to run. Then she looked at Jean-Luc, so vulnerable, so sweet. She touched his face then handed him the ring to slip on her finger.

Jean-Luc tucked her into bed, pulling the duvet up to her neck. "I wish I could stay with you, but Maman would never approve."

"I understand," she said and she did. Grace, in the same situation, would have been exactly the same.

He kissed her on the forehead as he would a child.

Leah dreamed that Michael came to her bed, sitting next to her. "My Indian Girl," he said taking her hand. "Don't marry him."

In her dream, Leah felt herself prop her head on one elbow and caress Michael's knee. "You're jealous."

"I would love to see you happy. Just not with him."

Putting on the light, Leah snuggled under the duvet. The room was cold, but not ghost cold.

There was no heating at night. She let the lamp burn until dawn.

CHAPTER SIXTEEN:
CULTURE CLASH
GENEVA
1970

"You mean it?"

When Jean-Luc nodded, Leah threw her arms around his neck. They sat on her bed in his Geneva château. At least she thought of it as her bed, since she had moved there. The open door satisfied Madame Perroset's sense of morality.

"Of course I mean it. We'll spend most nights in our room, but you need your own space. Decorate as you please." A breeze blew through the open window, barely moving the lace curtain.

"You can buy furniture or check out the attic." He hugged her. "Or keep what is already here."

Leah looked at the room. Not more than a two-foot area was free of furniture. Every surface had figurines, vases, do-dads and artifacts. "I'll start tomorrow. No, the day after. Tomorrow I've another housekeeping lesson from your mother."

Leah opened the door to the dining room. It was empty. The wooden table glistened. A mirror lay under a vase in the middle reflecting the jonquils on top.

"I'm in here, Leah," Madame Perroset called through the open kitchen door. As usual her hair was perfect. Her gray dress was perfect. Her shoes were perfect. Leah wondered if she slept fully dressed for it was impossible to imagine her in a rumpled night dress.

"Here, dear. This one is for you." The older woman held a plain gray-blue smock identical to her own. She helped Leah into it, adjusting the sleeves so her dress was protected. Madame Perroset then buttoned her own.

On the counter next to what Leah called the walk-in stove, masses of silverware lined up, so many soldiers marching to an unheard melody.

"What is our project today?" Leah understood why Madame Perroset had insisted she move to Geneva in April, two months before the wedding.

"Silver. When you're chatelaine, I will retire happily to my apartment in the left wing," she said.

"I don't want to drive you out," Leah said.

The idea of being the new chatelaine, the person in charge of the domesticity of this huge building, terrified her. She had tried to tell Jean-Luc that it was never her goal to be a homemaker. All she had ever wanted to be was an artist.

"You can still paint," he had said. "But every woman wants to be a wife, and how many women would ever get a chance to . . ."

"But . . ." she had interrupted.

"Mrs. Shleppi will be here. Then there is the day staff. Maman can always advise you until you get used to it. You will see. The house will almost take care of itself."

"Your taking over will give me time I've never had before." Madame Perroset patted Leah's hand. Leah felt the cold skin and observed the raised veins and age spots. "Now, there are many things too important to leave to servants—like caring for the silver. I spend at least two hours a week doing it to make sure it is done properly. Usually on Thursdays." Madame Perroset lectured like Leah's fourth grade teacher.

Leah calculated doing the figures twice to make sure she hadn't made a mistake. The total hit her like a little electric shock. "That means you've spent 177 days of your life polishing silver, give or take."

Madame Perroset's hand stopped from picking up a fork and went to her neck. Her pearls hung over her smock. She fingered one of them. "I never thought of it that way. But, yes, I suppose you are right. And look how lovely it is."

For the next two hours Leah took polishing lessons: hold the fork this way, get into the crack like this, rotate the cloth, no, not like that, like this.

"Preserving lovely things is an art," Madame Perroset said for the fifth time. "And when they've been in the family for generations . . ."

"We've pieces of furniture from my great grandmother," Leah said.

"How nice. I am looking forward to your parents' arrival."

Leah wasn't. When she'd telephoned the States to give them the news, her mother had said, "Oh dear, not another foreigner. What do you have against your own kind?"

Leah took the attic key. Had she fallen into water, the weight would have sent her to the bottom. The château was 250 years old. Electricity had been added in 1925, but the sixteen stone steps leading to the big wooden attic door were unlit. Leah directed her flashlight to the keyhole. This is like a horror movie, she thought. Maybe a crazy wife is locked inside. "Hello, Mrs. Rochester, I'm coming."

Leah needed both hands to turn the key and her full weight to open the door. She considered the creak it made almost obligatory. The attic ran the length of the building. Dust floated in the sunbeams pouring through porthole-shaped windows.

A mouse scurried across the floor, which didn't bother Leah in the least. In fact, she found them cute and all the cartoons of women standing on chairs screaming as the small fuzzy creature terrified them more than a little silly.

Armoires, old chairs, some in the need of repair, a rocking

horse, a doll house, skis, roller skates, ice skates, ski poles, several dressers and two cribs, were stacked so that there was little room to move. Some furniture had been decoupaged, but most was plain wood: oak, cherry, walnut. Any antique dealer would think he had found nirvanna, she thought.

Several bed boards were stacked in a corner. She found a single bed in oak, which she moved to the head of the stairs.

Walking behind a pillar supporting the roof, she looked at trunks labeled with names of Perrosets she'd never heard of: Francine, Pierre, Alain, Paul, Elisabeth, Madeleine. She opened them in turn to find clothes, hooped petticoats, corsets and bustles, top hats and waist coats. At least one Perroset woman had been a flapper. When Leah had children, she'd send them here on rainy days to play dress up.

The narrow end of the attic held a safe, the walk-in kind found in banks. Must be good load-bearing beams or the safe would have crashed through the floor, Leah thought. She touched the door, leaving her hand print on the safe, then rubbed the dust on her jeans that she had not worn before. Jeans in the château seemed almost as welcome as the devil might on the altar of Notre Dame.

A covered garbage bin rested under a machine that looked like a giant electric parsley shredder. Opening the cover, she found shreds of paper.

"Too bad I don't work in paper maché." She pulled out a handful. "My kids can play ticket-tape parade." She read some words in French about gold prices on a piece that hadn't been properly destroyed, but mostly there were numbers. "*Committee de Dix,* committee of ten. Even the committees are numbered. Don't understand how Jean-Luc stands such dull work," she said to the mouse who had come out to watch her work. When she finished she went out into the garden. Leah approached the handyman/gardener as he scrubbed the fountain's circular rough stone basin. The water inside was murky from the Javel and scented the air with chlorine. "Casimir, would you please exchange the double bed in my room with the single at the top of the attic stairs, after I finish painting my room?"

It flashed through her mind that Jean-Luc did not know she was painting the room herself. She couldn't have explained why, but she felt it necessary to do it when he was in Toyko on a business trip and she made sure she brought the paint into the house at the same time as her future mother-in-law had her regular afternoon rest.

Casimir Shleppi continued to move the long brush, holding it tightly by the handle, attacking the green slime that accumulated during the winter when the water was still. Big white bubbles rose above the surface then popped.

"*Bien sure, Mademoiselle Stockbridge,*" he said.

Madame Perroset walked up. Leah had not known she was in the garden. The older woman held a dark brown woven basket filled with daffodils, which Leah guessed would be on the dinner table that evening. She dreaded another meal with each of them seated at the long table that would have been good for a dinner party, but dwarfed their threesome. A suggestion they take their dinner on trays in the library, had brought a long sigh.

"You certainly are excited about fixing up your room," Madame Perroset sat on the marble bench and put her basket on the grass. After pulling off her gardening gloves finger by finger, she placed them in the basket between the clippers and buds. "Jean-Luc's father, God rest his soul, had me do the same thing. He said couples needed time away from each other, as long as it was not too often."

Jean-Luc appeared through the white trellis garden gate. Leah, surprised that he was home three days before he was expected, ran up and hugged him. He kissed her then his mother: each three times on their cheeks. "What a beautiful day. How is the decorating project coming, my lovely bride-to-be?"

"I'll be done tomorrow." She slipped her arm through his. Unlike her perfectly dressed future mother-in-law, she wore jeans and a Mass College of Art T-shirt.

"And will I get a huge bill?" he asked. "Did you get more than one estimate from the workmen? I did forget to tell you that."

"Only for paint, the bed linens and a few lights. I found the rest of the stuff in the attic. And I did it myself."

"Really?" Madame Perroset said.

"Really," Leah said. Why should the woman who spent over half a year of her life polishing silver be surprised when Leah did something herself, but then Leah was beginning to take for granted that nothing she did would please her future mother-in-law.

He draped his arm around her. "I can't complain. I do not think even a Swiss girl would be as prudent. And they certainly wouldn't have done any of the work themselves."

Leah covered her single bed with the duvet folding it in two and fluffed the pillow. She did a quick inspection before opening the door to where Jean-Luc and his mother waited. "You can come in, now."

Madam Perroset entered, followed by Jean-Luc. They stood, their eyes running over each inch. Jean-Luc turned in the center of the room.

Gone were the four poster, dressers, night tables, the long chaise lounge. The pink wallpaper with shepherdess and shepherds cavorting around the walls and ceiling had been stripped. Light streamed in the jay-bird bare windows. The matching pink drapes and lace under curtains had disappeared.

The armoire remained against one white wall. A single bed was pushed against another. A bookcase held paints and brushes. The middle area was open. Track lighting had been fastened to the ceiling without disturbing the moldings. Casimir had helped her with that.

Leah moved her easel, showing them how she could adjust the lights to the time of day. "Isn't it wonderful? I've my own *atelier,* my own studio. And if I work late, or you're away, I can just collapse into bed."

Jean-Luc walked around the room. "It certainly is nothing like I thought you'd do," he said.

"The room looks so much bigger without furniture." Madame Perroset's voice was barely audible.

Passengers, came out the automatic swinging doors, pushing carts tottering under piles of luggage. Every time the door opened, Leah peeked to see if she could see her family before the automatic doors snapped shut.

A melange of Japanese men in blue suits, Arab women covered in black robes, Orthodox Jews with their curls, shawls and black hats were scattered among Europeans and Americans. Planes from Tokyo, Tel Aviv, Cairo, New York and London had landed within the last half hour. Leah only cared about the Boston flight.

When the door opened and closed for at least the fortieth time, Leah saw her parents talking to a customs man. Her mother waved before the door shut.

Minutes later her parents, Chucky and Abigail pushed a cart into the waiting area. Alexander followed and grabbed his daughter in a bear hug so that her feet came off the floor. The rest of the Stockbridges took their turn in hugging her.

Abigail took off her glasses and wiped her eyes.

As Leah started pushing one of the carts toward the exit next to the car rental booths, Grace said, "Thank God, you're here. I was so worried you'd be late. I wouldn't have been able to talk to anyone." Her traveling suit was rumpled.

Alexander had the beginning of a five o'clock shadow, although it was ten in the morning. "It's a long flight. My arm is permanently marked from where your mother grabbed it each time the plane bounced."

"Well, I found it exciting. I never thought I'd fly anywhere. And to think my first flight was all the way to Europe," Abigail said. She looked the least tired of any of them.

Leah directed them out to the curb where Casimir waited in the BMW. He had to arrange the luggage in the trunk several times before it all fit. He held the rear door for them.

"Chucky, ride in front," Leah said.

"Sis, can you call me Chuck? Chucky doesn't fit my status as a Harvard freshman next year."

Leah rumpled his hair. "Gotcha, Chuck."

As they turned away from the airport, Leah said, "That landing strip over there is in France, the others are in Switzerland." She pointed to the left and right.

"How will we ever talk with your mother-in-law-to-be?" Grace asked. "I bought a phrase book, but I can't ask her which window I need to go to because I want to buy a ticket to Lyon or how I need a size forty-two shoe."

"Madame Perroset speaks excellent English," Leah said.

"That's good news," Alexander said.

"And German, Swiss German, Italian, Spanish and a little Russian."

"Imagine that," Abigail said.

As they pulled into the driveway, Grace said, "What a beautiful house. I've always loved big stone houses."

"I thought the same thing, but that's where Casimir and his wife live—right, Casimir?"

"Oui, Mademoiselle Stockbridge."

"That's the house," Leah said. "Really, it's a baby château."

Grace said nothing. Alexander took a long look at his daughter and nodded his head a couple of times.

Chuck said, "Boy, did you luck out, Sis."

They left the dining room for coffee in the library—all the Stockbridges, all the Perrosets. The sisters and their husbands had gathered to meet Leah's family. The children had been fed early and sent to bed by the governesses that traveled with the couples. As the hour grew late, one couple after another drifted off murmuring *"Bonne nuit,"* and kiss-kiss-kiss.

"Thank you for a lovely meal and evening, Madame Perroset," Alexander said. He had shadows under his eyes, despite a nap in the early afternoon.

"You poor people, must be exhausted. It will be a hectic week until the wedding," Madame Perroset said.

Alexander shook her hand. When Grace approached, she gave a false start at the three-kiss salute. Abigail stepped in and did it smoothly.

Grace and Alexander were propped up in bed.

Abigail sat on the edge in her long nightgown. Her hair, usually worn piled on top of her head, was in a single braid down her back and tied on the end with a white ribbon. Everyone knew it would slip off during the night, and Abigail would pat around under the covers until she retrieved it. Although her room was across the hall, they were exchanging impressions of the evening as Leah poked her head in.

"Have everything you need?" she asked.

"Come sit down," Abigail patted the bed.

"What a night."

"What a meal," Alexander said. "Cheese after the meal. That

was a new experience."

"And salad afterwards, too. It was like everything was backwards," Grace said. She fiddled with the ribbons of her bed jacket.

"But so good," Alexander said. "If I ate like that everyday, I'd be fat as a pig. I'm surprised you're still thin, Leah."

"It was a little more elaborate than a normal evening meal, but not much," Leah said. "Our starters are lighter, like a cucumber salad or radishes with a little butter instead of the fish soup."

"Do you think Madame Perroset will give me the recipe for the red pepper mousse?" Grace asked.

"Imagine me serving it at a dinner party. Everyone will be so impressed."

"I'm sure the cook will write it out. I'll ask," Leah said.

"And those sweet little deer-shaped knife rests. Such a good idea for keeping the table cloth clean," Abigail said.

"But why didn't they clean the wine bottles?" Grace asked. "They were filthy." Her upper lip curled.

"They are supposed to be left dusty if you bring them from your private cellar," Leah said.

"Well, I still think it's disgusting," Grace said. "Lots of germs at the table."

CHAPTER SEVENTEEN:
CLIPPINGS
GENEVA
1976

Glue rested next to the notebook open on the desk. "This is for you to use to keep your reviews," Monique had said when she'd presented it to Leah the night before her wedding. "Don't let marriage and babies stop you painting."

They had.

Leah used the notebook with its marbled cover in soft blues for newspaper clippings, chronicling her private life for the last six years instead of art show reviews. Every time she picked it up she wondered what had happened to Monique. Her last letter to her four years before had come back, addressee unknown.

"People move on," Jean-Luc had said when Leah had told him that she was sad that she'd lost touch. "Besides, you have other interests."

"But we shared so much. Our work . . ."

"Your work is being my wife," he'd said. "And of course, your art, too. I really tell my colleagues how talented you are." How long ago had they had that conversation? One, two years ago? Leah turned to the first page of the notebook. On the top of the page Leah had written: FROM THE STONEFIELD CHRONICLE **June 17, 1970**

Local Girl Marries Swiss Banker
GENEVA, Switzerland—Miss Leah Stockbridge became the bride of Jean-Luc Perroset at St. Peter's Cathedral, where Calvin, once preached. The bride,

---

who wore a full-length silk dress with a dropped waist, is the daughter of Selectman and Mrs. Alexander
Continued page 4

Local Girl Marries Swiss Banker
Continued from Page 1
Stockbridge and the granddaughter of Mrs. Walter Gordon Holt.

The dress had a V-neck and was embroidered with seed pearls. The bride carried a bouquet of white roses and lilies-of-the-valley. Miss Monique Galy of Paris, France was the bride's maid of honor and wore a full length ice blue dress and carried a bouquet of roses dyed to match. Mr. Perroset is the son of the late Mr. René Perroset and Mrs. Veronique Perroset of Grand Saconnex, Switzerland. He was attended by his brother-in-law, Franz Huber. Maud Chatal, the niece of the groom, scattered white rose petals Master Matthieu Huber, the groom's nephew, was the ring bearer. Miss Chatal wore a dress identical to the maid of honor.

An outdoor reception for the 250 guests followed at the groom's home. The couple had a civil service the day before attended by the families only. Mr. Perroset was graduated from the London School of Economics in 1956. He holds a MBA from Harvard School of Business class of 1962. He heads his family's private bank. The bride was graduated from Stonefield High School in 1963 and holds a BA from the Massachusetts College of Art.

After a honeymoon in Tenerife, the couple will reside at the groom's estate in Grand Saconnex.

Leah felt her mother gloating. Why else would she have underlined "groom's estate"? On a visit home, Leah had heard more from the grocer, dry cleaner, pharmacist about the château and about her life than she knew herself.

Selectmen Eat Swiss Chocolate June 31, 1971
STONEFIELD, Mass—The selectmen enjoyed Swiss chocolate and Toblerone at last Monday night's meeting. Selectman Alexander Stockbridge brought back the goodies when he and Mrs. Stockbridge went to Geneva to visit their first grand child, Yves-Pierre, who was born in the Hôpital Cantonal in Geneva, Switzerland June 9, 1972. Yves is pronounced Eve. The proud parents are Mr. and Mrs. Jean-Luc Perroset. Mrs. Perroset is the former Leah Stockbridge.

"See," Grace had written when she'd mailed the clip. "No one has any idea how to pronounce the baby's name."

"Everyone here does," Leah had written back, although she'd hoped for a name that would fit in both America and Switzerland. When she'd been pregnant she had imagined herself being a perfect mother with a perfect baby, cooing on cue.

He would sit in his little swing and watch her paint. Instead her son had screamed for the first six months of his life causing havoc in the château. After he stopped crying, he started crawling and getting into everything. Two nannies had quit, worn out. The third was a tough bird who refused to give up.

September 14, 1973
Stonefield Loses Leading Citizen
STONEFIELD, MA—Mrs. Walter Gordon Holt (née Abigail Taylor) passed away in her sleep, Monday night in her 83rd year. The widow of former School Superintendent W.G. Holt, she was born in Stonefield in 1890 and graduated from Wellesley College in 1911. She was the mother of Grace Stockbridge, wife

---

---

of Selectmen Alexander Stockbridge. Her son, Walter Gordon Jr., was shot down over Germany during World War II. Mrs. Holt was active at St. Anne's Episcopal Church, the local League of Woman Voters and is a former president of the Stonefield Women's Republican Club. Besides her daughter, she is survived by two grandchildren, Alexander Charles Stockbridge, III of Stonefield and Leah Abigail Perroset of Grand Saconnex, Switzerland. She has one great grandson, Yves-Pierre Perroset.

Visiting hours will be Thursday and Friday night 7:00–9:00 at the Halpin Funeral Home. Services will be held Saturday morning at 10:00 at St. Anne's Episcopal Church.

Internment will be at the family plot at the Stonefield Cemetery.
In lieu of flowers, the family requests that donations be made to The Abigail Taylor Holt Scholarship at Stonefield High School.

Leah touched the clipping, and turned the page. Her grandmother, if alive, would ask her why she wasn't using the book for its original purpose. She'd ask why she wasn't painting at all.

How many days did Leah wake with good intentions before getting caught up in her list of "musts"? Although Jean-Luc put in long hours, leaving often before six and returning at ten when he wasn't on business trips, she found any free time left over from the children being taken up with obligatory social events.

"I've lost control of my life, that's all," she said to the notebook.

October 30, 1972
Second Child, a Girl, Born to Selectman's Daughter
GENEVA, Switzerland—Leah Stockbridge Perroset presented Selectman and Mrs. Alexander Stockbridge with a second grandchild, a girl, Claire-Lise. The baby weighed seven pounds, eleven ounces. The new arrival has a brother, Yves-Pierre. The family will visit Stonefield in the spring.

June 27, 1973
International Golfing Family Beats All Comers
STONEFIELD, MA—Selectman Alexander Stockbridge and his son-inlaw Jean-Luc Perroset of Switzerland took first place at the Stonefield Country Club Scotch Tournament last weekend.

Leah sighed. She'd had such high hopes for that holiday, but Jean-Luc had been back and forth to Washington and New York for meetings. Yves-Pierre had thrown tantrum after tantrum, wearing everyone out. The summer had been exceptionally sticky and the fans in each room had done little but rearrange the hot air.

"Terrible twos," Grace had said. But when Yves-Pierre was with Chuck, the little boy was an angel, following his big uncle around and doing exactly what Chuck suggested. "Come back with us for the rest of the summer and control The Monster," Jean-Luc said on one of his weekend trips to Stonefield. "We'll spend it at the chalet."

"Wow, Sis. I'll be Peter. You be Heidi," Chuck had said when they arrived at the chalet two weeks later. Yves-Pierre burst from the car, running in circles, sending the sheep stampeding to the other side of the field next to the chalet.

"Only we've lambs and cows in the fields where Heidi and her grandfather had goats." Leah pulled Claire-Lise from the car seat, breathing not only air smelling of grass but of cleanliness and freedom.

The chalet had been built by cowherds who spent summers in the mountains making cheese while cattle munched cuds. Although they had expanded and remodelled it, they kept the front door carvings of a lynx, bear, sheep, cows and a fox that looked as if they could have decorated a Neanderthal cave. Leah imagined some artistic herder bored on a rainy day using the same knife he used for whittling tracing the outlines.

What Leah loved best of all was the furniture made of rough pine—nothing formal.

Sitting on the terrace after the children went down for their naps, Chuck said, "It's incredible. Nothing else for miles."

"Jean-Luc uses this for bank meetings, because it's so peaceful. And of course, we use if for skiing. We're a half hour from Gstaad."

"Can we have fondue for supper?" Chuck asked. "I've never had it, only heard about it."

"You won't believe this," Leah said, "but we have to go to a restaurant. There's no fondue pot."

"Isn't that against the law for a Swiss not to have a pot?" Chuck asked.

"Usually fondue is made by the men. But Madame Perroset is convinced that the wine isn't strong enough to kill the germs of everyone dipping their forks into the cheese."

"You're kidding," Chuck had said. His sister's expression had confirmed it had been no joke.

> **La famille de**
> **Madame Veronique PERROSET**
> profondément touchée par tous les marques de sympathie et d'affection qui lui ont été témoignée lors du deuil qui l'a frapée, remercie vivement toutes les personnes qui l'ont entourée souitpar leur présence, leurs messages ou leurs dons et les prie de trouver ici l'expression de sa recconaisance émue septembre 1, 1976

Leah cut around the formal thank you for the expressions of sympathy that had appeared in the *Tribune de Genève*, without nicking the black border. She ran the glue over the back of the cutting and pressed it into the notebook with the rest of the clippings.

She looked up from the desk. The château was still. From the window she watched Madame Shleppi dust the terrace furniture. The laundress had called saying she had a sunburn. Nanny had taken the children to the park. Jean-Luc had gone back to work for the first time that morning since his mother's funeral. He wasn't expected home until late.

It was Thursday—silver polishing day. Leah went to the kitchen. Madame Shleppi had lined up several vases and candelabras, their turn in the regular rotation. Leah looked at the bud vase from the dining room sideboard. Her distorted but untarnished reflection looked back. Picking up the chalk next to the blackboard outside the pantry, she wrote a note asking Mrs. Shleppi to put the pieces away.

The door squeaked. Leah's room was hot from the sun pouring in. She opened the French doors to the balcony. Cool air rushed in.

Leah ran her fingers across her easel. She looked at the tips and thought how people called dust black when it was really gray. Her palette rested on a stool. When she pressed her finger into a red paint dab, the ridges of the crusted paint left a dent in her skin.

Picking up her sketch pad she blew dust off it. She choked as it swirled around, blown back into her face by the breeze coming in the window.

On the bookcase she spied the daily calendar pad Abigail had sent her. The message for the last day she had painted read, " 'Even if you win the rat race, you're still a rat.' Lily Tomlin."

The date was September 9, 1972.

How had she not painted for almost four years? She could picture Abigail saying, "One day at a time, that's how."

Chapter Eighteen:
The Stepford Wives
Fight Back
Geneva
1977

"Why can't Nanny stay here to take us to the park?" Claire-Lise asked. She held Leah's hand as they walked along the sidewalk.

Yves-Pierre ran in circles, picking up newly fallen chestnuts and hurling them into the street.

"Not at cars." Leah grabbed his hand in midair as a car stopped at a traffic light. He kicked at her. "Stop, or we are going home." The five-year old stared at his mother and then dropped the chestnut.

"Claire-Lise, we already talked about how Nanny had to go to London to help her sick sister." She spoke French to the children. Jean-Luc spoke German. Nanny spoke English, because Jean-Luc wanted the children to have an English accent, not an American one.

"You speak French like you had been born in Geneva, *Chérie*," he had said, stroking her face. "You're a marvel."

The children could switch from one language to the other without even a slight effort. "They are being well trained for their future," Jean-Luc had said.

The threesome entered the park. Claire-Lise broke loose from her mother and ran to a slide built into an incline. A girl, the same age, waited at the bottom. Together they clambered to the top and slid down together, Claire-Lise's arms locked around the other child's waist.

Yves-Pierre hollered "Adam!" and ran to a little boy dressed in blue jeans and a Pittsburgh Pirate sweatshirt. He pushed him. Adam pushed back. Without any visible communication, they were two airplanes—vroom, vroom, zooming around the plastic rocking elephant, their arms outstretched.

Leah settled on one of the benches. On the other was a woman, about her age. *"Bonjour,"* the woman said. *"Où est Nanny, aujourd 'hui?"*

"Londres. Sa soeur est malade. Do I detect an American accent?"

"You certainly do. Kathy Sullivan Doré. Once of Portland, Maine, now of Geneva."

"Leah Perroset once of Stonefield, Massachusetts now of Geneva."

"No wonder our kids get along so well. They're all half-breeds, Swiss-American."

"What are you doing in Geneva?"

"Came to Basel for art school. Met my husband. He has a design studio here. I raise kids, don't keep a spotless house, and have my own studio where I escape two days a week."

"You can't work at home?"

"If I even tried, I'd never create anything. It works. I've a show in a few weeks in Paris."

"The color of my heart is green," Leah said.

"You promised." Yves-Pierre stomped his foot. His soggy pajamas dipped, revealing his buns.

"That was before you wet your bed," Jean-Luc said.

"Nanny says I can't help it." The five-year-old's lip trembled, and his face was scrunched up.

"I'll speak to Nanny about it when she gets back."

"Mon Cher, lets talk about it," Leah said.

Jean-Luc turned and spoke over his shoulder. "There's nothing to talk about."

Leah followed him. "Lots of children wet their beds. Especially little boys."

He continued down the stairs and picked up his brief case. "Not my son. I was a bed wetter but my father shamed me out of it."

"How old were you when you stopped."

"Fourteen." He kissed her on the cheek and left.

"It's for you, Madame Perroset," Madame Shleppi said.

Leah still felt whenever anyone called her Madame Perroset they should be talking to her late mother-in-law. She finished her breakfast tea in a gulp and went to the bottom of the entrance hall staircase. Despite the size of the château, there was but one phone on each floor. Her hand rested on the marble banister that was so wide, she had slid down it once when she'd found herself alone in the château.

"We missed you at the park," Kathy said.

"Yves-Pierre's father grounded him for bed wetting."

"That's no way to handle it," Kathy said.

"I know, but I can't convince him."

"Well did he forbid him company?" Leah ran her hand through her hair marked with gray that she called streaks as if she wanted them and had paid a hairdresser to put them there. She hadn't, but she didn't want to dye them either.

"No, he didn't. So when can you come over?"

"Today after lunch?" Kathy asked. "If we were proper Swiss housewives we'd have to check our agendas and could plan it for sometime next year."

"How about you come for lunch instead?" Leah asked.

"This place is lovely." Kathy pushed her cucumber salad aside. They ate on the terrace overlooking the gardens where Madame Shleppi had set a table with china, crystal and the silver. The children ate *saucisson* and *pommes frites* picnic style on a red and green plaid blanket that Leah had spread on the grass before

159

the fountain. Its gurgles mingled with the children's giggles.

"Better enjoy this weather, while we can." To prove Leah's point a leaf floated down and landed in the middle of the cheese platter.

Kathy picked it out, held it in her hand twirling the stem in her fingers. "Do you have any examples of what you used to paint?"

Leah asked Madame Shleppi to watch the children as she led her new friend to her studio.

"What a wonderful room to paint in," Kathy said walking around in a circle.

"I wouldn't know. I can never seem to get to it." Leah picked up several small canvases. "This is what I did when I used to be me."

Kathy took them over to the window. She set them so the light was right and took a couple of steps back. She cocked her head. "You're good, really good."

Only when she exhaled did Leah realize how important Kathy's opinion had been. If she'd heard, "Very nice," said in a polite voice, she could think that she was right to pack her childhood dreams away.

"Do you really think so? I mean, I'm not hinting for compliments or . . ."

Kathy spent several reasons telling Leah why she thought that she was good by pointing out a highlight, a brush stroke, a balance of items. "I've an idea. Use my studio when I'm not there. Let's work out a schedule."

When Leah told Jean-Luc, they were driving to a dinner party. He patted her on the knee. "What a wonderful idea. Nothing will interrupt you that way as it does at home."

They pulled up to his sister's.

"The main person to pay attention to is Herr Karl Bauer. He

needs financing for a major project, and we want him to feel our bank is the only choice. He's proud of his English, so compliment him on his Oxford accent. And when we get home later, I've a surprise for you." He leaned over to kiss her.

"If I never eat again, it'll be too soon," Jean-Luc said opening their bedroom door and letting his wife go ahead of him. "But that bisque was exceptional. Have Madame Shleppi get the recipe from my sister's cook."

Leah kicked off her shoes and hugged him. "I'll check the children, and be back."

He slapped her bottom. "Hurry."

Opening the nursery door she noticed the toys were on shelves, exactly in the right place. Nanny was back in control after her UK trip. The moon lit the rocking horse and doll house that Leah had retrieved from the attic. Toy soldiers marched across one shelf. Yves-Pierre loved his soldiers. Leah refused to let him have guns so he made guns out of clay and shouted "bang bang."

The children's bedroom opened off the nursery. Claire-Lise slept on her back, a stuffed pink seal named Frédéric in her armpit.

Yves-Pierre slept in the twin cot. Leah slipped her hand under the duvet and felt a dry sheet.

Dragging her son to the child-sized toilet located in the alcove, she pulled down his pajamas. "Piddle," she said.

He did, barely opening his eyes. She felt a surge of love for the tiny blond boy. His stream of tinkle missed the edge of the toilet.

She led him back to bed and tucked him in. He was harder to love than his sister, refusing to be cuddled when captured or constantly being pulled from doing whatever was forbidden. His attention span was nanoseconds. Yet when she saw him curled

161

into a little ball, barely making a dent under the covers, she vowed to try and be a better mother, which she defined as trying to have more patience.

There were times she could see things from his point of view. If he were in the middle of a cowboy and Indian game, his tiny figures placed in perfect position for an ambush, why would he want to stop to wash his hands? And trying to stop the water in the fountain by stuffing leaves into the spigots last week also made sense when he explained how he wanted it to back up so he could find where the pipes were. He thought that they would burst out of the ground as they did on a cartoon he had watched the day before. But his temper tantrums wore her out. She had grown to recognize the signs, the scrunched up face, the raised fists and was able to head a small percentage off.

Smoothing her son's hair and dropping a kiss on his forehead, her nostrils were filled with the sweet sweaty smell mixed with shampoo that children have at night after a bath. She shut the door and went back to the toilet to wipe the pee from the floor.

Nanny appeared at the door. Her tightly permed hair stood in spikes. She wore a flannel nightgown and fuzzy slippers. "Is everything all right Madame?"

"I just wanted to give Yves-Pierre a chance to have a dry night and let you sleep. He missed the toilet, but the bed is dry," Leah said.

"I'll still get him up at 3:00," Nanny whispered.

"Better to be on the safe side."

"How are our beautiful babies?" Jean-Luc asked. He lay in bed, reading *The Wall Street Journal. The Financial Times* and *Le Bilan* were on the night stand next to the lamp.

"Beautiful." Leah lifted up the duvet. Jean-Luc put down the paper. He stroked her cheek with the back of his fingers rounding her chin with his forefinger and bringing it across her lips.

She kissed it. He slipped the strap of her nightgown over her shoulder in their private ritual.

The next morning he stretched awake first. Leah snuggled into him, enjoying the last precious moments of calm before the alarm clock startled them into a new day.

He kissed her forehead. "I forgot my surprise."

"Hmm?" Her shoulder was cool where the duvet didn't quite reach. She tried slipping further down in the bed, but his turning to put on the lamp sent cold air rushing down her body. She heard him open the drawer of the night table.

"Look." He handed her a Swiss passport. "You're now Swiss like the rest of your family."

Forgetting the cold Leah set straight up. "What? How? I never . . . I mean, I need to take a stupid test, you know about wine, grapes and government . . . stuff . . . I . . ."

"*Chérie*, when you know as many people as I, you can move Alps with a single phone call." He threw on his bathrobe. "I thought you'd be thrilled, but you seem upset."

"Upset isn't the word. My nationality should be my choice."

Jean-Luc set on the bed. "I'm truly sorry, *Chérie*." He fiddled with the tie of his robe and looked like Yves-Pierre when his feelings were hurt.

"I know you meant well," she said.

"Becoming Swiss is really difficult for the common people now. Of course, a few years ago you'd have become Swiss automatically when you married, but the law changed. Think how easy I made it for you."

"It's just I never signed anything, or gave you my American passport or . . . or . . ."

"I snuck it out of your drawer, just like I took a coat to make sure the mink I bought you would fit." He kissed her.

And I never wanted a fur coat either, Leah thought.

★　★　★　★　★

An electric coil rested in a canister of water. Bubbles bounced up to the surface. Kathy and Leah wore heavy sweaters against the early October cold. Frost patterned the inside of the studio windows. The fire in the fireplace was just catching.

Leah held one end of a large canvas, Kathy the other as they struggled to get it in the huge carton. As Leah sealed the carton with tape, Kathy made two cups of tea. "Well, it's warmed up so I don't see my breath anymore. What did Jean-Luc say about you coming to Paris to my show?"

"He thought it was a good idea, and he was even all for me coming here a couple of afternoons to paint. Things are looking up."

"What about Yves-Pierre wetting the bed?"

"Nanny gets him up every couple of hours. It leaves him crankier but drier."

The marine at the embassy metal rod gate stood at attention. Set on a quiet street in Neuilly, France, the building had an elegance as it glimmered in the rain.

"Why are you here, Ma'am?" he asked Leah as she started to go inside.

"I've lost my passport and need a new one," Leah said. "I'm an American." She noticed how the water ran off the visor of his cap that stuck out under his slicker that covered him from his head to his feet.

He turned to push a button. There was a click and the gate swung open. Leah walked up to the front door where a sign over an intercom box read "Push button." She did.

"What are you looking for?" the box asked.

"I've lost my passport and need a new one," Leah said. "I'm an American."

"Push the door when you hear the click and go to the first desk."

The parquet floor was protected with a long, narrow runner marred by muddy foot prints. Leah felt herself dripping. Her hair was smeared to her head like a china doll's painted hair. Another marine sat at the ornate antique desk in a splindly chair that looked as if it would break under his weight. He was reading *The International Herald Tribune*.

"I lost my passport and need a new one. I'm an American." Leah wanted to say, "This is a recording," but didn't.

"Fill this out," he gave her a form attached to a clip board. A pen was tied to the hole of the metal part. He pointed to a chair in front of a fireplace big enough to stand in. A fire blazed. Leah thought about taxpayer money going up in smoke, except she didn't pay American taxes.

The room was wood paneled. Rain formed rivers racing down the leaded glass windows.

As she started to walk to a chair, he called her back. "You'll need identification. And a police report on how you lost it. Also two photos."

"I've my driver's license and social security card. I'll bring the other things back tomorrow." The rush of gratitude that she had renewed her Massachusetts driver's license and that she hadn't changed her name to Perroset was so strong it almost knocked her over. It had been an accident that she hadn't had any identification with Jean-Luc's name when she went to the Massachusetts Department of Motor Vehicles on a trip home. Rather than bother, she'd just kept it and her passport as Leah Stockbridge.

"Well, finish the form anyway, Ma'am." He had barely lifted his eyes from the newspaper.

Leah took off her coat and turned it dry side out before putting it on a plush chair next to the fire. The form looked funny to her and then she realized that paper was 8 1/2 × 11, not A4, the European standard size.

Jean-Luc had his arm around Leah's shoulder. "Kathy, this show is wonderful. If I can get my wife to be a little less devoted to the house and kids, she could do this too." His eyes took in the room with so many of the paintings marked sold on a large red rectangle.

The gallery overlooked the Seine. Through the floor to ceiling window on the Seine side they could see a barge carrying coal floating down the river followed by a bubble boat filled with diners. The boats glowed against the black-purple night.

"I'm so happy. I've two commissions out of this. I'll treat you to dinner as soon as the gallery closes," Kathy said.

The waiter brought a plate of oysters and placed them on the tripod hovering almost a foot off the table. The shells were nestled in crushed ice and lemon slices. In perfect choreography they each reached for a shell, tipped them to their mouths and let the meat slither over their tongues.

"This is obscene, it's so good," Kathy said. A small drop of juice on her upper lip, shimmered in the candle light.

The waiter appeared with a bucket of champagne.

"I didn't order this," Kathy said.

"It's my contribution," Jean-Luc said. "I'm so glad I could get away to join you girls for the weekend. Did Leah ever tell you we met in Paris? Luckiest day of my life eight years ago, when I saw her painting near Sacré Coeur. I knew immediately she was for me." He stroked Leah's face with the back of his fingers and patted Kathy's hand.

The empty shells piled up.

Back at the hotel as they unlocked the door, Jean-Luc said,

"Kathy is talented. I just wish she wasn't so set on divorcing her husband."

"Sometimes it's the only answer," Leah said.

"Families shouldn't break up." He pulled her to him. "I can't imagine letting you get away."

CHAPTER NINETEEN:
HIDDEN AGENDAS
GENEVA
1979

Leah sat at the dining room table with her agenda open. Although she'd chosen it for its pink and violet flowered cover, the gentle pastel colors didn't lessen its tyranny over her life.

Through the open French doors the smell of apple blossoms mingled with her freshly brewed coffee.

"More, Madame?" The housekeeper asked holding the silver pot in her hand. It gleamed in the morning sunbeam, the housekeeper having freed Leah from responsibility for all silver maintenance.

"No thank you. Just put the pot next to the daffodils."

When the older woman left, Leah cut herself a third piece of bread. She figured if she cut three thin slices it equaled one fat, and she felt as if she'd eaten more. A raisin fell onto the table and she popped it into her mouth and held it under her tongue.

She looked at the agenda again, hoping that a miracle had happened and she would find oodles of free time. She'd drawn a line through every Monday, Tuesday and Thursday, her painting days. When Kathy had moved to Môtiers, Leah had sublet the studio. But written around the cross-outs were the words: hospital committee, lunch with Virginie, florist, caterers, musicians, historical committee, school meeting, interview headmaster for Y-P.

Her show at the Galerie Belle Rive was scheduled for the last week in September. Already two months behind schedule, she wasn't sure how to catch up.

This was the second showing she'd planned. The first one at Galerie Amélie had been canceled by its red-faced owner, who'd explained she hadn't checked dates with her partner. Leah hadn't known a partner existed. Walking past the gallery on the date of the canceled exhibition, and feeling masochistic for doing so, she was confused to find the walls empty and the lights off. However a poster in the window proclaimed an exhibition for the following month and that the gallery was closed for the annual holiday.

Kathy had pushed her to ask for an explanation.

Leah had refused. "It's not the Swiss way to make waves," she'd said.

"Screw the Swiss way. You're an American. We question, not accept," Kathy had said. When Leah began to protest, Kathy had added, "I don't care what passport you have. It's where you are raised that sets your character."

Leah went back to her agenda. She knew July would not be productive.

Jean-Luc had arranged for a holiday. She and the kids would spend two weeks with her parents while he flew to New York and Washington to meet clients. Then he would join them to fly to Fargo for a two-week covered wagon trip through North Dakota's prairie land. Yves-Pierre could talk of little else but being a pioneer. At night he slept with his toy Canastoga wagon, a birthday gift from his father, under his pillow. She might get some painting done while at her folks.

Her childhood friends had melted away into their own lives. She made no effort to contact them. If she met somebody while running errands for her mother, they would promise to call, but the calls seldom came, nor did she make any. The first few times she'd tried, she found she couldn't talk about Nanny when her friends couldn't afford a baby sitter. Complaining of having to go to Rome when they were lucky to get to Cape Cod felt cruel.

Back to the present, she thought. Going through her list, she tried to figure out what to cut. Not the five business dinners Jean-Luc had insisted they give. The charity committees were another must to fulfill her role as the Perroset chatelaine.

She didn't hear him enter until he was beside her. He wore slacks, an open neck shirt and cardigan, his Saturday morning uniform. This was the only day he went tieless.

He bent to kiss her head. "Morning, *Chérie.*" He poured coffee. "What do you think about taking the kids to a movie this afternoon?"

She picked up the newspaper next to his place. "*Kramer vs. Kramer* and *Grease* are about all there is. Let's take them riding instead."

"Good idea. It's too nice to be indoors." He buttered a piece of toast and peeled a tangerine. Its odor blended with the apple blossoms and coffee. "Let's compare agendas to make sure we haven't missed anything."

Twenty minutes later Leah's had two new entries.

The Perrosets walked hand-in-hand through the outdoor marché at Ferney-Voltaire. The stalls, with their tables and multi-colored awnings, stretched up and down the street. Voltaire's statue watched people make Saturday purchases. Leah now took it for granted to wander less than a mile from her home and end up in another country. Going to France for coffee or to leave her dry cleaning was as normal as going downtown to the center of Geneva. In fact, France was closer to her home.

From a table piled with baguettes and round bread, Leah chose a loaf of *pain du campagne* with its thick crust split on top. After sniffing the yeasty-fresh baked smell, she dropped it into her straw basket.

At the olive stand, Jean-Luc bought a hundred grams, asking the clerk to scoop some of this and some of that kind from the different red plastic dishpans.

"Don't close the container," he said. He picked a black garlic one with wrinkled skin and touched it to Leah's lips. She opened her mouth, and he popped it in. He took a green piquant for himself. Then he put the lid on and slid it into her basket.

The odor and sizzling of a rotisserie with chickens turning on a spit, their juice dropping on chopped onions, lassoed them. To the left was a huge paella pan almost four feet in diameter.

"Oh, that looks good," Jean-Luc said inhaling the spices.

"Let's get some. Save Mrs. Shleppi cooking tonight," Leah said.

"Good idea," said the man behind the pan. His thick handlebar moustache quivered when he talked. While Jean-Luc paid, Leah bought a dress for Claire-Lise's Barbie and a model airplane kit for Yves-Pierre at a toy stall.

They stopped at the puppet lady, as Jean-Luc called the woman who waved to them. She wore her black hair cut like a little Dutch boy and her black eyes twinkled. All kinds of puppets and marionettes hung from the back, awning and sides of the stall: the three pigs, two wolves, a grandmother, a girl in a red hood, Kermit, Miss Piggy, Oscar the Grouch, a swan, fox, Snow White, and a duck that was a poor imitation of Donald.

The woman smiled. "Monsieur Perroset, I have it. At last."

She reached under the table for a long box. In slow motion she took off the cover, pulled back green tissue paper like florists use, to reveal a puppet in medieval dress. She had little pink circles on her cheeks, a little pink mouth and her long blond hair was tied back with a criss-crossing ribbon the same green/brown as the dress.

He put his right hand under the head holding it as if it were a patient in need of a drink of water. "Maid Marion, I've waited a long time for you," Jean-Luc said. He lifted the marionette carefully, supporting her rear end with his left hand. Then he sat her down as if she were a baby and reached for the cross sticks with the strings leading to her arms, legs and head. He walked the puppet across the table then made her curtsey. "She is beautiful," he said and tipped the puppet's head as if she were flirting with him.

"She's over 100 years old. I've the vetting certificate," the woman said. "The dress is new. The original was in tatters, but I copied it as best I could."

Walking back to the car, Jean-Luc kept grinning.

"Now, I've finished my Robin Hood collection. Marion will hang between Friar Tuck and Little John."

The couple arrived home just before the children were due back from Saturday morning classes. All the windows and doors were opened, letting spring air circulate through the château.

"Give the paella to Madame Shleppi and tell her to take the rest of the day off," Jean-Luc said. "I'll put my Maid Marion away. I can hardly wait to see how she looks with the others."

As Leah took the basket, she said "Drop the kids' presents on their beds, will you please?" and handed him the airplane kit and doll dress.

"Mummy, we're home." The children dashed into the hall followed by Nanny. Leah held her arms out. They dropped their book bags on the chair next to the stairs. Claire-Lise snuggled into her hug while Yves-Pierre squiggled out of reach.

Looking over their heads Leah thought how much younger Nanny looked without her glasses, although she could not begin to guess the age of the woman. Over forty was close enough. She made a mental note to drive her to the optician on Monday to get a replacement pair for the ones that Yves-Pierre had broken last night. One more thing for her agenda.

As Leah released her daughter, Jean-Luc thundered down the stairs. Without a word he grabbed Yves-Pierre leaving the child's shoes, still untied, where they fell. Claire-Lise ran behind her mother. Nanny stood open-mouthed. Jean-Luc carried his screaming son up the stairs.

"Take Claire-Lise to the kitchen," Leah said to Nanny and ran after her husband and son. The screaming had stopped.

When she reached the nursery door, she saw Jean-Luc holding Yves-Pierre with one hand in the middle of his back as the child bent over a chair. His pants were bunched around his ankles. Her husband's belt was in his other hand and that was raised over his head. Red welts striped the child's bottom. He made no sound. Leah grabbed Jean-Luc's hand before he could bring it down again.

"Enough."

Her voice was soft, but her look penetrated through him. His color slowly returned to normal. He threw the belt across the room and left the nursery slamming the door.

Yves-Pierre stood. With his face scrunched up, he restored his clothing.

Leah looked at the yellow marks on the unmade bed. She reached out to comfort her son.

"Leave me alone," he said.

Leah sat on the bottom stair, the phone in her lap. Outside a pea soup fog lent an eerie glow to the windows. Leah could just make out the silhouettes of trees, reminding her of the cut-outs she'd done as a child.

The spring weekend had been stolen by a winter Monday morning. The children were in school. Jean-Luc was holding a committee meeting at the chalet and wouldn't be back for the rest of the week.

Leah resisted telling Kathy about the weekend. She had done what she could to comfort Nanny for not seeing the stains. Jean-Luc refused to speak to his son, until he had written, "Only babies wet their beds," one hundred times.

Instead she said, "I should be able to paint, Kathy, but there's such a list of things to do for those damned parties." As she talked she twisted the receiver's cord around and around her hand.

"Leave the kids with Nanny and come to Môtiers for a week. I promise to feed you and leave you alone," Kathy said.

"I can't." Leah said.

"Why not?" Kathy asked.

"The dinners must be perfect," Leah said.

"Have you ever noticed, how whenever you want to paint, Jean-Luc suddenly increases your social life?" Kathy asked.

"He's the first to encourage me," Leah said.

"Have it your own way, but the offer stands. You've only four months until the exhibition."

"How's the restoration coming?" Leah asked.

"The important rooms are done: my studio, kitchen, bath, the kids' bedrooms. Who cares about the rest."

After hanging up, Leah sat on the stairs thinking. She needed to change into a dress and heels from her pants and sweater before meeting with the caterer.

She continued mentally to run through her to-do list. Because the housekeeper wore house slippers, Leah felt Madame Shleppi before hearing her.

"Madame Perroset, I think you better come with me."

Leah followed her to the room where Jean-Luc kept his puppets.

"Look," Madame Shleppi said. "It's unlocked."

"It's never unlocked." Yet Leah pushed the door, which was

ajar leaving a sliver of light on the carpet, and went in. Jean-Luc had arranged the puppets by categories. All his fairy tale puppets were together. The animals were grouped separately. His antiques were in one case, the Thais on a wall. Over five hundred puppets were displayed in that room. One thousand puppet eyes stared at her. Leah imagined them coming alive and pulling each other's strings.

"Probably Monsieur Perroset forgot. I'll get his key and lock up," Leah said. In their bedroom she opened the top dresser drawer where he kept the keys to the attic, puppet room and wine cellar on a large ring. They were in their proper place under his jockey shorts.

Before she locked the door, she went in. Nothing seemed to be missing. Maid Marion hung next to Friar Tuck, a sparkle in her eyes created by dots of white paint. Leah picked up her hand. A finger tip was missing from the elaborately carved hand. Leah was sure she'd been perfect when they bought her.

Friar Tuck swung next to Marion. He wore a happy expression and carried a chicken leg, missing a bite. His belt didn't look the same to her. The rope was unravelled and retied about his well-stuffed waist.

Leah looked at the other puppets. Each one had a small nick, a button cut off a piece of clothing, a flower missing petals.

In Yves-Pierre's room she examined the waste paper basket. It contained the box from his model airplane, a preliminary homework paper that he had probably copied into his exercise book, and his covered wagon in pieces.

Nanny came out of her adjoining room where she had a television. Although she was free to leave during the children's school hours she preferred to do needle work in her room.

The Perrosets kept her to baby-sit and to save Leah from running back and forth to the schools, which were on different schedules and meant eight trips back and forth daily as the children came home for lunch which they often did.

Leah had been surprised that Jean-Luc wanted them in the public schools rather than the private or even the international, but he explained he wanted them to see ordinary life. When they were twelve he would send Yves-Pierre to boarding school in England or to Rosay, depending on which would be the best for him at the time. Claire-Lise? Well he was looking into Swiss boarding schools for her.

"And my opinion," Leah had asked.

"Dear, you don't understand our local education system, you were raised in New England. Were we living there, I would defer to your wisdom."

"What are you looking for, Madame?" Nanny asked and Leah jumped.

"Nothing," Leah said.

Chapter Twenty:
The Guilty Party
GENEVA
1979

Leah pushed the kitchen door open with her elbow. Her arms were filled with laundry.

Madame Shleppi sat at the table, her head down between a pile of unsnapped green beans and an empty colander. Her shoulders heaved. Casimir stood over her, his hand rubbing her back.

Leah couldn't remember ever seeing the housekeeper react with great emotion. She smiled, never laughed, lowered her eyes, but didn't frown.

Dropping the clothing near the laundry room door Leah asked, "What's wrong?"

Casimir looked up, an expression of surprise on his face. "Nothing," he said.

Lifting her head, Madame Shleppi dabbed at her eyes and said, "Nothing."

Lie to me, but don't insult my intelligence, Leah thought after several more questions produced only a back-bone stiffening resistance.

After dinner with Madame Shleppi, her face immobile, serving silently, Jean-Luc threw his napkin on the table and went to the liquor cabinet. "Mirabelle?"

Leah shook her head and watched her husband pour the clear liquid into the crystal liquor glass.

"Let's go into the library," he said. Without waiting for her answer he left the room.

She followed him.

He shut the door and sank on the couch. Taking out his pipe and tobacco pouch, he took great care in filling its bowl then tapped the leaves. The pipe, bought at Davidoff's, had been handmade for him. The tobacco was a special mixture that smelled of cherry. Imagining all the tobacco leaves beaten into submission, Leah took her place in her winged chair next to her knitting basket and picked up the Irish knit sweater she was making for Yves-Pierre. She had marked the last row, the one before she needed to twist every so many stitches to make the cables.

She would have preferred to go upstairs and paint, but Jean-Luc wanted her with him on the few evenings he was home. A few weeks ago she'd tried to place a chair and reading lamp for him near her easel, but each time they went there after dinner he would twist and sigh, go downstairs, bring back a book or some papers, then twist some more. Thinking of all she still needed to do for her exhibition, she began purling.

The smell of pipe smoke perfumed the room. Jean-Luc took the latest issue of *Bilan*. The magazine's cover had a photo of a Swiss drug company president. He and his wife had been their dinner guests about a year before. Leah had found him worse than boring, treating her and his wife like children, always suggesting that the women go and talk about clothes and jewelry while the men folk discussed business. Leah had felt mentally patted on her head. She shifted the unfinished sleeve to start the knit row.

Jean-Luc puffed on his pipe, then put the magazine down. "We may have to let the Shleppis go."

"What?" Leah dropped a stitch. She quickly put a spare needle through the loop before it slipped more. "Why?"

"I think Madame Shleppi damaged my puppets."

"That's crazy."

Jean-Luc puffed slowly. "Every one has a little defect. New defects. Even Maid Marion."

Shit, Leah thought, but said, "It makes no sense. She's been with your family since you were a boy."

"She has access to the key. Who else could do it?"

"But why?"

"Maybe she resents being a servant. You never know with the lower classes."

"I'm sorry Jean-Luc, but I don't want her fired."

He moved to the footstool in front of her. Taking her hand, he said, "You are so gentle, so good. But you have to be strong when things are clearly right."

"I won't be gentle if you fire them. I don't have time to find new help much less train them. Promise me, you won't do anything."

"You're wrong, but I will humor you . . . this time." After stroking her cheek, he went back to the couch. Periodically he stopped to read parts of the article about the drug company president to his wife.

"Yves-Pierre, I want to talk with you," Leah said. Her son had come in from playing, his football under this arm. His face was streaked with dirt and his hands were filthy. Leah sat at her desk in a straight backed chair.

Her son bounced the black and white ball on the parquet.

She caught the ball and put it on the desk. Leah spoke to him in English instead of the usual French, hoping he would realize that this would not be an ordinary conversation. Now that the children were comfortable in three languages, the whole family used French together. Yves-Pierre, more than Claire-Lise, had inherited her ear for languages, thus the few times he spoke English to his mother he mimicked her Bostonian accent replacing *r*'s with *h* sounds. When he spoke with others, his English was flawless and his accent was that of a British public school boy.

But her son, instead of answering in English, spoke with the flat tones of the Genevois, *"D'accord, et le sujet, Maman?"*

Leah debated correcting him because Jean-Luc insisted the children speak Parisian French and use certain French phrases not Swiss. Ninety had to be *quatre-vingt-dix* and not *nonant*. And you are welcome could never be the Swiss *service, à votre service* or *de rien* but a firm *je vous en prie*.

Rather than make an issue, Leah ignored it.

"Don't touch the material," she said to her son as he rested his hand on the arm rest. The cover had been needlepointed by her mother-in-law in light pastel. She resisted rubbing where he'd left a mark.

"D'accord," he said pouting.

"I want to talk to you about your father's puppets." She rejected the idea of mentioning the pout in favor of sticking to the important issues.

"Pourquoi?"

"You know why."

"Pas de tout." He picked her letter opener that was shaped like a sword and thrust it at an imaginary enemy. *"Je veux regarder la télévision."*

"Not until you tell me why you damaged your father's puppets."

"Je ne l'ai fait pas." He turned and started to leave the room.

"Stop. Your father wants to fire the Shleppis. He thinks Madame Shleppi did it."

He stopped. *"Peut-être elle l'a fait."*

"I doubt it. I know it was you."

Yves-Pierre had a way of lifting his chin whenever he was caught doing something wrong. He turned and lifted his chin.

"Ce n'est pas mon problème."

Leah thought of all the lectures her parents had given her on responsibility to others. Editing some she repeated them to her son who rolled his eyes.

"Pourrais-je sortir?"

"Yes, you can go." She watched him leave the room. Maybe spending time with her father would be good for Yves-Pierre. The last holiday home, Alexander had taken the boy fishing and golfing. They went to court and to meet the other selectmen. Men things. Things that Jean-Luc had less and less time to do. Things that taught values by example.

"I wish I knew how to be a better mother," Leah said to no one. Maybe it was already too late. Yves-Pierre would go away to school in September. In many ways she felt like she'd lost her son, but how and why she couldn't figure out.

CHAPTER TWENTY-ONE:
THE SHOWING
GENEVA
1979

"I don't see why you need to leave for the entire month of June," Jean-Luc said watching Leah pack sweatshirts and jeans.

"Because I can't work here." She stepped over his feet, which stuck out onto the rug from where he sat on the edge of the bed. He made no move to pull them out of her way.

"That's your fault. You should arrange your time better. You've Nanny, two studios, household help. What more do you need?" He pouted.

Tel père, tel fils, she thought, like father like son.

"Time." She threw in underpants and several pairs of thick socks. Kathy's house was drafty. Heating was minimal and it was always colder in the Jura. She opened the door to their bathroom and took her toiletry bag from the drawer under her sink.

"Visit me weekends."

"But the children . . ."

"Yves-Pierre is away on a class trip for three of the weeks I'm gone. Bring Claire-Lise with you."

He looked at his hands. "Kathy's house isn't comfortable. She doesn't have any furniture in the living room."

"And the kids love roller skating in there."

"That's not normal. *She's* not normal," he said.

Leah didn't want to defend her friend yet another time. Jean-Luc would never understand a woman who didn't want to be married or who cared nothing about her home. Kathy was a painter and a mother and sometimes a mother and a painter depending on who needed what more. Leah was looking forward to a house where laughter wasn't an exception.

"I don't like it," Jean-Luc said.

Leah jumped on the bed, pulled him down and kissed him. He didn't kiss back. "I know you don't. But this show is important to me." She licked his ear. "I've been so busy with those dinner parties and damned committees that I couldn't work. It's my turn." She ran her hand down his chest. "We've time. Even if it's not Saturday night."

"I think I can vary the pattern a little." Jean-Luc took her in his arms.

Leah couldn't explain why, but instead of turning onto the Lausanne auto route, she took a right and drove through the tunnel to Ferney-Voltaire. As usual the border guard waved her through as just another Swiss bringing money to the French economy. Unlike Geneva, Ferney-Voltaire was a village hoping someday to be a town: farms and old homes melded with new houses and block apartments.

Leah headed for the center. She decided if she found a parking place, she was meant to do it. If not, she'd continue to Kathy's in the Vals de Travers. Six spots were free outside the bank and the PTT. That's my answer, she thought. She angled her car between a Deux Cheveaux and a Renault.

After renting a post office box, she nodded at Voltaire's statue before entering Crédit Agricole. Someday she would forgive that cranky old man for writing the things she had to read for her French classes back in Stonefield.

Three bank tellers sat at desks. She chose the middle one. Using half the money Jean-Luc had given her for her visit to Kathy, she opened a bank account.

In Switzerland, she'd have needed his permission. She pushed her receipt with its green and red logo into the lining of her bag next to where she'd hidden her American passport in her maiden name that she had used for the identification demanded by the teller.

"A girl needs a nest egg," she kept telling herself as she began the nine hairpin curves up the last mountain before arriving at the Vals de Travers. She hated that stretch of road. Drivers accelerated too fast, often passing where they had limited vision.

In most places there was no guard rail. She imagined going over the edge, her car tumbling and twisting into the valley below. Relief flooded through her when she arrived at the straight Ste. Croix road which lead down the mountain to Môtiers and Kathy.

Clanging woke her. Leah rolled out of her sleeping bag on the floor and rushed to the window to see thirty cows, each wearing a bell, strolling by Kathy's barn toward the pasture at the foot of the mountain. A man in high boots ran behind with a stick, hitting the strays except for one that he let drink from the beige stone fountain in the middle of the street. No moving cars were visible, but a spotless truck filled with hay was parked by the barn covered with cowbells and horseshoes.

Kathy, in a flannel night gown, came into the room scratching her stomach and yawning. Môtiers was high enough in the Jura to be cold even in late spring.

"Better than an alarm clock, those damned cows," she said. "Get dressed and get to work."

Leah looked at her watch—6:30. She slipped on jeans and entered the kitchen. Adam and Jennifer, still in pajamas, rubbed their eyes.

Kathy, in jeans buttoned a paint-splattered shirt over a turtle neck before grabbing a milk can.

"Light the fire. I'll be back with milk and bread."

Leah found a taper and opened the ceramic stove that covered half the wall. The tiles were forest green. The kindling that Kathy had arranged before they went to bed, snapped and crackled before shushing into flame.

"Get dressed, kids," Leah said.

The children disappeared.

Kathy was back within ten minutes to find Leah brushing Jennifer's hair. She set the milk and bread on the table. One was warm; one from the cow, the other from the baker's oven.

"She's gentler than you are Mama," Jennifer said. Leah's hand held the child's head in place, so she had to look sideways.

"That's 'cause she's not your mother. Mothers are always nicer to other people's children. It's a rule." Kathy poured some milk into a pan and rested it on the ceramic stove. She filled a bottle with the rest then put the empty can in the soapstone sink. After spooning chocolate powder into four bowls and cutting bread, she said, "Eat."

"I want *confiture*," Adam said.

"So open the refrigerator and get it. I'm your mother not your slave." Kathy ruffled his hair.

Adam got the jam himself. The jar was sticky and he wiped his hands on his pants.

By 7:30 Leah was in the studio working. Kathy painted next to her, stopping only to bring them sandwiches at noon. Dinner was canned spaghetti and salad from the neighbor's garden.

After the kids were asleep, the two women walked to Môtiers' one café. They had not changed from their paint-splattered clothes. Leah picked a black-eyed Susan. She absent-mindedly pulled a petal off at a time. She didn't think; he loves me, he loves me not. She thought; my show will be great, it will flop. The last petal was a prediction of greatness.

"The reason I live here is this village has 600 people, 6000 cows, six million flowers and—most important—six other artists," Kathy said as she stopped at the café's door. Light glowed through the thick yellow glass panes. "Seven, now you're here."

"I don't feel like an artist anymore—just a pretend artist."

"Wait till your show is over. You'll wow 'em." Kathy pushed the door. "Sometimes Tinguely is here."

As they entered three women and a man waved her over. The Swiss sculptor wasn't among them, but Leah absorbed their conversation. Instead of finance and politics, she found herself talking about color and line, topics she had not discussed in a group since she'd left Paris. Only when the waitress began closing at 10:00 did she realize how much she'd missed her own kind, whatever her own kind was.

"It's still Switzerland. At one time that café closed at 8:00 p.m., but we persuaded the owner to stay open longer," Kathy said as they walked home. The only sound was the fountain's gurgle.

The mountains loomed around them in the moonlight, although the sun had just set. All the houses were shuttered, the people inside asleep.

Each day the women rose early, painted as soon as the kids left and took turns getting meals, with a quick stop at the café before bed. Leah, freed from responsibilities, found her brushes took on a life of their own. She thought of the paint books she had as a child that when you added water the color appeared.

"Work shouldn't be this easy," she said.

"You've been around too many Calvinists," Kathy said. She looked at Leah's canvas. "God, you're good. I could strangle you for not having any confidence in yourself."

Their routine stopped Saturday when Jean-Luc arrived with Claire-Lise, who hugged her mother then ran off with Jennifer.

"She really missed you," Jean-Luc said, his arm around his wife's shoulders.

186

"I can see," Kathy said. "It's obvious the way she's clinging to me."

Jean-Luc glowered.

"Come look what I accomplished." Leah lead him into the studio.

"You have made real progress," he said holding first one miniature than another to the light. "I'm proud of you."

The life Leah wanted resumed when the Perrosets' car pulled out of the driveway Sunday afternoon.

On Leah's last night, Kathy suggested a walk to Mauler & Cie, a winery where local grapes were turned into champagne. Located in a 13th century abbey, the tasting room had been the monk's refractory. The two women stood at the long oak bar in the wood paneled room and tested a dry, sweet, semi-dry and pink. The overweight woman behind the counter wrapped the bottles with a white towel as she pulled them from individual ice buckets to half fill the flutes in front of Kathy and Leah. An empty bucket sat on the bar to throw away any of the undrunk champagne.

"Let's get the semi-dry. My treat," Leah said.

They carried the bottle back to Kathy's. "If we don't finish it, we can always put a spoon in it so it doesn't go flat," Leah said.

"We'll finish it to celebrate how much you got done." They clinked their glasses together. They weren't flutes but old mustard glasses decorated with Smurfs.

"Jean-Luc would have a hemorrhage if he saw this," Leah said.

"I won't mention it if you don't." Kathy held her champagne to the light and watched as the bubbles caught the reflection in their race to the surface.

The Perrosets deplaned at Cointrin Airport on the morning of

August 1st, the 689th anniversary of Switzerland's birth, making it the world's oldest democracy as Jean-Luc was forever pointing out.

The children, who'd slept most of the flight that brought them home from their holiday, stretched out on two seats each, rubbed their eyes as Leah steered them through customs.

Monsieur Shleppi met them outside the airport as close to the arrival door as he could park. He had the trunk and both right side doors open. "Nice holiday?"

"Fantastic," they all said at once as they got into the car.

Nanny and Madame Shleppi waited at the front door of the château. "I think you've grown a foot, Yves-Pierre," Nanny said as she hugged both children.

"I'm going to get some sleep," Jean-Luc said.

"At least a nap. Then we can go to the bonfire and fireworks tonight."

"I'll be up in a minute," Leah said. The idea of sleeping in a bed instead of a covered wagon had definite appeal. She dialed Kathy.

"How did it go?" Kathy asked.

"Fantastic. I got three more canvases done at my folks'. I still don't have enough."

"Come out again. Bring the kids. I'll shove 'em outdoors with mine. We can pretend they don't exist."

"Good," Leah said. "You saved me from inviting myself."

"This one or this one?" Leah held a black dress then a navy blue in front her. "Or this?" She took a pink silk and adding the black and blue to the pile on the bed.

Jean-Luc took her by the hand. "The show is for your paintings, not your dress. You never make a fuss about what you wear . . ."

"This is different . . ."

"It is. By the time you decide what to wear your show will be over. Put this on." He picked out the pink silk. She slipped it over her head, and he zipped her up. His fingers had difficulty manipulating the small pearl button at the neck.

The children knocked at the door. "We want to see you before you go," Claire-Lise said. She held out a drawing of a woman at an easel. "For good luck." Leah kissed her daughter and son as Jean-Luc held her coat for her.

The windows of the *Galerie Belle Rive* glowed. Along the quai across the street, people boarded a dinner boat. The *Jet d'eau* shimmered in its spotlight as it shot into the night sky.

Jean-Luc held the gallery door open for Leah. "Well, time to greet the ocean liner," he said. He was talking about the gallery owner, not the ship on the lake.

"Be kind," Leah said although she never saw Madame Castilini without thinking of an opera singer.

Madame Castilini was directing the bartender on how to arrange the champagne glasses. She served real champagne from France. There were small slices of bread with smoked salmon and caviar, arranged so the red and black made a checkerboard. As soon as she saw the Perrosets, she floated over to them.

"Check how I've reangled the lighting." She towed Leah behind her. "Now, don't be angry, but I exchanged the mushrooms and squirrel. It's better, don't you think?" This was the tenth arrangement the two women had done. Before Leah could comment, the first guest arrived.

The night became a blur of remarks. There were the polite comments of the couple's friends.

Madame Castilini sidled up to Leah and, holding a lace trimmed handkerchief over her mouth, whispered, "You've three sales." She paused; "And one from a very fussy client, a very, very fussy client." Then she careened off toward another client.

Leah's sister-in-law, Anne-Joëlle, stood in front of an arrangement of four still lives of children's toys. They were priced as a set. Leah excused herself from a woman who had been telling her how she had always wanted to paint someday. She resisted saying what Kathy would have said to the woman which was, "So paint."

Anne-Joëlle kissed Leah three times. It was more of her cheek pressing against Leah's than lips touching skin. "This must have taken you so long. No wonder you kept deserting my poor brother and the children."

Leah did what she usually did when she talked to her sister-in-law. She smiled and listened.

Kathy arrived late and disheveled on the arm of a man. Systematically she walked him around the room, gesturing at each painting and waiting for him to look more closely. He took out a magnifying glass.

What's he doing, Leah wondered as she talked with Arnaud Savary, art critic of *La Suisse*. Savary signaled a waiter as Kathy walked up and put her arm around Leah's waist.

"Meet Peter Ainsworth, head critic of *American Artist Today*. I got him to fly over just for this."

Savary took a flute of champagne from a tray offered by the waiter.

Peter picked two glasses and gave them to the two women before taking one himself. "And Kathy spoke the truth. You're very talented. Very distinctive style."

"I agree," Savary said. "I'll admit that I wasn't too excited about seeing miniatures. Usually don't like them, but I'm converted."

"Bask," Kathy said as they watched Madame Castilini put another sold sign on a painting. "This show is a hit."

Leah opened her eyes. Jean-Luc's arm rested heavily across her waist as they spooned each other. It had been well after midnight when they'd crawled into bed. He'd made gentle love to her as he had not in years. Leah wondered if pride drove him.

The fluorescent hands of the clock read 10:30 a.m. Because the shutters were closed and drapes drawn, no light permeated the room. She slipped out from under his arm and the duvet and put on her robe then tiptoed down the stairs. Normally, no one went around the château in anything but complete dress. *La Suisse* and the *Tribune de Genève* were at her dining place as she had asked they be.

Madame Shleppi appeared. "What would you like for breakfast?"

"Coffee, bread, thank you." Leah spread the *Tribune de Genève* on the table and saw the headline. She alternated between holding her breath and shallow gasps as she picked up the newspaper.

Exhibition at Galerie Belle Rive Not up to Expectations
Many housewives just take care of their children. Madame Jean-Luc Perroset paints. Maybe she should spend more time with her family, for her work is amateurish, although at the top level of an amateur.
Complete review, page 30

The rest of the review was in the same vein. Leah forced herself to read through each word.

Shaking, Leah found Savary's review in *La Suisse*. It was worse.

Jean-Luc found his wife in tears, her head in her arms. After reading the reviews, he gathered her into his arms. "I'm so sorry, *Chérie.*"

"Telephone, Madame," the housekeeper said. "Madame

Castilini." Leah honked into the handkerchief Jean-Luc handed her. Breathing in several times quickly, she took the phone.

"I've read what those snakes wrote in the paper. If I'd a gun I'd shoot them. Two-faced devils. Oohing and ahhing last night then today the knife in our backs." The gallery owner sputtered on. Leah imagined her with her hands waving, pacing back and forth with the phone tucked under her chins.

"Monsieur Poulain called this morning. Remember? He bought the book and glove painting last night."

"I suppose he wanted to cancel." Leah's voice quivered.

"No. He called to say he wanted to buy another, the one of the bread, boiled egg and banana. He also suggested shoving those critics in the lake."

"Who is Poulain?" Leah asked.

"A Parisian. A client. He has a good eye for new talent. You should have heard him rage against the provincial Swiss . . ."

"I appreciate your call," Leah said, wanting to hang up, but it took another five minutes before the gallery owner finished venting.

"*Chérie*, every artist gets bad reviews at some point. Remember that," Jean-Luc noted.

Leah sighed. "I'm going back to bed."

A tapping woke her midafternoon. Leah's eyes felt as if they'd been sealed with Velcro then ripped apart. She thought of the game that some of the ex-pats played called name five famous Swiss. The invention of Velcro always came up, even if it was a thing and not a person.

"Kathy's on the phone," Jean-Luc almost whispered. Leah went downstairs. There was no sign of the children or Nanny. "I sent the kids to the park with Nanny," he said.

Couples living together a long time don't need language, Leah thought as she reached for the receiver.

"We just got back from the hospital," Kathy said. Her voice wasn't natural, quavering instead of her normal matter-of fact delivery.

"Hospital?"

"On the road to Ste. Croix a car going like a bat out of hell nearly knocked us into the valley. On the fifth curve." Kathy started to cry.

"You must have been petrified," Leah said.

After several deep breaths Kathy said, "He totaled our car and went off the edge himself. He's dead."

"Oh my God." Leah sat on a stair.

"What happened," Jean-Luc mouthed.

"Accident," Leah mouthed back. "What happened, Kathy?"

"Peter wasn't wearing a seatbelt and he hit the steering wheel full force and his broken ribs ripped into his lungs. He bled to death. My face is only cut. Not from the windshield, but from the makeup mirror. I've a broken rib where I hit the dashboard."

"Ask her if she wants us to go out there," Jean-Luc whispered.

"We're coming out," Leah said.

"Would you?" Kathy asked. "I need you. Really need you."

A month later Leah shuddered as she drove the hairpin curves to Môtiers. The last of the leaves had been washed off the trees, making the road even more slippery. As she passed the spot of Kathy's accident she wished she were Catholic so she could cross herself. But even if she were Catholic, she'd still be too afraid to loosen her grip on the wheel.

Kathy welcomed her with a bowl of tea. "I still get twinges if I move too fast," she said. They sat by the ceramic stove in the kitchen, Kathy in a rocking chair she'd found in the trash and repaired.

Leah, sitting cross legged on a giant cushion, asked, "Any news on the accident?"

"Take your pick on bad news. The car was stolen. The man driving it had a false passport. Because Peter didn't have his seat belt on, the insurance won't pay for his hospital. They're billing me. However, you know what they say about blood and stones."

"Shit," Leah said.

"I'm alive," Kathy said. The wind gusted and blew a branch against the window. "So if it doesn't make sense, who says it has to? What are you up to? Loosely translated that means how's your painting?"

Leah took the two bowls to the sink and rinsed them. "I'm not. We've been going to the chalet almost every weekend. There's the committees and this dinner and that."

"You know what they say about falling off a horse? You gotta get right back on. Same thing with bad reviews."

Leah stood motionless at the sink. "Maybe the critics are right."

Kathy snorted and had to blow her nose. She made gentle little puffs into the piece of tissue she'd pull from her pocket. "Still don't dare do this with any gusto. It hurts too much. Back to the subject. It's like people who can't do stuff, teach: people who can't paint become art critics."

"You are certainly Miss Cliché today. But even Peter's magazine wouldn't review me."

"Well he had called in the review to meet their deadline before the accident, but another friend of mine who works there said someone bought the magazine and made a new policy that they'd only review American artists working in the States," Kathy said.

She got up and put her hand on Leah's shoulder. "Lately the stars are working against us, but don't worry. They'll come our way again."

★ ★ ★ ★ ★

The sixth straight day of rain left Leah feeling mildewed. Even with fires in all the fireplaces and the central heat on, the château held the damp. She wore tights, heavy socks, jeans, a turtle neck and sweater and still shivered. She hoped she wasn't getting Nanny's flu. That poor woman had been in bed the better part of a week.

Jean-Luc hated it when she dressed like this, but that morning he had been all smiles and told her how beautiful she was with her graying hair.

"You're wonderful. Business is wonderful," he'd said. She never remembered hearing any businessman say anything but, "It's hard, very hard now."

On Wednesdays the children had no school. Claire-Lise played with a friend. The two girls appeared in the den where Leah was trying to read as close to the fire as she could get.

"Can we play dress up?" Claire-Lise asked. The girls followed Leah to the attic.

The heat had risen so it felt toasty. I should read here, Leah thought. Water sheeted on the windows. Rain battered the roof. Leah moved two trunks. When she opened the larger, a musty smell escaped. Leah sneezed.

Claire-Lise pulled out a hat with a feather. Françoise, her daughter's friend, grabbed a boa which she draped around Claire-Lise's neck. The original white fluff was thick with dust and both children sneezed. The next garment was a beige silk dress from the 1920s. Leah still could not imagine a Perroset flapper.

She was at the bottom of the attic stairs when she heard Claire-Lise say, "Look at all the paintings."

She started to walk away, but her curiosity was piqued and she climbed the stairs once again. Several dresses and a coat lay on the coarse floor boards. The girls had another trunk open,

195

and it was filled with her miniatures—not her new work, but the paintings she had exhibited in the Paris restaurant right before Jean-Luc proposed. Searching the other trunks, she found everything that had been exhibited her entire time in Paris.

Leah had no trouble finding a parking place near the bank. The rain kept shoppers home. The Rhone had risen to almost the top of its banks, the highest in years. Not bothering to either lock the car or open an umbrella, she stormed to the bank's door and rang.

The 18th century building had a very modern locking system that could only be activated by a guard after the applicant for entry had been approved by security. No one dropped into this bank. Appointments were made, hotel arrangements were set up and often clients were delivered, not in limos, because that would have drawn attention, but in the bank's two-year-old Mercedes. Understated elegance, not ostentatious.

When she heard the click unlock the door, she slammed her weight against the heavy oak. Had there not been a stopper from the wall, the wall would have been dented.

"Madame Perroset," the doorkeeper said, but Leah stomped by him, ignoring how she dripped on the oriental rugs. The bank's lobby was a huge wood-paneled room dominated by a cherry wood table, elaborately carved with twenty-four equally elaborately carved chairs around it.

A floral centerpiece was taller than Claire-Lise. It looked more like a five-star hotel lobby than a bank where there were no tellers for withdrawal and deposits, but only secluded offices to arrange large transfers of funds.

A large marble staircase, leading to the private offices, contrasted in time with an iron bannister carved in Art Deco style. Leah took the steps two at a time.

Madame Picard, Jean-Luc's secretary, sat at her desk outside his door.

"I want my husband." She brushed by the elderly woman.

Madame Picard, jumped up knocking her chair over. She barred the door with outstretched arms. "He's in a meeting. He can't be disturbed. Those were his orders." The older woman's glasses were slightly askew. Her lips trembled.

"You've two choices. Move, or I'll knock you out of my way," Leah said.

The woman hesitated three seconds. Leah pulled back her arm, her hand in a fist. Madame Picard stepped aside and brushed her skirt much like a cat washes when it is embarrassed and wants to cover up by saying, "I really wanted to do this all the time."

Jean-Luc's desk was positioned about twenty feet into the room at the end of an oriental runner. He was framed by a floor-to-ceiling window with both sheer curtains and then elaborately hung maroon velvet drapes. The two maroon leather chairs in front of the desk were occupied by men Leah had never met. They had been in the middle of a laugh when she'd burst into the room.

Jean-Luc stood. "Leah, what are you doing here?"

Mrs. Picard followed wringing her hands. "She didn't give me any choice, Sir."

"Would you excuse us gentlemen? I need to talk to my husband," Leah said with a pretend smile. She caught a view of herself in the gilt mirror over the marble fireplace where a fire was in full glory. Drowned rat would have been a complimentary description.

"Gentlemen, can you wait in the waiting room?" Turning to his secretary, who looked as is she were about to cry, he said, "It's all right Madame Picard. Shut the door, please." As she was almost out of the room, he added, "And Madame Picard, get them another coffee please."

"I don't know what this is about, but can't it wait until I am home?" Jean-Luc asked.

Leah walked to his desk. On it she saw papers covered with lists. She swept them off, hitting the chalk board where the suddenly rising price of gold was marked. "We'll talk now."

Leah watched Jean-Luc turn a red that clashed with the brocade drapes. "What the hell do you think you're doing? You barge in here dressed like some hippy, create a scene . . ."

"Shut up. Why are all my paintings in the attic?"

Jean-Luc sat down. "I see." He folded his hands in a steeple.

Leah went to the couch in front of the fireplace ablaze with a log bigger than her waist. A few raindrops fell down the chimney; they made a sizzle, a small sizzle, a sizzlette that distracted Leah for a second. Rain beat against the window.

She grabbed one of the leather pillows from the sofa and threw it at him. Reaching up, he picked it out of the air as it soared by his left ear.

"I thought they were sold. Why? Why did you do it?"

He came around from the desk and put his arms around her. She stiffened. He tried stroking her face, but she snapped at his hand, which he pulled away before she could sink her teeth into his skin.

He took her by both shoulders and shook her. Then he shoved her on the couch. "Calm down."

He went to the door and told his secretary to bring his wife a cup of tea. He went around behind Leah and began massaging her neck. She let him, but instead of relaxing her muscles, his touch caused them to tighten.

Within minutes, Madame Picard knocked. Jean-Luc reached through the door and took the Victorian rose cup. Jean-Luc walked back to Leah and held out the cup and said, "I'll give it to you, if you promise not to throw it at me."

"I promise." She wondered how he made her feel as if she were being unreasonable. When she took the cup it rattled against the saucer. "I can't imagine what you can tell me."

He pulled up a chair in front of her. She lifted the cup to her mouth. The liquid burned her tongue leaving it as if it were coated with fuzz. She placed the tea on the end table next to the sofa.

The fire behind her crackled as a log shifted and thumped lower in the grate. They both jumped.

"*Chérie*, it's not like you think." When Leah only glared he continued. "I knew I was going to ask you to marry me, but I wanted you to come because you wanted to, not because you feared you wouldn't be successful as an artist. I thought if your show was a success, you'd be confident enough to move to Geneva."

"I thought I was a success because three people bought everything."

"I wanted you to feel that way. That was my point."

"And that was the one consolation I had when my exhibition failed last month. That in Paris, someone, three someones, liked my work enough to buy a lot of my work. Years of hope were built on nothing."

"You sold many paintings here," he said.

"That's not important. What matters is you lied to me." Leah felt so cold.

"I didn't lie to you. I never said that I did or didn't buy those paintings." His words faded although his mouth kept talking. Leah put her hand over her mouth and cried, but when he tried to comfort her, she wouldn't let him.

CHAPTER TWENTY-TWO:
THE STRANGER
GENEVA
1981–1982

"I told everyone, absolutely everyone, to look for you, but no one saw you," Grace said. The international line crackled and there was a noticeable time pause between Grace's and Leah's speech. Leah sat on her bottom stair in the château's entry as she spoke to her mother. With her free hand she held her place in *The Stranger*, which she'd been reading when interrupted by the overseas call. The house had been deliciously quiet with Jean-Luc in London, Yves-Pierre at Rosay Academy and Claire-Lise sleeping over at a girl friend's.

"There's no reason the cameras should notice us. We aren't royalty or anything. We weren't even presented to the Queen." She didn't tell her mother that Jean-Luc had had several meetings with Margaret Thatcher and was still meeting with her advisors. First it was supposed to be a secret and second she couldn't bear to listen to how wonderful President Reagan was, which was where that topic would lead.

Jean-Luc had almost turned somersaults when Reagan's victory was announced. "Good for business," he'd said. "Sometimes things work like they should."

Leah figured she was the only person in the world who didn't trust the American president.

"I still can't believe my daughter was invited," Grace said. "Tell me everything. Don't leave out a single detail."

"I don't suppose you want to hear how bored I was between the time we had to be in the church and when Lady Di arrived." Leah felt mean torturing her mother, but the words fell from her mouth before she could stop them. Some day Claire-Lise will pay me back, she thought.

"No, I want to hear about the dress, the flowers, and does she really have a beautiful complexion?"

Without saying that her mother probably saw more on television than the Perrosets did tucked in the corner of St. Paul's Cathedral, Leah launched into the things her mother wanted to hear. "After the wedding, we saw *Cats*. It was incredible. Fantastic stage set, costumes."

"Maybe Daddy and I can meet you in London. Take in a few shows."

Leah smiled. Her mother, who once wouldn't go into Boston, now made at least one trip a year and sometimes two to Europe.

"That would be nice."

When she hung up, she called Kathy. She'd tried several times since she'd been back but there was never any answer. She'd probably taken the kids camping, she thought, but then realized that school had started. She went upstairs and settled into the chaise lounge to read.

Leah drove into Geneva. She wasn't sure where she was going, but without Jean-Luc, without the kids, it didn't matter. A yellow VW van let her into traffic. She parked the car under the Gare du Cornavin and was surprised when the van parked at the opposite end of the underground area. Coincidence, she thought. She mounted the stairs quickly.

Although Geneva was considered a safe city, she was glad other people were around. As she walked down the street, she looked behind her. No one followed. How silly I am, she thought.

An Officer and a Gentlemen was playing at the Rialto. She bought a ticket for the v.o., *version originale*. She had never learned to like dubbing where the voices went on well after the mouth stopped moving. She was often amused by the French subtitles, however, especially after a long, long speech and the words flashed on the screen were something like, "Of course" or "I don't think so." And sometimes she found the translation inaccurate. She never did understand why in one movie the name Ethel Merman had been translated as Judy Garland.

After the movie, annoyance at Richard Gere sweeping Debra Winger into his arms as music played and the other factory workers watched, niggled at her. Fairy tales were for books and movies.

Grace said that Leah led a fairy tale life. If she did, then why didn't she feel it? The least she could do was to be grateful for a life that others only dreamed about living. She could just imagine Abigail saying, "If you want sympathy, you'll find it under S in the dictionary."

She passed a man sitting in front of an easel painting the church across from the train station. He had dark curly hair so much like Michael's that Leah had to go around to check out his face. It was nothing like her first husband's, but her heart continued racing.

She went to a tea room to recover. Several women sat at tables in pairs. Leah examined the many pastries in the case. The coffee eclair looked good, but so did the apricot tart. In the end she chose a rectangular tart with perfectly sliced apples, the last one of its type. As the waitress brought it to her table with a pot of tea, Leah felt stupid at her reaction to the artist.

Would Diana and Charles really live happily ever after? Would Richard Gere and Debra Winger? Would she?

"I never thought that I'd be bored. I always had too much passion, too much to do," she said. A woman at the next table stared. Leah blushed to have been caught talking aloud to herself.

As she broke into her tart a few flakes of confectioner's sugar fell on the gold speckled Formica table top. As she brushed them away, she could imagine Abigail Holt sitting across from her, saying, "If you're bored, it's your own fault." This is my day to remember the dead, Leah thought.

"Telephone," Madame Shleppi said. Leah put a tissue in *The Stranger* to mark her place and left the book on the sofa. She shook her hair away from her ear before saying, "Hallo, Madame Perroset ici." She'd never gotten used to answering with only her name as most Swiss did. It felt too abrupt, too cold.

"Hello, Mrs. Perroset," a flat midwestern American twang said over the phone. "You don't know me, but I'm Kathy's mother. Dorothy Sullivan. There's been a terrible accident."

Leah grabbed the banister. "What happened?"

"The beam in the living room broke. Load bearing. Kathy was trapped in the rubble for hours until they could dig her out. She's at the Vals de Travers Hospital. In Couvet. She's just out of intensive care."

"The kids?"

"Both fine. It was their weekend with their father."

"I'll be out as soon as I can."

Within an hour Leah landed her car in the hospital parking lot. Without bothering to lock it she ran into the main entrance and stood at the main desk. The receptionist thumbed through records filing a card here and there when something matched.

"Madame Katherine Sullivan?" Leah asked.

When Leah took the pass, her hands shook.

"Room 302. Elevator is to the left."

Leah pushed the button with the up arrow, but when the doors opened, the elevator was filled by two nurses and an empty gurney. Instead of yelling, get out and let me in as she wanted to do, she took the stairs two at a time, wishing that rushing could help her friend and hating that it couldn't.

Although the room had four beds, Kathy was alone. The other three beds had blue wool blankets folded neatly in identical compact squares on top of the pillows.

However they were all on the bottom not on the top of the beds. Kathy's head was turned to the window that looked onto the Jura yellow with fall leaves. A lightning bolt flashed through the gray sky and rain drops splattered the glass.

When Leah approached, she saw her friend was asleep, her chest moving slowly up and down almost imperceptibly. Her face was cut, her head swathed in bandages. A jagged scar ran down her left cheek.

Settling in the green plastic chair next to the bed, Leah watched an IV drip into Kathy's arm until she, too, fell asleep.

"When did you get here?" Kathy's voice was weak, but loud enough to jar Leah awake.

She rubbed her eyes and glanced at her watch. "About an hour ago. Your mother called me."

"Hmmm." Kathy half-heartedly pointed to the IV bottle. "They give me stuff to keep me in La La land. Make 'em stop. Mom doesn't speak enough French." Then her eyes closed and her breathing became short little putts.

Leah drove to Môtiers from the hospital, a distance of less than a mile down postcard perfect streets. The workman who was repairing Kathy's collapsed roof, his hair plastered from the downpour, packed up his truck. Seeing part of the house caved in, made Leah shudder as she imagined Kathy trapped inside. She went to the back door and let herself in. An older woman, who looked like Kathy might in another thirty years sat in the kitchen.

"Mrs. Sullivan, I'm Leah Perroset."

The woman got up and extended her hand. "I've heard a lot

about you. Kathy said you're a real good friend." Mrs. Sullivan, who insisted Leah call her Dorothy, showed her the damage. "I want it fixed before my daughter gets home. Then we need to have the ramps installed."

"Ramps?"

"She's paralyzed from the waist down," Dorothy said.

"Oh, my God," Leah said.

Leah spent every afternoon at the hospital.

Mornings she drove Dorothy wherever she needed to go: picking up groceries, selecting a safety rail for the shower, buying supplies for the carpenters.

A month after the accident, two months after the royal wedding, Leah walked in to Kathy's room to find Rolf Doré sitting by his ex-wife's bed. Her friend had been crying. When Rolf patted her hand, Kathy pulled it back from her ex-husband.

"Excuse me, I'll come back later," Leah said.

In the cafeteria she sat at a table with a cup of espresso. The floor-to-ceiling window had the same view of the Jura as Kathy did from her hospital bed. There were fewer leaves on the trees now. The top of the mountain had its first dusting of snow from the night before.

She wondered how long to stay out of the way. She was the only one in the room, except for the woman behind the cash register.

Rolf solved her problem by coming in. He stopped at the espresso machine before sitting at Leah's table. Leah could hear the machine gush as he filled his demitasse. He was tall and spoke French with the sing-song accent common to Swiss Germans. "My ex-wife is a stubborn woman," he said. "I want to convince her the children are better with me. At least short term."

"What do *they* want?" Leah asked as she watched him stir

sugar into the beige foam.

"To see their mother. I wanted to check her out before I exposed them." He emptied the demitasse with one gulp.

"They're good kids. They'll be able to take it."

"But will Kathy?"

"She's doesn't need legs to talk to them."

Leah didn't know a lot about Rolf. Kathy hadn't discussed her marriage break up nor hashed out his transgressions. Her only comment was that she was the guilty party, because she couldn't handle art, husband and kids. "Rolf is the most dispensable of the three," she'd said.

"Maybe you can make her see some sense." He gave Leah the ritual three cheek kisses before leaving.

She put their cups with the other dirty dishes on a cart outside the entrance to the hospital kitchen and took the elevator to the third floor. Kathy was no longer alone. A woman from Fleurier, the next village, was recovering from a knee operation. Leah had never seen her, because the curtain was always pulled around the bed. She could hear Johnny Halliday singing through the fabric. The volume was several decibels lower than Yves-Pierre would have played the rocker's records.

Kathy's face was blotched. "He wants the kids."

"I know. What do you think?" Leah asked.

More tears dampened Kathy's cheeks. She opened the drawer of the stand next to her bed and pulled out a packet of tissues. After she stabbed at the plastic wrap ineffectually, Leah took the package from her. Using a fingernail to break the seal, she handed one to Kathy.

"I can't walk. I don't need legs to parent."

"That's what I told him."

"Maybe you could talk to Rolf," Leah said to her husband. She was in bed, dressed in a highnecked flannel nightgown for the first time that fall. Her feet were on the hot water bottle. Jean-Luc liked to pre-warm the bed.

He aligned the creases of his pants suspended on the hanger before slipping on his pajama bottoms. Undoing his tie, he hung it in the closet. He folded, then rolled, his dirty shirt before putting it in the hamper. His order of undressing never varied.

Once under the covers he said, "I don't like interfering with other couples. I'm not sure Rolf is wrong. Kathy was strange enough before her accident. The kids might benefit from a good bourgeois home."

"Rolf is busy with his agency. He's not home very much," Leah said.

Jean-Luc picked up the financial report he'd put on the night table and reached for his reading glasses. "We still shouldn't get involved, and you should be spending less time running back and forth. By the way, have you heard from Yves-Pierre?"

"Changing the subject?"

"Checking on our son." He kissed her nose.

She glanced at the title on the paper which read, General Rios Montt. She'd met him at a party at the Guatemalan Consulate. "Are you financing something in Latin America?"

"*Chérie,* the bank has interests all over the world. I'll worry about business; you worry about the family."

Leah pushed Kathy's wheelchair down the hospital hall and out the front door. "Freedom, Lady," she said.

Dorothy followed with Kathy's suitcase. One by one the nurses stopped to kiss Kathy on the cheeks and called out their farewells.

"Keep up the exercises."

"Come back and see us."

"Wish all our patients were as great as you. Maybe we can

get you to come back to give a course in patient manners."

Kathy acknowledged each comment.

As Leah and Dorothy manipulated Kathy into Leah's car, Leah saw a yellow van with Geneva plates pull in. Yellow vans are common, she thought.

Adam and Jennifer waited for their mother. They'd tied a yellow ribbon around the front door and had made a sign saying, "Welcome home." They'd solved the custody problem. "We belong with Mom," Adam had told Rolf.

"She needs us. I mean she's not just our mom when things are okay," Jennifer had said.

Rolf had reported all this to Kathy and Kathy had passed it on to Leah. "He makes a pretty good ex-husband," Kathy had said. Leah agreed.

Dorothy had decided to stay on for a while, claiming she hadn't felt so useful for a long time.

"Good," Jean-Luc said when Leah told him about the homecoming. "You can spend more time with your own family."

The Perrosets picked up Yves-Pierre at school then drove to the chalet for the Christmas holiday. The formal Christmases had ended after the death of Leah's mother-in-law and were replaced by a skiing holiday at the chalet with just the core family.

After the children went to bed Christmas Eve, Leah sat on the floor in front of the fire. When the children were little the couple could never have lit a fire for fear of being accused of trying to singe Santa. Although neither child believed in Père Noël, they still wanted their parents to wait until they were in bed to set out presents. Leah, having finished all her chores, watched Jean-Luc stuff her stocking, the last thing to be done. He held out each box before dropping it in and said, "Guess," but he wouldn't tell her if she were right or not.

She'd poured them each *vin chaud* that she'd made earlier. *"Sante!"* she said holding her cup high. She took a sip. The hot wine had just the right amount of orange, clove and cinnamon.

"Santé, I'm glad you started the idea of stockings," he said. "It's a nice tradition." After he sat next to her his back against the couch, he leaned over to kiss her. They made love, knowing the children wouldn't peek until daylight. When he and Leah went to bed, hand-in-hand, she found herself humming "I saw Mommy kissing Santa Claus."

Two days before New Year's Eve as the family stacked their skis against the entrance, they heard the telephone ring. Yves-Pierre burst into the chalet first. They locked the door only when they were gone overnight.

"Papa, it's for you. Some man with a Spanish accent," he called as the others stomped their feet to shake the snow off their boots.

"Merde," Jean-Luc said. He took the phone. Spanish shot from his mouth like gun fire as he turned his back on the family.

The children disappeared upstairs to get out of their snow clothes. He slammed the receiver down.

"I don't believe it," he said.

"What?" Leah asked.

"I have to go to Guatemala, then DC. Can you drive me down the mountain to the nearest car rental? No reason for you and the kids to give up the next few days."

When Leah got back it was almost dark. A few flakes of snow fell, but it wasn't serious snow. She went inside. The kids were in their rooms. She dialed Kathy. "How'd you like to spend New Year's Eve in Valais?"

"Can I bring mother?"

"Bring whomever you want. Even a Môtiers cow."

"I don't believe this," Dorothy kept saying. "It's like a dream, a postcard, a . . ." She stood at the chalet window watching the four kids make a snow army. Five snowmen stood on each side of a bunker sparkling like diamond dust in the moonlight.

Leah boiled potatoes. She took a half wheel of cheese from the refrigerator.

Kathy whirled the wheelchair around to the refrigerator putting pickles and cocktail onions in separate dishes. "Are you missing Jean-Luc?"

"I'm like Dorothy," Leah said. "I'm having a wonderful time. Let's get the kids inside."

The house smelled of wet snowsuits as the two families sat at the table waiting for *raclette*. The apparatus under which Leah placed the cheese looked like a letter *H*. The bar of the *H* held a heating element. As the cheese melted, she scraped it onto the potatoes in turn, starting with Dorothy who held her plate out. The adults sipped Fendant, but the children had hot tea.

"No Coca-Cola, it sets the cheese in your stomach," Leah said.

"My God," Kathy said, "you really sound Swiss."

After dinner, as the dishwasher hummed, the kids went to the loft to play Monopoly.

Dorothy said, "Even if it is New Year's this old lady is going to bed. She can't wait to get under those feather duvets. They must be a foot high. Then she's going to look out that little window and pretend she's Heidi." She kissed everyone good night. As she went upstairs she paused, turned and said, "This little girl is on a big, big adventure."

"Just then she sounded like an American Lieutenant I met in Jean-Luc's office before Christmas," Leah said. "He kept saying things like, 'This lieutenant is pleased to meet you Ma'am.' "

"That's the first time Mom ever talked like that. Thank God. Must have been the Fendant." They watched the fire. "I thought your husband only had ultra rich clients."

"He may not have been a client. I didn't give it much thought except for the stupid way he spoke." Leah added a log to the fire. "How are you really doing?"

"I'm feeling lucky. I'm alive. I've kept the kids. I can still paint. Mom's been wonderful."

"No bitterness?"

"Anger, Leah. I don't think it was an accident. Neither does the carpenter who'd been working on the living room."

A shiver ran up Leah's spine. "Maybe he was just trying to cover up his own slipshod work." She picked up an afghan and folded it.

"Maybe."

"Besides, who'd want to kill you?" Leah asked. "People don't go around trying to murder artists."

Kathy paused. "I wondered about Rolf so he could have the kids and get out of the child support, but he's not paying all that much. I earn an OK living. Again, I'm one of the lucky ones."

"Also, he's basically a nice man," Leah said. She allowed her friend a right to her fantasies, especially if it helped her adjust. As they watched the flames, a light snow fell outside. Leah wondered if she'd be as strong as Kathy in the same situation.

"You know what would have made me bitter?" Kathy asked.

"If you couldn't have continued painting?"

"You know me very well. How about tea to toast the New Year in?"

Leah got up. "You've got it, Lady."

"G stands for Geneva, Genéve, Genf. G stands for gray, gris, grau, which is how Geneva is in January no matter what

language you put it into: day after day of gray," Leah said thinking of how sometimes it snowed, but usually it rained, with the
snow visible at higher elevations.

Jean-Luc had called Leah from D.C., Miami, New York and
now from the Cayman Islands, stops he'd made after he'd left
Guatemala. Each time he complained about how hard he was
working. Leah wondered if he had a lover. If he did, she figured
his mistress would have to be one hell of a woman to draw her
husband away from the reports which were never far from his
hands.

Claire-Lise was curled up on the couch in the living room,
next to Leah. "At school, they dip the needle like this instead of
wrapping yarn around it like you do." She demonstrated needle
dipping.

"What can I say? I knit like an American." Leah was making
a deep purple sweater for her daughter.

Claire-Lise giggled. "Then you should only use red, white
and blue yarn."

"And you can only use red and white if you dip instead of
wrap."

"Tell me when you were a little girl," Claire-Lise said. "Tell
me about the dancing school party and the snake."

As Leah began imitating M. LeRoyer's accent, she thought
how much she enjoyed her daughter when it was just the two of
them. If she had let herself, she would have felt sad that she was
never able to enjoy Yves-Pierre in the same way. With each *"Enfants, enfants,"* Claire-Lise giggled.

Claire-Lise no longer went to the public school, but to a
private one in Versoix with six other daughters of Geneva's
leading families. Jean-Luc had given in on boarding school,
because neither Claire-Lise nor Leah wanted it. Besides learning the normal subjects and three languages, they had comport-
ment lessons. Leah suspected these lessons were why the child

loved the dancing class stories so much. Leah drove her daughter there every morning and picked her up every evening. Several times while going back and forth Leah had thought she spotted the yellow van, leaving her itchy. For a second she wondered if Jean-Luc was checking to see if she were faithful to him. No, she decided. He had no reason to doubt her. Jealousy wasn't one of his bad traits.

"Mum, I've dropped a stitch," Claire-Lise said.

Leah brought herself back to the present and took the project to fix the problem. If only she could fix her life as easily.

CHAPTER TWENTY-THREE:
DISBELIEF
GENEVA
1982

After dropping Claire-Lise at school, Leah pulled into the boulangerie parking lot to buy a Three Kings' Day cake. Gilt paper crowns stacked in the window reminded her of Burger King.

Homesickness swept through her. "Burger King isn't something that should make me homesick," she said. "We do have them here and McDonald's too." She felt a slight concern on how often she had been talking to herself lately.

Then she caught a reflection in the glass as a yellow van turned into the Alfa Romeo dealer across the street. The driver didn't get out to look at cars. Leah entered the boulangerie.

"Bonjour Madame Perroset," the woman behind the counter said. In her late thirties, she wore a dress, heels and stockings as usual. Leah had always wanted to ask if her feet hurt at the end of the day. Like most of her temptations she resisted, opting for the polite Swiss housewife role.

"Bonjour, *une Galette des Rois, s'il vous plaît.*"

"For how many people?"

"Five."

The clerk opened the glass case and took out the cake, which resembled a circular sweet bread. She plucked two crowns from the window display and put them on top of the cake. "Do you want to choose the king and queen?" She held out two boxes filled with ceramic figures, each no larger than a fingernail. Leah took a painted king from one box and a white-gowned queen with a pale pink face from the other.

Looking out the window, she saw the yellow van's exhaust drop smokily to the pavement. "Should I put the figures in the cake, or do you want to do it yourself?" the clerk asked. When Leah didn't answer, she repeated her question.

"Excuse me?" Leah asked. When the clerk asked for the third time, she said, "I'll do it."

She half-watched the woman drop the king and queen in a small bag, put it in the center of the crowns and fold it all in paper before handing it to her. The rest of her attention was on the van.

In the car Leah put the cake on the passenger side, started her engine and pulled into traffic. Glancing in her rear view mirror she saw the van two cars behind. A black BMW and a green Fiat were in between. She passed the entrance to her driveway to continue down Route de Ferney until she came to the UN entrance at a five way intersection.

Turning left without signaling, she cut off a number eighteen bus. Screeching brakes echoed. The UN guard came out of his booth and thrust his hand, palm up, next to her window, "Identification, please, Madame."

"I don't want to go in, I just want to turn around." In her rearview mirror she saw the van turn right and park next to the dolphin fountain in front of the World Intellectual Property Organization building. She leaned over to pick up the galette that had slipped onto the floor.

"Lucky you didn't cause a multi-car pile up," the guard said. He cocked his head and smiled.

"I know. Can you help me out of here?" At thirty-six with gray hair that Jean-Luc didn't want her to color, Leah felt too old to flirt with a security guard young enough to be her brother.

He tipped his hat and walked into the intersection to stop oncoming traffic. The yellow van stayed on the sidewalk as Leah accelerated up the hill.

At home she went to her desk and found her agenda. She added the letters YV under January 6th. Thumbing through the pages, she noticed that whenever the YV appeared, Jean-Luc was away.

He must have hired someone to watch me, she thought. But why? I never was unfaithful. Maybe he's checking to see how much time I spend at Môtiers. But my agenda is open for him to see. It doesn't make sense. She forgot the yellow van in preparing the galette and hot chocolate for afternoon tea with Claire-Lise and her friends.

When an overwhelming urge to read something in her own language attacked, Leah decided to go to the American Library downtown. She pulled her hood over her head as she left the front door. Sleet frosted the trees. When she slipped and almost fell on the ice, she vetoed the idea of driving in favor of taking the bus. The number five, which stopped just outside the château's gate, came almost immediately. As she mounted the steps she noticed all the orange plaid plush seats were empty. Looking out the dirty window, she saw a yellow van pull out from a side road.

"How dare you," she said to the van. Her foot tapped. She unbuttoned her coat although the bus wasn't heated. "God damn Jean-Luc for not trusting me. I'll show him." At the Vidolet stop, she jumped off the bus, dashed to the van, pulled open the passenger door and hopped in.

"Why are you following me?" she demanded.

"I don't understand?" the man said. "Who are you?"

For one second she wondered if she had the right vehicle. "You know who I am. Go park under the station." To her surprise he obeyed. As her breathing slowed to normal, she realized what a stupid, stupid thing she was doing. This man could be a murderer, a psychotic, albeit a handsome one. Even nuts could have dark flowing curls and black flashing eyes.

He parked in a dark corner of the underground garage. Leah could see no one. I need to get where there are more people, she thought. "If you want to ask me anything, go ahead. But stop following me."

"You're crazy." He shut off the ignition.

"You're bluffing. You've been following me for weeks. I've a God damned right to know why." She shivered as he stared at her, his eyes slightly narrowing.

"You were brave to jump into my van."

Leah was shaking. "Stupid, is another word."

His eyes bored into hers. She held his gaze, not flinching for a second. He looked away first. "I'm not going to hurt you, but yes, I've been following you."

"Let's get a cup of coffee," she said, wanting to go anywhere there might be people around.

He nodded.

They walked to a small café in the Pâquis district, not far from the station. Despite the sleet and the early hour, a woman in fishnet stockings and heels higher than Tina Turner's stood in a doorway. Her coat hung open. Her blouse displayed cleavage.

The man followed Leah into the Café Valais. She pushed aside the entrance's heavy blanket that protected patrons from drafts each time the door opened.

Two women in shorts and boots sat at a table smoking cigarettes. One had lemon yellow hair that frizzed from her black roots to her waist. Leah couldn't see her face, but guessed it was excessively made up.

She chose a table near the window.

"What do you want to drink?" the man asked.

"*Renversée.*"

He went to the bar and brought back a small cup of espresso and a glass mug. Frothy milk coated the top of her coffee. Leah added two sugar cubes and felt the grains crunch under her spoon as she stirred. The taste was like hot coffee ice cream. Drinking it calmed her. "Are you a detective?"

"Reporter. And I'm not going to hurt you." He reached into his pocket and pulled out his visiting card. It said Raphaël St. Jacques, *La Suisse,* with the newspaper's address and phone number. He handed her forty centimes. "Call. They'll verify that I work for them."

As Leah got up to use the telephone, he said, "They'll also tell you this is my day off."

When she returned to the Formica table she said, "You're right. They described you as a Julian Clerc look alike."

His face broke into a smile as he looked at her out of the corner of his eye. "I've even had teenagers ask for my autograph. I always sign his name. As long as they don't ask me to sing, I can get away with it."

Leah caught herself before she smiled back. "Why are you following me? Did my husband send you?"

"Anything but." He fidgeted in his chair and stirred his empty cup. Realizing there was nothing to stir, he shook his head. "I don't know if I can trust you?"

Leah imagined pouring the *renversée* over his head and banging his skull with her empty mug and thought how good the sound of glass against bone would be to hear. "Y-y-ou trust *me?* I . . . I could have you arrested for annoying me. My husband . . ."

". . . certainly has the power to have me fired or arrested. I know that." He looked around and then he leaned toward her. "Please calm down. Our conversation has to be confidential."

Leah sat back in her chair so hard the front legs came off the floor a millimeter. She thought, this must have been how Alice felt in topsy-turvy Wonderland.

"It's reporters that are suppose to keep confidentiality, not the people they talk to."

"In this case, it's for your own good. I want to ask you some questions, but if anyone knew we were talking, it would be dangerous for both of us. That includes not telling your husband."

I am with a mad man, Leah thought. At least she had the barman polishing glasses behind the counter and the two hookers for protection.

"I'm serious, you can't tell anyone, especially your husband," Raphaël said.

"If it's so dangerous, why would you take the risk to follow me, of all people?"

He fidgeted more in his chair. His curls, matted by the sleet stuck to his forehead. "Oh God. I don't know if I should risk it. But if I don't I'll never get any further." He sighed and looked around the room. Then he sighed again. He pulled his chair around to Leah's side of the table and whispered, "I'm on the biggest story of the century. It's not official, but if I break it, I'll make your Bernstein and Woodward cracking Watergate look like child's play."

A man walked in and said something to the woman with the lemon frizzy hair. She put on her coat and followed him out.

"I can't imagine what you want with me. I'm just a house-wife."

His lips twitched their way into a half smile. "If you tell me what I need to know, I'll stop bothering you. I promise."

Leah swallowed a mouthful of her *renversée*. It had cooled. "Shoot." Shoot may be a bad word to use with a madman, she thought.

"Have you ever heard of the Committee of Ten?"

Leah shook her head.

"Did you get a lot of presents last year after the price of gold jumped ten times over?"

"I didn't know it did, jump that is." She paused. "My husband and his associates are always talking the price of this and the price of that."

"Don't you read the papers?"

"Not the business pages. Business, politics never really interested me all that much."

"You used to be an artist . . ."

Leah felt chilled by his words and her failure.

"What about it?"

"Why did you stop?" he asked.

"I wasn't any good," she said.

"I saw your exhibit. You were more than good. That idiot Savary writes what he's told. He pushes some galleries, not others."

Leah said nothing for a moment working up her courage. "What was he told to write about me?"

"He was told to trash you," he said. "I was there. He'd written a good review and the editor told him to go back and do it again."

"But why did the editor care?" Leah asked.

"It came from higher up. Your husband is good friends with the publisher."

"You mean your publisher was taking a grievance out on Jean-Luc through me?" she asked.

"Or was told by your husband."

Leah shook her head. "Impossible. Jean-Luc always encouraged my painting."

"Have it your own way. Does the name Ollie North mean anything?"

Leah's mind was still worrying over why anyone would want to ruin her art career. That Jean-Luc would be guilty was too far fetched for her.

"Ollie North?" the reporter repeated.

"Never heard of him," Leah said.

"What about General Rios Montt?" he asked.

"I met him at an embassy event. Why?" she asked.

"Because there's going to be a coup in Guatemala this year. Soon," he said.

"Any banana republic could have a coup at any time," she said.

He drank the dregs of his espresso and took a yellow package of Mary Long cigarettes. He offered her one, but she refused. "May I, then?" After she nodded, he lit one. He pulled a piece of tobacco from his tongue with his thumb and forefinger. He looked at her and didn't say anything for a few minutes. His silence was broken only by the tinkle of the barman rearranging the glasses.

Finally, Raphaël said, "There's more to it. But I can't prove anything. And I wouldn't want to put you in danger." He got up for a second espresso and *renversée* although she hadn't finished her first.

She thought about a man Kathy had dated twice who said he was with the CIA and wanted to recruit her for some secret spy work. Kathy had stopped dating him, but they'd laughed that his line was more original than asking about astrological signs.

The second woman left after throwing change on the table. The metal made a ringing sound as it spun and fell. The man behind the counter picked up the change and cups before wiping the table. The rag looked so dirty, Leah wouldn't have been surprised if it had left muddy streaks. "You're not very good in following people. A yellow van is really obvious," she said.

"I can't afford another car. I spent all my money going to the States, London, etc. I can't do all my research here. Sometimes when I follow your husband, I rent a car. It gets expensive."

Leah swallowed the words, "Life is tough all over," but she

didn't believe it. Her life overall had been blessed. With the exception of a little boredom here and there, she had things most women only dreamed of. Today was at least a break in her boredom. She watched him drink his coffee.

"You really don't know anything, do you?" He hit his fist onto the table. "Raphaël, you're such a dope." He slipped his arms into the sleeves of his raincoat without getting up. "Keep my card. I won't follow you anymore, but if you ever need help, call me."

Leah picked up the card from where he had tucked it under the ash tray. A drop of espresso stained the upper left hand corner. She fingered it for a moment before putting it in the lining of her bag under her passport and Crédit Agricole bankbook.

"You must promise me you won't tell anyone about our meeting. Not your husband, not your kids, not your friend in Môtiers." He hovered over her.

"I promise," she said. It was a promise she'd keep, not because she believed him, but because she didn't want anyone to know that she'd jumped into a stranger's van. Even more she didn't want to deal with even a remote chance that Jean-Luc had sabotaged her showing. No, she thought, my husband even keeps buying me art books and paints. They stayed in her château studio for she had given up the space she had inherited from Kathy.

As he stood up and dropped a red ten franc bill on the table, he said, "You seem like a nice person."

Leah wanted to say, "I am," but didn't.

"I've a very traditional life. Traditional American, traditional Swiss. I take care of the children, oversee the house. My husband works." She shivered.

"What's the matter," he asked.

"Probably the cold." She cupped her hands around her mug, but the warmth only penetrated her body, not her soul. All she could think of was, that's exactly the type of life her mother had lived—the type she had intended to avoid.

He paid and left. The words *what a nut,* ran through her mind. It gave her comfort.

CHAPTER TWENTY-FOUR:
MEETING A PRESIDENT
GENEVA
1987

"Casimir, let us out here, please," Jean-Luc said.

The black BMW sedan pulled to the end of a tunnel of light, which made Leah think of all the stories about near-death experiences. Jean-Luc got out of the back seat and held out his hand to help her, but instead of reaching the heavenly gates, her dress-sandled foot struck gravel. The lights blinded her so she could not see the mansion that she knew from too many boring dinners was at the other end of the driveway. When her eyes adjusted, she saw two United States Marines, not St. Peter, standing at attention in front of the ordinary iron gate that sealed the property off from its neighbors during normal times. Rifles rested next to them, definitely not an item for any heaven where she would want to spend eternity.

A small shelter had been erected just inside. More than a hundred people with video and still cameras, microphones and note pads mulled around. Several flashes went off.

When Leah focused again, she noticed one reporter staring at her. For a moment she thought it was the man who'd followed her. She hadn't thought of him for years. Not that it mattered. He'd never annoyed her again. Probably a young kid anxious to make a name for himself, she thought. He'd been right about the coup, though, but no earth-shattering story had ever come out.

She broke eye contact first, deciding it was a different reporter just trying to place who she was. Jean-Luc whispered in her ear,

"You look beautiful," as they walked through the gate. He presented their Swiss passports to the guard seated at a table under the shelter. The man examined the photos carefully then compared their names to a list in a plastic sleeve.

"Pocketbook, please Ma'am," a third marine drawled, his voice laced with magnolias. Leah had decided long ago when she talked to people from the American south that it was as foreign a country to her as was England or Hong Kong. Leah handed it to him, glad that it wasn't the one where she kept her American passport, bankbook and the reporter's card. There had been a series of pocketbooks over the past few years with slit linings hiding her secrets.

Another marine, taller than the rest, picked up an electric circle like airline security personnel used and ran it up and down Jean-Luc's body. When he finished, Jean-Luc adjusted his cummerbund. A woman marine stepped forward and did the same to Leah. It beeped. Leah wondered if it would lead to a body search. She had no desire to remove her blue silk evening dress that had been so hard to zip. A diet was in her future, for she had no desire to go shopping to replace her clothes with a larger size.

"Empty your pockets please," the woman said.

Leah pulled out a set of keys.

The marine checked her again. "You can go ahead," she said giving back the keys and handing the electric circle back to her partner.

Leah held tightly to Jean-Luc's arm. The spotlights on either side of the driveway hurt her eyes. Gravel wormed its way into her open-toed sandals. Twice she stopped to empty stones. "I'll make a great impression as I limp through the reception line. I can say, 'Mr. Gorbachev, you have a birthmark, and I've a limp. And Mr. Reagan, you have no heart.' "

"Leah . . ." Jean-Luc's voice vibrated the same way it did

when he threatened the children.

"I promise to be good. I wonder what would happen if we ducked behind these spotlights."

"Probably the FBI, Secret Service, CIA and U.S. Marine Corp would shoot us."

"What about Gorby's guards?"

"Nowhere as spectacular. I wish you'd worn your mink."

"I don't like having dead animals on my body." She touched his face to soften her criticism of his gift.

"But you wear leather shoes," he said.

Although there was a logic, he was missing the point. How often had she asked him for a book and gotten a necklace, requested a puppy and received a watch? Once when it hadn't been close to her birthday, Christmas or their anniversary, she asked him why he never got what she asked for.

"But they're so simple, you can get them for yourself," he'd said. "Besides, wives want valuables."

The wives Leah knew did. Her sisters-in-law were always plotting on how to get more jewelry or antiques. Leah had never decided if it were because she had frugal New England Yankee genes cruising in her blood or if she were just strange that these things didn't interest her.

The mansion where the reception was being held belonged to another banker, a close associate of Jean-Luc's. The owners had moved out while Reagan and Gorbachev used the place for their conference. The Perrosets were no strangers to this house, but had never been there at an occasion like this, although meeting top leaders was not a novelty for Leah.

As soon as they entered the front door, a black-uniformed maid took their coats. Another, dressed identically except for a lace trimmed white apron, offered them a choice of California wine or vodka.

Leah pictured someone carrying wine cases off Air Force

One and vodka bottles off Gorbachev's Aeroflot flight. World leaders never carried anything but their coats, if that. Although she never drank anything but wine, she took the vodka. It burned her throat. She breathed in quickly so as not spit it out.

Leah recognized the other guests: bankers, businessmen, the mayors of Geneva and surrounding communes, presidents and general managers of businesses and secretary-generals of government and non-governmental organizations. This is a Who's Who of Geneva, just as I expected, she thought.

Her sister-in-law, Anne-Joëlle, came up behind Leah. "Your hair looks lovely. I've never seen it like that. Where did you get it done?" She kissed her three times alternating cheeks as she talked. Leah finished the vodka and rested the glass on a passing tray. "I put it in a French twist myself with one of those metal do-hickeys." As her sister-in-law's face swirled, Leah wished she had drunk the vodka more slowly. Jean-Luc would kill her if she embarrassed him.

Anne-Joëlle leaned forward. "Can't you just feel the power in this building. We're here with the world's two most powerful men."

"Sometimes, my dear sister, power is wielded behind the scenes." Jean-Luc took each of the women by the arm and directed them toward his brother-in-law.

A man entered the hall. "Ladies and gentlemen. We're ready to start the reception line. Please line up. Give your name to the first man in line. He will introduce you."

"That's the protocol officer," Jean-Luc said.

The line moved quickly. In most cases Mr. and Mrs. Reagan and Mr. and Mrs. Gorbachev merely shook hands, saying nothing other than, "Nice to meet you" or "We're pleased you came."

The Gorbachevs both had firm handshakes.

Mr. Reagan's hand was warm. He beamed at Leah and passed her on to Nancy. Leah thought she heard Mrs. Reagan whisper to Jean-Luc, "Please stay to dinner," but decided that the vodka had not only gone to her head, but given her auditory hallucinations. She should have eaten before she came, but Jean-Luc had promised to take her out to dinner after the reception.

As they left the reception area, which really was a small ballroom where the owners invited people to listen to chamber music, Jean-Luc and Leah were cut out of the line by the protocol officer. He ushered them into the library. "Please wait here," he said and left them alone.

"Do you think we should call the restaurant? Change our reservations?" she asked her husband as she looked around the room smelling of old paper and leather. All the wall space was covered with books.

"They'll hold them for us." He picked an economics book off a shelf. He sat in the leather chair next to the fireplace where a fire smoldered its last leaving gray ash with a few glimmers of red.

Leah ran her finger along the titles. Everything was history, finance, or political science. She wondered if the wife ever read anything at all. When they came to this house to dinner the men talked about business. The wives talked about their *femmes de menage,* their children and shopping.

This was typical of most of their business dinners. We don't have any just social friends, only business contacts, Leah thought. The realization hit her like a basketball thrown too hard at her chest. Before she could say anything to her husband, the protocol officer returned.

"Good, you've made yourself comfortable. Mr. Perroset, everyone is waiting upstairs. I'll see your coat is delivered, Mrs. Perroset," he said. "I was told to say that you would be here the rest of the evening, Sir." He spoke with the short vowel sounds of someone raised in New York City, but who had tried to cultivate the neutral accent of television newscasters.

"May I use the toilet first?" Leah asked, knowing she wouldn't reach home without an accident.

"Of course. I'll have someone show you where it is."

"I know, thank you."

"I still have to accompany you. Security."

Adjusting her dress as the water swirled half-heartedly in the bowl, Leah thought that even with the world's two most powerful men in the house, the toilet still didn't flush properly. She watched her waste wash away, realizing that all evening as she touched the hands of two world leaders her body had been loaded with shit. Probably so had theirs, physically and politically. She found the idea amusing, putting the idea of such power into perspective.

She dried her hands on the guest towel. As she came out she bumped into President Reagan. Literally.

"Excuse me, Sir."

"Are you hurt, young lady?"

"No. Are you all right? I didn't hurt you, I hope?" She looked over her shoulder expecting to be wrestled to the ground by the Secret Service, but it was just the two of them.

"No, I'm looking for something."

"May I help?"

"I don't know what it is." He tipped his head in her direction and walked away. A security guard appeared at the door and ignored her eyes.

A few minutes later she whispered the conversation to Jean-Luc.

"You must be tipsy. Or it's your overactive imagination. Don't forget to call the restaurant. I'll make it up to you later," he said as he helped Leah into the car. "Casimir, don't worry about picking me up. The Secret Service will drop me home." He tapped the roof of the car and Casimir started the motor.

★ ★ ★ ★ ★

"Bizarre," Kathy said. "Are you sure it wasn't your imagination?" She rolled her chair a few feet to throw another log into her ceramic stove, which because it was wedged between kitchen and the living room walls heated both rooms.

Stifling an urge to help, Leah allowed Kathy to do things herself, especially in her own home. When she visited in Geneva, then Leah might be allowed to wait on her, but not in Môtiers.

"Not impossible. Entering that damned house was like walking through a near-death experience, but God wasn't the light at the other end of the tunnel. And the vodka did go to my head. But I wasn't drunk or anything."

Sophie walked into the kitchen, her hands covered with clay. *"Bonjour,* Leah. Staying for lunch?"

"Sure."

Two women artists and their children lived with Kathy at her invitation. Sophie, a potter, and Florence, a sculptor, had moved in four years before.

"It doesn't make sense that all of us should battle alone what with raising our kids and all," Kathy had said to Dorothy and Leah. She'd redesigned the house so the adults had small sleeping spaces.

The kids were put into a dormitory. The barn had been converted to studio space for everyone. They shared cooking areas and chores.

It had gotten off to a rocky start, not because of the women, but because the girls kept fighting over each other's clothes and the boys over their toys. Once the mothers left the kids to battle it out, things settled down.

"Can I help with lunch?" Leah asked.

"Naturally. No free lunches in this artistic kibbutz," Sophie said, and handed her some comma potatoes and a scrub brush.

Kathy set the table, spinning her wheelchair around between

the dish cabinet and silverware drawer. "How many are we?"

"Leah, you, me, your mom, and I'll see if Florence wants to quit work to eat," Sophie said.

Leah washed the last potato. "I'll go."

Sophie handed her a burlap bag. "Pick up some chestnuts. We'll roast them to eat with Dorothy's apple pie."

The tree was to the left side of the house and the chestnuts were hidden under the fallen yellow leaves. Within minutes the bag bulged. She carried it through the garden where their luncheon potatoes had grown.

The studio was down a path about thirty feet behind the house. Unlike the studio where Leah had painted for her show, which was now the boy's dormitory, this studio was huge, having once held twenty head of cattle. No remnants of compost or cow urine remained, although a collection of cow bells hung outside the door as a reminder of earlier occupants.

The stalls had been torn out, walls insulated, sheetrocked, and painted white with large floor-to-roof windows. Skylights let in more light and made the space far airier and brighter than any cow had ever experienced. Space had been divided into work areas. Sophie's pottery wheel stood in one corner. Three vases sat on the counter, waiting to go into the kiln for a final glazing.

Leah walked to Kathy's three easels with their half-finished canvasses. She was doing a series, experimenting with laying the pigment thickly over other materials: cloth, newsprint, plaster. The paint smell attacked Leah in the same way the smell of pipe tobacco or shaving lotion recalled an old lover.

She picked up the palette and brush and pretended to mix paint and touch the canvas, stepping back to check her imaginary work.

Behind a spun-lemon yellow curtain, Leah heard the steady tap of Florence's hammer against stone. That was where the others stuck the sculptress so stone dust wouldn't mix with their oils and clay.

Shrugging, Leah put everything back where she had found it and interrupted Florence.

Lunch was a discussion of techniques, information about exhibitions, fellow artists, both their work and their love lives, the kids punctuated by laughter. Leah listened more than contributed, feeling like she had crossed a desert and had ended up at an oasis.

After the last dish was done, with everyone but Kathy back at work, Leah looked at her watch. "I should get back to Geneva," she said.

"I'll accompany you to the car," Kathy said.

Knowing better than to push her, Leah walked next to the chair. "I like what you're working on."

"I'm really pressed to get enough for the next show. I can't believe I've finally got a New York show."

"You deserve it." Leah dug into her purse for her keys. When she didn't find them she started patting her pockets. "Ahh," she said when her hand pushed through the hole in the lining her jacket and touched the key ring.

"When are you going to try again?" Kathy asked.

"Try what?" Leah double checked for her glasses.

"You know what. Painting."

"I don't know," Leah said. And I don't think I ever will, she thought.

"I'm not going to give up nagging you," Kathy said. "You're too talented."

Leah leaned over and kissed the top of her friend's head.

CHAPTER TWENTY-FIVE:
THE DYING TIME
SWITZERLAND AND MASSACHUSETTS
1989

The clay spinning under Leah's fingers conjured up memories of silk teddies against her nipples, the softness of her children's skin when they were babies, and chocolate melting on her tongue. Café au lait–colored water oozed over the wheel as she shaped the pitcher, narrowing it at the neck then enlarging its rim. Her foot slowed on the treadle. Taking a string, she pulled it under the base, releasing it from the wheel.

To Leah's right Sophie glazed a bowl. Kathy's wheelchair creaked as she rolled along the length of her six-foot long canvas. She held a brush creating a bright blue stripe. Florence's tapping behind the curtain could barely be heard over the CD player. "Ella, Ella." Sophie sang out of tune with France Gall's recording. The other women had become immune to Sophie's voice, which only was on key by accident.

Dorothy, wearing an apron that hid her clothes from her neck to her shoes, appeared at the door. "Anyone feel like lunch?"

The tapping stopped. Florence, her hair gray with stone dust, peeked from behind the curtain.

Leah washed clay from the ridges of her fingertips. Kathy dropped her brush in a can of turpentine.

The women followed Dorothy into the house like four ducklings waddling after their mother.

Dorothy ladled corn chowder into unmatching bowls. Grabbing the baguette, Sophie cut several slices while Kathy passed beetroot salad.

The phone rang. Florence pushed back her chair to go answer it. "*Excusez-moi.* I do not speak English," they heard her say.

Leah went to the alcove where the phone was kept. "May I help you?"

"Oh, I'm glad it's you, Sis."

"Chuck?"

"Your housekeeper gave me this number. I've got bad news."

Leah leaned against the wall.

"It's Dad. He's had a heart attack. How fast can you get home?"

Leah stood in the foreigners' line at Boston's Logan Airport.

Claire-Lise held both red passports with their white crosses. "Papa and Yves-Pierre are shits. They should be here with us." Claire-Lise spoke with the same authority as Pope Jean-Paul II on most subjects these days.

Leah's annoyance at her husband's reaction matched her daughter's. When she'd called him after hanging up from Chuck, he'd said, "Honey, can you manage on your own? I have this huge meeting. Then I should go to Nigeria, but if you really need me . . ."

As if reading from a script called *The Good Wife,* Leah had said. "I suppose I can do without you. I'll have the children."

Then she'd called Yves-Pierre. After a long wait he arrived at the phone in the headmaster's office. When she told him, her son had complained, "But Maman, we've an important football match. If Papi is so bad, he won't know if I'm there or not."

But I will, Leah said to herself. To be fair, she thought as she inched forward in the line, Jean-Luc had arranged for Swiss Air to hold the plane until she could pick up Claire-Lise and get to Cointrin airport.

"I've two tests coming up, Maman," Claire-Lise had said when she'd been pulled from class, but before Leah could lose her temper her daughter continued, "so clear it with the head-mistress."

Leah shook herself into the present and moved up to the booth where the customs official took their passports.

"Reason for the visit?" he asked.

"My father. He's dying. He lives in Stonefield."

The man slapped their passports on the counter in front of them.

They passed into the baggage retrieval area. Three carousels, like gigantic inverted cups, were surrounded by passengers from the Geneva and Paris flights that had landed within minutes of each other. A single suitcase circled on the third carousel until an attendant pulled it off.

Claire-Lise ran to get a cart, then came back. "Almost all airports have free carts, but no, the dumb Americans expect people to arrive with quarters. Probably think everyone carries American money."

"How many do you need?" Leah asked. She was too tired to remind her daughter that most Swiss train station carts required coins too.

"Four."

As Leah dug into her wallet, she dropped her pocketbook. French, Swiss, and American coins rolled across the floor among tickets, make up, car keys and breath mints. Leah began stuffing everything back into her purse before giving Claire-Lise the change.

A bell sounded as bags began bumping down the chute. Other people retrieved theirs and disappeared. Leah's were last, although they should have been first, having been the final ones loaded. Pushing the overloaded cart, Leah headed for the customs inspection line. Claire-Lise walked next to it keeping the bags balanced.

The customs man in his mid-thirties pointed at the blue

suitcase. "Open it." Fumbling in her bag, Leah found the key zipped in the lining pocket. She lifted the case to the table. The lock stuck. When she gave a sharp turn it opened but the key broke in the lock.

"Passports and landing slip." He compared their photos and faces. Leah had declared they were bringing only personal possessions.

"Are you sure you've nothing to declare?" he asked.

Leah knew that asking him if he practiced his growl each morning would only delay them further.

"Nothing," she said.

He took each piece of clothing, checked the pockets and felt the seams. Mrs. Shleppi had put tissue between the layers of clothing. He held the paper to the neon light overhead. The pile of clothes grew. He took the shoes and tapped the soles. Then he massaged the lining of the empty case.

"What are you looking for?" Claire Lise asked.

The customs official glared at her. "Drugs."

"If my father . . ."

"Claire-Lise. The man is doing his job," Leah said.

"But Papa . . ."

". . . is in Switzerland."

"Why do you speak English so well?" the customs man demanded.

"My parents are American," Leah said.

He flipped through the pages of Leah's passport, frowning. Then he signaled another man, who had been standing to one side, his hands behind his back. When the man walked over the first official pointed to the passport.

"Look at this, Fred. Better question her." Their luggage was bustled off by a third official who appeared from nowhere to pile clothes and shoes on top of the other suitcases. He then disappeared.

236

Mother and daughter followed Fred into an office scarcely more than six by seven feet. Its table, file and three chairs left almost no free space to move. He indicated they should sit. The baggage cart stayed outside the door.

Fred looked through Leah's passport. "This says you were born here. Why don't you have an American passport?"

"I became Swiss shortly after I married," Leah said.

He flipped through its pages. "You've been to Russia, Romania, Syria, Jordan, Kenya, South Africa, China, England, Germany, East Germany, Sweden and," he paused and if possible his frown deepened, "Cuba. Americans aren't allowed in Cuba."

Choosing to ignore the Cuba issue, she said, "My husband is a banker. Sometimes I go with him on business trips. Not often. My visas are kept up to date in case he wants me with him at the last minute."

Fred picked up the phone and said, "We may have a Commie here. Ya better come down."

"I want to call the Swiss Consulate," Leah said.

"We've the right to a phone call," Claire-Lise said.

"Shut-up. You've seen too many movies," he said lighting a cigarette without asking.

"My uncle, an American lawyer, is outside. Get him," Claire-Lise said.

"Claire-Lise, please be quiet," Leah said.

A man about fifty came puffing in. He was bald. His stomach hung over his belt. His name on a tag on his shirt pocket said David Flannagan.

"I want to get a message to my brother or be allowed to call my consulate. I've done nothing wrong," Leah said.

Fred handed Flannagan the passports. "Look at those visas."

Claire-Lise said, "Everyone we know travels like that, for business, for the UN. I don't see your problem. If my father

237

were here . . ." she stopped after she glanced at her mother's face.

"Now tell me really why you don't have an American passport?" Fred asked. "No one in their right mind gives up their American nationality."

Leah couldn't say, "I have one hidden at home," so she said, "I married a Swiss. My life is there. I've the right to call my consulate."

"You threw your rights away when you surrendered your passport." Fred hovered over her, his face frozen in its hostility. Leah stood up until her face was within inches of his. Without flinching, she lowered her voice and said, "I demand to call the Swiss Consulate. Now."

Flannagan had been watching, his arms folded.

"Let her," he said.

"I'll dial it for you." Fred looked up the number in a phone book he pulled out of a drawer and pushed the buttons of a speaker phone.

"Swiss Consulate," a woman's voice said. "I want to speak to the Consulate General," Leah said. "I'm Madame Jean-Luc Perroset. I am having a problem at Logan Customs."

Within seconds, she heard the receiver being picked up. "Leah, are you in Boston?" The voice came through the receiver. Leah thanked the heavens the times this member of the diplomatic corp had eaten at her table and also how he always chose to speak English with her because his mother tongue was German. Although he would only admit it in whispers, he didn't like French despite being fluent in it. The two customs officials exchanged looks.

"Yes. I'm being detained at Logan. Can you do something?"

"Give me your phone number. Stay there. I will make some inquiries and call you back."

Stay there, Leah thought. Right. Where else could she go?

"Mrs. Perroset, perhaps we can make you more comfortable while we wait for some response from the Consulate. We are always concerned when we find people who've traveled to enemy countries," Flannagan said.

The clock on the wall ticked. No one said anything. Twenty minutes passed. A third customs official rushed in the office. His skin color gave credence to the cliché pale as a ghost. "Jesus H. Christ what are you guys doing down here? The White House just called. The goddamned Secretary of State was in the Oval Office."

Leah took great pleasure in watching the men grovel as they accompanied her to the exit.

Within minutes the automatic doors opened. Chuck swept Leah into his arms. His Irish knit sweater felt rough on her cheek.

"What took so long?" he asked.

When she told him, he said, "How the hell did the White House get involved?"

"Jean-Luc's connections, I'm sure," Leah said.

They went directly to the hospital. Leah only half noticed the fall leaves or the changes along Route One. Only when Claire-Lise said something about the life-sized cows at the Hilltop Steak House being tacky Americana, did she realize she was home. The idea of putting herself in a metal cylinder on one continent, being hurled across the ocean and a few hours later getting off on another made her feel as if she had achieved time travel more than geographical.

As they entered the intensive care waiting room, Amanda, Chuck's wife, stood up. She'd been needlepointing a cat next to a vase. She kissed Leah and held Claire-Lise at arm's length. "Your hair has grown, but you're the same height," she said.

Leah willed Claire-Lise not to roll her eyes. The telepathy worked.

"Auntie Amanda, yours is different too. The gray is gone."

"Clairol's honey brown. Instant youth," Amanda said. "The next time Dad Stockbridge can have visitors is in fifteen minutes. We told him you were on the way so the surprise wouldn't, well, you know."

"Usually only one person is allowed in," Chuck said. "I'll check and see if Claire-Lise can go in, too." He was back in minutes and gave two thumbs up.

The walk from the patients' family waiting room led them into a large area with a nurses station in the middle with a bank of monitors to one side. Cublicles, rather than rooms, each closed with a curtain rather than a door, ran off in every direction. When they came to the one with the sign "Stockbridge" posted outside, Leah drew a deep breath before she let Chuck pull back the curtain to enter.

Tubes ran from Alexander Stockbridge's nose. The monitor's beeps sped up as Leah and Claire-Lise approached the bed. Leah appreciated her daughter's iron clasp on her arm as she took her father's hand. It was icicle cold. She swallowed until she could speak in a normal tone.

"Hi, Daddy. I love you," Leah said.

He nodded. His eyes washed first Leah's then Claire-Lise's face. Tears ran down all three faces.

"None of that Daddy." Leah kissed him on the forehead. "If you get upset, they'll kick us out."

He nodded.

Leah brushed his still-thick white hair back from his forehead. His skin was gray. Too soon, the nurse bustled in to tell them their time was up.

"What's the prognosis?" Leah asked back in the waiting room. She held a cup of coffee in a Styrofoam cup that Amanda had procured from the machine just outside the door. After sipping it, she controlled an automatic response to spit out the weak coffee.

Chuck poured himself a cup of coffee and sat next to his sister. "Not good. He needs a quadruple bypass. The mitral valve is not working right. If they operate there's a good chance he'll die on the table. If they don't operate, he'll die within a few days."

"What does he want?"

"The operation. He's worried about Mum. Feels she needs him."

"Mother's sick too? *Merde.*" Jean-Luc's mother, had she been there, would have changed the words to the more refined "*Cambronne.*" Perroset women weren't allowed even mild profanities.

Chuck took her hand. "We were about to call you anyway when Dad had his attack."

Amanda sat down on the other side of Leah. "Mother Stockbridge has been acting strangely for about six months. Forgetting dates, names, things like that. Last week she went downtown in her nightgown. The druggist called us. He's an old classmate of yours, Peter Pronk? Remember him?"

Leah nodded. "Alzheimer's?"

"They think so."

Things keep getting worse and worse, she thought. When will it all stop.

Paige opened the door. "Hi, Auntie Leah," the eight-year-old said thickly. They followed Paige's halting gait into the living room. Leah remembered when she was only home in late October for three days while Jean-Luc had a New York meeting watching Amanda's face when Paige at age five and dressed as a witch carried a trick-or-treat bag and climbed her grandparents' stairs for the first time. It had matched a mother's whose child had won an Olympic gold medal.

Leah hugged her niece, shocked by how homesick she felt in the middle of her own family. Letters and phone calls were not the same as being able to drop in for a cup of tea. The events of the day swirled around her. She sank into a chair too tired to stand.

"Can I get you something to eat?" Amanda asked, adjusting a painting a millimeter to the left.

"I'd just like to go to bed," Leah said. "We've been up forever."

"Me, too," Claire-Lise said.

"You're in my sewing room, Leah. I opened the couch. Made it up before we went to the hospital. Claire-Lise, you're with Paige." She led them to their rooms.

Leah slipped into a flannel nightie and brushed her teeth. When she went back into the room, Chuck sat on the bottom of her bed. "Need anything else, Sis?"

Leah's eyes felt as if the upper and lower lids were magnets. "I'm glad I don't have to deal with Mother tonight."

"I know, it's weird," Chuck said. "Paige says Mom called here tonight and asked what time Dad would be home from the office."

"What time are they operating tomorrow? I'm too tired to remember." She lay down.

"Seven. He's first." Chuck pulled the quilt up to her neck. As she fell asleep she realized it had been years since someone tucked her in. How strange that she felt safe in this house belonging to her brother and sister-in-law. She dreamed that she'd heard the phone ring and someone said, "We'll tell her when she wakes."

The morning sun streamed through the window. For a moment Leah didn't know where she was. Amanda's sewing machine in the corner seemed like an alien being under its protective blue-flowered cover. Then she saw her suitcases on the floor. She dug through it, found her bathrobe and went to the kitchen.

Chuck sat at the table while Amanda scrambled eggs. "The hospital called," he said. "Daddy died in his sleep last night."

Claire-Lise handed the stewardess her headphones as the plane's crew prepared for landing. "Grandma was really strange at the funeral."

"It's part of her illness," Leah said. She tried not to think how odd her childhood home had felt at the after-funeral buffet. Between her father's leather-patched sweater hanging on the coat rack and her mother asking people to stay until he got back, she'd almost begun expecting his arrival herself. Instead of this flight to Geneva banishing the memories, they were exploding in such detail she could taste the tuna sandwich she'd choked down as she and Amanda had washed dishes after everyone left.

"Ladies and gentlemen, Please fasten your seat belts and return your trays to an upright position for our descent into Geneva. Swiss Air would like to thank you for flying with us."

"Mum, could we go to the chalet for a couple of days?"

Leah adjusted her table and pulled her seat upright. "You've already missed a week of school."

Claire-Lise looked at her fingernails, each a different color. "I know, but I feel funny. Whenever I go to the mountains, it's like, you know, I touch something inside me."

Leah understood. "Your father wouldn't approve."

She pushed the flight magazine in the pocket of the back of the seat in front of her.

"But he's on a business trip. I'll only miss Friday. Just one more day. I'll go back Monday. I promise. Please."

The plane bounced twice as it touched down on the Geneva runway.

The fog gave way to sunshine as Leah's car climbed the mountain. In the last village before the chalet, Leah and Claire-Lise stopped at the grocery store. Claire-Lise threw canned spaghetti sauce and Knorr soup mixes in the cart which filled the aisle.

"Don't want you cooking, Maman."

Glancing at her daughter, Leah noticed the muscles on her face were more relaxed than they had been since before they left for the States.

"I'm glad you talked me into this," Leah said. The mountains would help her sort out the feelings hop-scotching around each other.

"You're a soft sell." Claire-Lise held up a bottle of Coca-Cola, which was on Jean-Luc's forbidden list.

Leah added it and a second one to the cart. Winking, she said, "No, I'm not."

The last twenty minutes of the drive they saw no other cars. The road, twisting and turning, was only wide enough for one vehicle. A few cows with bells around their necks stopped grazing to watch them pass. Mother and daughter entered a pine forest. When they emerged they saw the chalet against the blue sky. Claire-Lise opened the window to inhale the clean air.

"Look Maman, there are ten cars. One's Papa's."

"Strange, your father didn't say anything about being up here. He said he was going to Nigeria."

Parking behind the cars, she got out. Claire-Lise followed her. The front door was unlocked. Leah set the grocery basket on the pine kitchen table. The smell of cigarette smoke and sweaty clothes permeated the room.

"Maybe everyone's hiking or something," Claire-Lise said.

Then she froze, her eyes fixed on the window. Leah followed the direction of her stare.

In the field where the sheep grazed were Jean-Luc, Yves-Pierre and several men, most of whom she did not know. One brought his club down on a lamb's head. Leah reached her hand out as if to stop the brains splattering as the bone gave way. The man pounded the fallen animal until its wool was red.

Jean-Luc grabbed the sheep with the one black ear. Leah had warmed her by the fire and fed her with a bottle the night she was born. Her husband held it as her son ran his knife across the throat. At the other side of the field, another man threw an axe. It caught a ram in the back. They heard its scream through the walls.

Why? why? Leah thought as she grabbed Claire-Lise. She pressed her daughter's head to her own chest.

"Make them stop," Claire-Lise cried. "Maman, do something."

Leah didn't understand why her feet were glued to the floor—why the only action she could take was to protect Claire-Lise. I'll wake in a minute, she thought. When Claire-Lise pulled away to vomit, something inside her switched on.

She ran to the back door. "Stop," she screamed. "Stop! Stop! Stop!" Her voice broke through the men's bloodlust.

Jean-Luc raised his hand and everyone threw down their weapons. He walked to his wife. Standing inches away, his face contorted into a stranger's, he demanded, "What the hell are you doing here?"

Leah screamed. "I can ask you the same question. You were supposed to be in Africa." Vomit projected itself out of her mouth and mixed with the blood on his shirt.

"Jesus, watch it." Jean-Luc jumped out of the way.

"Why is our son here?" She wiped her mouth with her shaking hand.

"None of this is your concern. Go back to Geneva."

"Go back to Geneva? Just like nothing happened?"

"You heard me." He grabbed her hand, pulled her inside and slammed the door. At the sink he took the sponge to wipe his shirt. "This is a man's activity. It has nothing to do with you and Claire-Lise." He picked up her keys and propelled them out the door. "We'll talk when I get home."

Leah's hands shook so hard she had trouble getting the key in the ignition. Claire-Lise, her body slumped on the passenger side, moaned over and over, "I don't understand. I don't understand." At the end of the forest, Leah parked among the trees to hold her daughter until Claire-Lise cried herself out. As they drove back to Geneva, the child fell asleep, her face swollen and blotched.

Leah glanced over as often as she could. The joy in her son's smile as the sheep died at his feet closed her heart. She knew she'd never go to the chalet again.

CHAPTER TWENTY-SIX:
NO REAL EXPLANATION
GENEVA
1989

The moon, a half circle, shone in Leah's bedroom window. Her arm prickled with pins and needles, but she was afraid pulling it from under Claire-Lise's head would disturb her. The child slept breathing through her mouth. Her face was swollen from crying.

Never had either child been allowed to sleep in her parents' bed, but Claire-Lise had been afraid to stay in the nursery with Nanny away. Besides, Leah did not want to sleep alone. Yet her daughter's breathing could not keep the visions of blood mixed with wool from her mind.

"What am I going to do?" she asked the moon.

It didn't answer. I've outgrown the moon, Leah thought. I've outgrown feeling.

Claire-Lise whimpered and rolled over. Leah rubbed her arm and felt her nerves complain as the circulation was restored.

The following Saturday, Jean-Luc and Yves-Pierre came into the house, their laughter preceding them. They dropped their suitcases at the foot of the stairs. Both wore sweatshirts against the unseasonably late summer cool.

Claire-Lise had been reading in the library. When she saw them through the door, she threw her books to one side and ran up the stairs screaming, "You filthy murdering pigs!"

Leah, who had been in the dining room, came in, drawn by Claire-Lise's screams. When she saw her husband and son, her movements stopped. They looked so normal to her, so unlike the people in her recent nightmares.

The laughter stopped. "Go upstairs," Jean-Luc said to his son.

"I didn't do anything," Yves-Pierre said.

"I want to talk to your mother."

As the boy thudded up the stairs, Jean-Luc went to his wife. He put his arms around her but she stayed log-like in his embrace. "What's the matter?"

Leah pushed him away. "What's the matter? I find you and my son engaged in brutal slaughter of innocent animals, and you ask me what's the matter?"

"Oh, that." Jean-Luc pulled off his sweatshirt and tied the sleeves around his neck. "I thought you'd have forgotten. You had no business being there, you know?"

Leah had often heard of people being speechless. She had never experienced it until then. Phrases jumbled over themselves like a film with many scenes cut quickly, faster even than an MTV video. Bits and pieces tumbled in her head: the family chalet, her son's face filled with glee, blood spurting, Claire-Lise's vomiting, her hand-raised lamb dying, and again Yves-Pierre's expression, that of a stranger, that of someone she wanted to stay a stranger.

"*Chérie,* that's something the Committee does each year." His words faded out. "Nothing to get this upset about."

She imagined him saying to one of the other blood-covered committee members, "Women!" in that tolerant, amused tone that men get when they consider what a woman says of no consequence. When she still didn't speak, he said, "You do eat lamb chops. Where do you think they come from?"

"Animals can be slaughtered gently," she said. As she left the room, she wondered what she was going to do.

Chapter Twenty-Seven:
Attics and Reporters
Geneva
August 1990

He's still throwing money at our problems, Leah thought pulling the curled red ribbon. The paper crackled as she unwrapped the palm-size box. Lifting the lid, she found a Royal Oak watch.

"Happy birthday, *Chérie*," Jean-Luc said.

"It is beautiful," she said.

He took the box from her, removed the wooden watch with the diamond hands and strapped it to her wrist.

The lake sparkled at the end of the terrace. A waiter sidled around a bucket of champagne. He carried a tray above one shoulder and put it on a small table next to the bucket. With gloved hands he took an empty plate in one hand and a fork and spoon in the other and served five filet de perche from a silver platter, added rice, a stuffed tomato and placed it in front of Leah.

"May I warn you that the plate is hot, Madame."

He repeated the process for Jean-Luc. *"Bon appetite."*

"Has it been a good birthday?"

"Thank-you," Leah said.

"Too bad the kids couldn't be here."

Leah rejected saying that Claire-Lise stayed far away from him. She'd transferred to a boarding *lycée* last January and decided to work in a holiday camp during the summer. As for Yves-Pierre, Leah had trouble overcoming her dislike for her own son. She didn't need a shrink to tell her the meaning of her recurring nightmare about her son smiling against a background of blood.

"There'll be no divorce," Jean-Luc had said, when she asked for one a week after he'd returned from the chalet. "My family doesn't divorce. We'll work it out."

And as he had explained again that the lamb killings were a tradition, her stomach had convulsed as her throat fought to keep the nausea under control. Grown men beating up on helpless animals each summer wasn't her idea of sharing and building comradeship even if it had gone on for generations.

"You can kill animals kindly," she'd said, feeling like a needle stuck on a recording.

"Dead is dead," he'd said.

She and Claire-Lise had gone to Stonefield for Christmas. Jean-Luc had complained, but had given in. When he'd dropped them at the airport, he made her promise to come back. To make sure she did, he'd shown up for New Year's and accompanied them back to Geneva. Claire-Lise refused to sit with them. When he pulled into their garage, Leah saw a green Honda two-seater convertible tied with a large red bow. Grinning, Jean-Luc handed Leah the keys. Since then, she'd received so much jewelry, so many clothes, books, flowers, she could have opened a department store. What he couldn't buy her was peace of mind.

"How is your fish, *Chérie?*" he asked. "Mine is seasoned just right."

The fish was tender, the batter crisp. He picked up her hand and kissed the palm.

She pulled her hand away. Watching him chew she thought, what a farce this is. I dislike my husband, and God forgive me I dislike my son. I even dislike myself.

Leah found a note from Madame Shleppi by the telephone

when they returned from the restaurant.

"Your daughter called. She wants you to send her tent." Jean-Luc had gone upstairs ahead of her. Just as well he hadn't seen the note. They fought too often about Claire-Lise's refusal to come home. They fought about Yves-Pierre. What Jean-Luc called hardness that would be useful in business, Leah called ruthlessness and cruelty. She'd phone her daughter tomorrow.

Walking into the den she opened the drapes, windows and shutters that they kept closed to keep the heat out during the day. The brocade rustled, signalling a breeze that had been missing for a couple of weeks. That is all it was, a breeze, not the *bise,* the wind which churned up the lake and sent tree tops careening back and forth.

She turned on TF1 to see *Columbo* fill the screen. Peter Falk's raincoat looked no better for his speaking dubbed French. Dick Van Dyke had done something criminal, but since she'd missed the beginning she wasn't sure what. Her eyes grew heavy. As the breeze increased, she pulled up an afghan.

Jean-Luc woke her to the test pattern.

"Come to bed, *Chérie.*"

Fully awake in bed, she listened to him snore, his arm heavy on her waist. She lifted it off, slipped out of bed and stood by the window.

The moon shone on the stables and the orchard. The breeze had died. Everything looks so peaceful, she thought. What a lie. Everything is so wrong. If only I knew what to do. Or where to go.

"Where will you go?" Leah asked the next morning. The sun streamed in the window. She spoke on a portable phone that she kept next to the bed. Jean-Luc had bought it, one of his guilt gifts.

"Lake Como, Maman. Heather, Solange, Mylène and me."

"Your father is upset because you're never here." Leah walked to her desk and watched the gardener mow the lawn. The fresh cut smell drifted through the window along with the odor of the roses.

"Tough shit. I won't spend time with him or that cretin of a brother."

"But Claire-Lise . . ."

"Look, Maman. You may buy that ritual and rites of passage shit, but I don't want to be with anyone who kills helpless animals. I don't care if it's my brother and father. Good God, if it were something noble like a lion like the Africans do, but a lamb? I mean, get real."

Leah didn't want to reprimand her daughter for saying things she, too, felt, nor for the American slang she'd picked up from Heather. She wanted to say, "Maybe I should get real." What she did say was, "You have to come home sometime."

"No, I don't. At the end of this holiday, school will be starting."

"But we need to get your wardrobe ready," Leah said remembering Grace saying exactly the same thing to her.

"No, you don't. Last year's is fine. I don't want to take anything more than I have to from that pig."

"You take tuition," Leah reminded her daughter. "And your board and books and . . ."

"Only until I'm eighteen then I'm going to the States. Uncle Chuck said I could get my American passport because of you. He'll help me. I already asked him."

Why didn't he tell me? Leah wondered.

"Don't get mad at him. I swore him to secrecy. Client-lawyer privilege. I paid him."

Leah shuddered. She's like I used to be before I lost myself, Leah thought.

Mounting the attic stairs after hanging up, Leah saw dusty

footprints left by two men from the bank. They had carried several metal lockers up the week before. They'd arrived in an armored truck. She must remind Madame Shleppi to sweep when the weather cooled down.

Jean-Luc had gone to the attic a couple of times after the delivery to shred the contents. He'd come down shortly after, his face bright red and sweat running in rivulets. He'd put the key in his dresser drawer.

Opening the attic door, Leah understood why he hadn't wanted to work up there. The heat, so unusual for August, that stayed trapped under the eaves was stifling. Leah could barely breathe. She opened the porthole-type windows for the little good it did. The trees outside the window were as motionless as if in a painting. Even the birds had given up their songs.

The last time she'd seen the camping supplies they were between the shredder and safe. Leah felt her clothes glue themselves to her body and her face prickle. Sinking onto a locker, she picked up a navy blue folder to fan herself. She recognized the Friedman Pharmaceutical logo. The CEO, someone she had liked a bit more than many of the top people she was required to entertain, had been a dinner guest often. She thumbed through the pages expecting columns of boring figures. They were there, but it was the words that caught her attention. By the time she finished reading, she wanted to vomit.

What else in God's name was there? she wondered. She tried opening one trunk marked with the bank's name. It was locked. She tested three others. They, too, were locked, but the next one flipped open when she wiggled the mechanism. Folders and computer printouts with holed borders still attached filled the space. With shaking hands she read as much as she could.

Some made no sense. She wished the rest did not.

She tried regulating her breathing.

Putting everything back as exactly as she'd found it, she went downstairs to the bathroom. The shower had never flowed strongly but she turned it as hard as she could and stood under the nozzle.

She remembered a poster she'd seen years ago saying, "I felt sorry for myself because I had no shoes until I met a man with no feet." Since her father's death and the lamb killing, she'd had no shoes. Now someone had cut off her feet. She scrubbed her skin raw. A voice came through the door. "Want company?"

"No," she said.

Wrapping herself in one towel and a second around her wet hair, she went to greet her husband.

Leah shoved her phone card in the slot. A faded visiting card, stained with espresso, rested on the shelf next to her pocketbook. Looking out the side door through the yellow circle with the yellow phone that marked all PTT booths, she saw shoppers passing by. She dialed *La Suisse*. It rang several times before the newspaper's operator answered. "He no longer works here. He's reporting for TSR," she said.

Leah thumbed through the phone book until she found the television station's number. When the operator picked up on the first ring, Leah asked for Raphaël St. Jacques.

"He's not in. Can I take a message?"

"No, I'll call back."

Before Leah could say good-bye, the operator said, "Don't hang up, he just walked in."

"Hello," a voice said.

"I don't know if you remember me. I'm Madame Perroset."

"I remember you. When we had coffee in Pâquis, you wore a blue pea jacket and ordered two *renversées.* "

Leah hadn't remembered what she wore or what she'd drunk, but that was her usual order on a cold day, and she had had a navy pea coat then. "Can we meet? I need to talk with you."

"Where?"

"Outside Geneva?" Leah said. She heard him ruffling pages. "I'm suppose to go to City Hall this afternoon. Tomorrow?"

"Now."

"Hold on." He must have put his hand over the phone, because Leah heard muffled conversation, but she couldn't make out the words. Then he came back on. "Still there, Madame Perroset?"

"Yes."

"There's a restaurant, *La Flambé* in Gex. Know it?" the reporter asked. "Can you be there in an hour?"

"I'll find it. I'll be there."

The restaurant was half way up a hill on a corner in the tiny French village. A thin man, carrying menus, greeted her. Two businessmen drank espresso, and three women ate strawberry tarts.

"Am I too late for lunch?" Leah asked.

"Not at all," the man said.

She noticed two rooms. The windows of the main room faced the street on two sides. The second room to the left of the bar had a wall hiding people from view. "I'd like to be back there. I'm expecting someone, and we'd like to be private."

He winked and said, *"Ah bon,"* in a tone that sounded as if he could hardly wait to see who her secret lover was, then led her by a plant-filled sleigh. He held the chair for her on a table set for four. He left two menus, but removed the two extra place settings.

Raphaël St. Jacques arrived three minutes later. The waiter held two thumbs up as if he were approving their affair. The reporter had aged only a little, although his sideburns had been shaved. He looked less like Julian Clerc than she remembered but how much of that was bad memory she couldn't decide. A glistening of sweat covered his face and there were dark marks under his arms. He wore a short-sleeve gray and white striped shirt.

"A beer, please," he said to the owner.

"Iced tea," Leah said. With the glasses beading moisture, they sat looking at each other. "I don't know where to start," Leah said. "When I first met you, I thought you were nuts. Now I need to know what you know."

He picked up his beer glass and gave her a salute. "I gave up on the story a long time ago. Lack of proof."

"What were you after?" Leah's touched the tea glass to her forehead then to the back of her neck before sipping. The white stucco walls seemed to close in. Maybe I shouldn't be here, she thought. Although in theory she could turn back—her private life no longer mattered. She watched him play with the paper coaster under his glass.

"It sounds so stupid now." He took a long drink of his beer and ignored the froth at the left corner of his mouth.

She resisted picking up her napkin and wiping it as she would have done with her children when they were little. "Tell me."

The waiter came over. "The kitchen is closing, if you wish to order."

"Two daily specials," Raphaël said. He hadn't looked at the menu. "The story sounds like a bad script. Something Ludlum or Clancy would reject."

Leah leaned forward. "Maybe not."

"There's so many plot theories, but for a long time I thought that your husband headed a group called The Committee of Ten, made up of the richest men in the world. I thought they controlled almost everything: politicians in all the countries, the press, the money supply. They encourage wars, hatred, religious fanatics. No one even knows that these men are wealthy. They've existed for centuries with the jobs being handed down from father to son. Sounds stupid. Doesn't it?"

"Does Friedman Pharmaceuticals mean anything to you?"

"It's a small group in Basel made up of good scientists. They lease their discoveries to drug companies for royalties. I had thought the president was on the Committee, but I could never prove it."

"I've seen some evidence that they created the AIDS virus. In our attic." Leah took a long drink of tea to steady herself.

Raphaël leaned across the table to hear. "Can you repeat that? The virus is in your attic?"

"No, I found the documentation in our attic. There *is* a Committee of Ten. It was in the documents."

He raised his hands in a Rocky victory salute. "I knew it, I knew it. I love being right." He lowered his arms. A frown replaced his smile. "But why would they create a disease endangering the world?"

"To release in Africa."

The waiter brought their salads. Leah put her napkin in her lap and picked up her fork, then put it down again. "You don't believe me?"

"After my earlier research, I believe. But why? What could they get from it?" He bit into his lettuce.

"Think how rich in resources Africa is. The objective was to strip Africa of its people and take it over. It got out of hand. The virus mutated so the vaccines they developed to protect Europeans and Americans no longer worked. *They* is Friedman."

He blinked several times, then shook his head as if hoping the ideas would fall in their correct slots.

"And that's not all," Leah continued. "They've a follow up plan if they can't kill the population fast enough, fast enough being mid-decade. They plan to release a fungus called *aspergillus flavus* into the corn and grain."

"Jesus, Mary, Joseph. What does that do?"

"I don't understand all the terms but it creates a toxin that destroys tissues in babies, reduces fertility in adults. It will make the AIDS virus look simple," she said, remembering how the words on the page had seemed so simple that they were almost impossible to comprehend.

"How . . . ? How . . . ?" Raphaël asked.

"I stumbled across the documents before Jean-Luc could shred them," she said.

"I wish I could have seen them." He sighed.

"He still hasn't destroyed them. It's been too hot to go up in the attic," Leah said. She pushed some of the lettuce around her plate. Raphaël opened his eyes wide. "Can you get them to me?"

Leah shook her head. "Too many. And how could I explain their disappearance."

He nodded and played with his glass. "Photograph them?"

"How?" she asked.

The music of a carousel melded with laughter of children as she followed Raphaël into his apartment in the Vielle Ville. He stopped by a plaque saying that George Eliot had once lived in the building.

After unlocking the front door he led her up two flights of stairs. Clothes and boxes were everywhere. A mattress, small table and two chairs were the only furniture in the main room. An office had been set up in an alcove. In contrast to the chaos of the main room, the computer, desk and files were arranged in precise order. "My wife kicked me out about six months ago. Being married to a reporter isn't much fun," he said. "Always late, always preoccupied."

Leah saw a photo of three kids on a window sill. He saw her looking at it. "I miss 'em. They come for weekends, but it's not the same." He went to a box and began digging through. Socks and underwear went flying. It was empty. "*Merde,* where did I put it?" He took another carton from a pile. That one was filled with papers. Six boxes later he stood up. "Eureka."

"What is it?" Leah asked.

He held out a miniature camera that fit in the palm of her hand. "To photograph the papers. Do you dare? Does it make you feel too disloyal to your husband?"

Leah didn't know if the rest of the stuff about the committee was true. It didn't matter. Enough evil had been reported in that single trunk without anything else. Leah thought of the people who'd withered away, and those who'd loved them and who'd watched them suffer. She thought of the lamb with the axe in its back. There was no decision for her to make.

"Show me how to use it."

He had her load and unload the camera. He showed her how to focus. She tried it both with and without her glasses. "You realize that he'll know it was you. Your life will be in danger. Have you a place to go?"

Suddenly she sank to her knees. How the hell had she gotten herself into this? Why had she called this man? He lifted her into a chair and pushed her head between her legs. Within seconds she felt a cold cloth on the back of her neck.

"Are you all right?" he asked. "Can I get you anything else? Do you want to lie down?"

She took several deep breaths and willed herself to regain control. She opened and closed her mouth several times because she could find no words.

Kneeling in front of her, he took her hands. "I know this is the greatest story I could ever break, but if you want to walk out of here, I'll crack it another way. You can go back home and pretend nothing happened. At least now I know I wasn't crazy and there was a basis to what I thought."

The words slapped her into reality. Pretending time was over.

"Let's go over how I use this damned camera again," she said trying to make her voice sound strong.

As Raphaël let her out of his apartment he handed her a bag containing the camera and several rolls of film. On the street when she looked back at his window, she saw him watching her. He gave her a thumbs up. As she walked across the cobblestones to the Mont Blanc underground garage, she said a silent prayer. Her hands shook as she started her car.

"I have to plan," she said to herself.

Driving across the border she emptied her Crédit Agricole account.

Leah found Claire-Lise's tent near Jean-Luc's rifle and the rest of his army equipment. He was on inactive service at his age, no longer required to do the annual duty. Long ago she had noted that the status of his employees in the bank mirrored their army rank. She placed the tent at the head of the stairs.

The heat was worse than the day before. Sweat poured down her face. Her clothes were soaked as if she had run through the sprinkler watering the lawn. Going back to the trunk, she put the papers in what she hoped was the best light possible. The clicks of the camera clapped in her ears. She shot 100 documents before running out of film. She slipped the camera inside her pocket.

Carrying the camping equipment downstairs, she ran into Madame Shleppi. "I had a terrible time finding this."

"In this heat, you must have roasted, Madame Perroset," the housekeeper said.

"Hmmm. Could you wrap this, and I'll mail it off to Claire-Lise before the PTT closes." She handed Madame Shleppi the tent.

"TSR can't develop these. They don't have the equipment,"

Raphaël said when she telephoned. He told her where to meet him.

Leah paced up and down the sidewalk in front of the address he had given her. The building was old, but then what wasn't in downtown Geneva? She watched the *Jet d'eau* spurt into the air over the rooftops housing stores and apartments. The spray drifted and she imagined it misting her face. She wished she could jump into the lake and swim away, never to return.

Children ran up and down the walk, eating snow cones and tugging on their mothers' hands. One little girl wearing a dress to her ankles was with an older woman. Leah would probably never be able to bring her grandchildren here to play.

When Raphaël came up behind her, she jumped.

"I'm sorry, I didn't mean to startle you."

He directed her to *La Suisse*'s offices two blocks away. The receptionist kissed him and a sea of faces surged forward, greeting and teasing him about being a big-shot TV reporter who was slumming at his old paper. He pointed to a seat. Leah sat as he went into the editor's office. She saw him gesturing through the window, but when he came back he was smiling.

"Old François always comes through." Taking her by the hand, he ran up the stairs and knocked on the darkroom door. A small man wearing a black rubber apron came out.

"Raphaël."

"Peter. Can I use the room? Alone."

"Bien sur," the man said. "Time for my break anyway." He disappeared down the stairs.

The red light cast shadows on Raphaël's face. He used tongs to swish the contact sheets through the banana-smelling developing fluid. Taking a magnifying glass, he held it to the sheet. "Shit. They're blurred." One by one he examined the sheets. "Shit, shit, shit," he kept saying.

"I'm sorry, I'm sorry, I'm sorry." Leah kept repeating.

"Nothing we can use," he said. He turned in a circle and ran his hands through his hair. "I thought we trapped the bastards. Shit, shit, shit."

They sat on the bench overlooking the lake. Mont Blanc rose in the distance behind the rugged ugly rock ledge of the Saleve, a contrast in natural beauty and natural ugliness. Their shoulders were hunched, their faces locked in frowns.

"So near and so far," Raphaël said. "It's my fault. I know how hard that camera is to focus. I should have taken more time to show you." He leaned forward and held his head in his hands.

Leah's hand hovered over his back then let it drop on his shoulder. "I can try again. We don't have much time. As soon as it cools down, Jean-Luc will shred them."

"No. It's too risky for you. Is there a way I can get inside?"

The fear that had sealed Leah's rectum for the past two days, tightened and ran up her intestine.

She had never understood the term "scared shitless" before. She did now.

"Have you thought what you will do with the documents? I mean if he's so powerful, will any paper publish them?"

"Someone will. Maybe *The Washington Post.* Maybe *The New York Times* or *Le Monde.* I'll find . . ." He ran his hand through his hair. "Please just get me inside. After I have the proof we can worry about how to get the information out. Right?"

"Right." She sat still a moment. Then she straightened. "We're going to a dinner party tonight. I can give the Shleppis the night off. I'll leave the keys where you can find them. Give me your notebook." She sketched a map of the château. She showed him how to approach through the field behind the stable. "I'll leave the keys in the stables, here." She drew another sketch and pointed to a place next to the first stall. "Go in through the kitchen, there will be no one who can see you at all."

"Let me unzip you," Jean-Luc said. He kissed Leah's bare shoulder. "You get more and more lovely," he said. "So different from the little Bohemian I found painting in Paris." He ran his hand down her hair then stroked her cheek, bringing his fingers over her lips. "Isn't it time we make love again?"

Leah put her arms around his neck. He felt muscular under his dinner jacket. There was the memory of someone she'd once loved under her fingertips. This would be the last time, she thought. She remembered overhearing her mother talking to a friend and how she had said that when she made love with Alexander she wrote mental shopping lists. It had shocked Leah not only that she did it, but that she'd discussed it within hearing distance of her daughter.

She now understood, because as Jean-Luc nibbled her neck and worked his way down to her nipple she wondered if Raphaël had gotten the pictures. She wondered where she'd go or when. Maybe she could wait until the story broke. As Jean-Luc's tongue sought her clitoris, a bang ruptured the calm. "What's that?" Jean-Luc asked. "Sounds like it came from the attic."

"When I got Claire-Lise's tent, I opened the windows. Probably one slammed. Look." Several shards of lightning flashed through the sky. "The heat wave is breaking."

"You're shaking," he said as she wrapped her hand around his penis.

"It's been so long since we've done this." Her voice was hoarse. She hoped he'd think it passion, not terror.

Jean-Luc climaxed just as the heavens opened. The drapes stood straight out, and the rain almost drowned out the thunder rumbling across the sky. The smell of newly wet earth poured into the window along with the rain. Jean-Luc hopped from bed and shut the window. Grabbing a robe he said, "I'll check the other windows."

Leah grabbed her robe. "I'll do it."

"We'll do it together." They ran around the château closing it up.

"I'll get the attic." He went to his dresser drawer and opened it. "The key is gone."

"I may have left it in the door," Leah said.

"That's careless," he said.

"Who'd go in?" Leah prayed that Raphaël had left.

"Still," he said, "one mustn't ignore small details. I'll be back." He kissed her on the nose.

Leah grabbed the first outfit she could find, the pale blue suit she'd worn earlier. The rain was tapering off. At the bottom of the attic stairs, she heard Jean-Luc talking.

Then she heard Raphaël's voice. "Put down the rifle."

A shot.

Jean-Luc clattered down the stairs. He raced by Leah without seeing her standing in the shadows. She ran in the opposite direction and out the back door. Keeping to the woods she doubled back until she came to the bus stop and caught the last bus into the city before public transportation shut down for the night.

Chapter Twenty-Eight:
Cutting the Strings
Argelès-sur-Mer, France
1994

"Anne-Marie, I'm sorry," the voice on the telephone croaked. Leah had answered to her new name for so long that it no longer seemed fake. Her old life no longer seemed any more real than a nightmare did an hour after waking.

"Can you cover for us tonight?" the voice asked.

"Sure, Jacques," Leah said. "Don't worry." She took the kettle off the burner and put the freshly picked mint leaves in a container. She went to Madame Perez, who sat in a wheelchair in front of the television.

"Jacques called. He has laryngitis. I have to work the artists' market tonight."

"Hmmm." The old lady tapped her cane. She no longer used it, except as a weapon. The walker stood in the corner. The old lady refused to let it be thrown away, swearing that one day she would exchange it for the wheelchair where she spent all her waking hours. "About time that man married you. Artists are all the same. Irresponsible. Like my son." Scowling, she picked up her newspaper.

"You're son isn't an artist," Leah said.

"He might just as well be, he's so irresponsible."

Tap, tap went the cane.

Leah glanced at her watch. "I need to be there in half an hour. I'll get you into bed and leave your supper tray on the night table."

"Desert me. See if I care," Madame Perez said.

When Leah looked at her with one eyebrow raised, she added, "I know. You don't do guilt trips. You've told me enough times."

"I'll ask Jacques to look in on you."

"And give me all his germs?"

"I'll ask him to gift wrap them." She spun the wheelchair around and pushed it to the bedroom.

Leah rode her bicycle down the dirt road holding tightly to the handle bars as it bumped over the ruts and stones. She turned left behind the vineyards with their stubby stocks thick with unripe fruit. The grapes were so hard at that point in the growing season they could have been used for marbles. Several weeks would need to pass before they would soften and the skins would break open, letting their juices seep out.

After reaching the small cottage at the end of the lane, she dismounted, leaned her bike against the post and walked through the graveled yard.

A man dressed in a T-shirt and shorts waited at the door. *"Bonjour."* His voice was a whisper.

Leah caressed his face, and brushed by him. "Everything ready? By the way, if you've a cold, standing on cold tile in bare feet, won't help."

"I feel better than I sound," he said. "Everything's packed in the van."

"Good. I'm glad you're not sicker because I promised Madame Perez you'd stop by."

"You'll pay for that."

She took the car keys off the nail next to the door and blew him a kiss as she left.

The artists' market was a parking lot a block from the beach and was open every night during tourist season. Within twenty minutes she had the table ready. On one side were displayed Jacques' sculptures and the other were her hand-painted scarves and ties. A straw mannequin to the left of the table modeled a sample T-shirt.

Other artisans arranged their paintings, pottery and jewelry before the crowd started wandering through. The woman who made doll furniture waved at her. The wood carver asked about Jacques. The woman jewelry designer invited her and Jacques to dinner the next week adding, "That is if the witch will let you out."

It wasn't the witch that kept Leah secluded. It was fear that she'd see someone whom she'd known in Geneva. Although she'd put on twenty pounds and still wore her hair like Anne-Marie's photo, she didn't want to take any chances. It was no longer a constant fear, more a niggling. Probably Jean-Luc had remarried, forgotten her, given her up for dead. If she hadn't bothered him for four years, he had to assume that he was safe from her, as if she had the power to do anything to him anyway.

Despite Mrs. Perez's demands, the desire to paint had entered Leah's system like a drug, forcing colors and designs through her mind. Her hiatus where she'd fooled around with pottery had changed not only her style but her medium. Cloth painting had replaced miniatures. While her palette had never been strong, her colors became delicate, almost Japanese in feeling.

In 1991 Leah had decided to exhibit her winter's work at the artists marché held on the beach nightly during tourist season. Although she had real reservations about sitting there night after night, she'd put on dark glasses and risked it. A woman, on holiday from the UK, had bought fifty scarves for her London boutique. Leah had found a steady customer. The woman demanded that each be an original. Leah happily separated her commercial and her artistic work.

Although she could have afforded to quit Madame Perez now, she preferred being hidden away. The seclusion of the caravan, which she still thought of as her cocoon, brought a sense of security. She liked painting. To a degree she even liked

Madame Perez. Their sparring was more ritualistic than sincere.

She liked Jacques as a man to talk with, to make love to, but never again would she surrender control of her own life to another.

Feeling satisfied, she smiled as a tourist stopped to look at her table.

"How much is this?" the woman asked. It was a scarf with a farm house and tree. The motif had been repeated four times, depicting each of the seasons.

"Eight hundred."

"Do you take credit cards?"

Leah produced Jacques' credit card machine.

At 11:30 Leah glanced at her watch. A half hour left. There were clouds. A light wind blew from the direction of Spain, a sign of a weather change.

A young girl walked by. For a moment, Leah thought of Claire-Lise. That loss would always be a gaping hole. Covering it with a lid was the best she could hope for. But then there were moments like this when something would trigger a memory that would rip off the hole's cover leaving Leah with an overwhelming feeling of sadness. It sometimes amazed her that in finding herself, she had lost her daughter.

At midnight she packed up the unsold merchandise.

Her pieces filled a box, but Jacques' work took three. She loaded them in his van along with the collapsible table, chair, cash box and credit card machine.

"Time for a glass of wine, Anne-Marie?" the jewelry designer asked. He pointed to the bar across the street under the mosaic of the Catalan man and woman dancing which covered the outside wall of the hotel above its terrace. All the tables were occupied and tourists stood with their glasses of wine outside, talking and swaying to the music blaring from speakers on each side of the entrance.

"Another time. I want to get home before the rains hit," she said.

Outside Jacques' cottage Leah debated just leaving the van until she saw a light in the kitchen. He sat at a table, a bowl of tea in front of him as he molded a piece of clay.

She walked in and kissed his head. "Good night for business. You sold the church and angel. I sold two scarves and four ties."

"Madame Perez was bitchy as ever," he whispered.

He took Leah by the hand. "Want to stay over?"

"I better get back. Besides, you need your sleep."

He got up and hugged her. As she turned to go, he grabbed a dish towel and slapped her on the rear with it. When she turned he smiled and said, "That's for passing up the chance to sleep with me."

She pedaled down the dirt road, stopping first to put the bike in the shed just as a few drops of rain fell. I'd better check the old lady, she thought. Madame Perez's snores penetrated the walls as she entered the house. Leah checked the doors, shutters and back door before leaving.

The goat was chained to the stake near the barn. When Leah turned the flashlight on his yellow eyes with the bar-shaped pupils, he blinked. "Sorry," she said untying him and moving him to where he would be sheltered in case the sprinkles became a real storm. After pulling a carrot from the garden, she fed it to him and giggled as his lips tickled her palm.

Running down the path, she almost laughed she felt so good, so happy, so free. She opened the door to her cocoon and flipped on the light. Despite the electricity, the caravan was dim.

"Hello, Leah."

She screamed.

"It took me a long time to locate you. Five years, in case you forgot. Or should I call you Anne-Marie?"

"H-how did you f-find me, Jean-Luc?" She did not recognize her own voice, it was so soft.

He rose from the chair to caress her cheek with the back of his finger. "You look different." He touched her hair, feeling a strand between his fingertips. "Why did you run away?"

His musk aftershave, a smell she'd once loved, choked her breathing passages. It took all her will power to keep from hitting his hand away from her. Her voice shook as she said, "I had no choice."

"I want you to come back. I want to forgive you."

"How would you explain my reincarnation? I'm officially dead."

His face and body became immobile. "How did you know?"

"I read my death notices. Eerie sensation."

"I imagine," he said. "Sit down."

Leah settled on her bed, willing herself to breathe normally. My brain needs oxygen to think, she said to herself. All she wanted to do was scream. No one would hear her. Jean-Luc's face glowed for a second as a lightning bolt flashed outside, followed by a clap of thunder. She tried swallowing, but her muscles were frozen. He sat at the table.

"How are the children?" she asked.

Goose flesh ran up and down her arms, although the caravan was at least eigthty-five degrees. Such a natural question she thought, as if I'd just come home from shopping. What I really want to know is what is he going to do to me?

"Yves-Pierre will get his degree in June. London School of Economics. He'll do an MBA at Harvard eventually, but I want him working with me for a while."

"Claire-Lise?"

"With your brother. At Boston University. She hasn't spoken

to me since your funeral. It was a nice funeral. You'd have liked it."

"Closed casket, I presume."

He nodded. "You always had a sense of humor, didn't you? Not always appropriate, however. You know I'm going to have to kill you? I don't want to." His words were monotone.

Her mind raced. Should she pretend regret? Ask forgiveness? He wouldn't believe her. She saw a gun in his hand. "Why not just go back to Switzerland? We've ignored each other for all these years, why not forever?"

He smiled. "You'd like that. So would I. However, you know too much."

Keep him talking, she thought. "Only bits and pieces. I haven't said anything to date, why would I now?" A second lightning flash was followed by another roll of thunder. A few rain drops hit the caravan. She jumped.

"Nervous, *Chérie?* I am too. I loved you, you know, but you weren't like other wives. You had this wild streak that I couldn't control. You know how I hate not being in control."

He wore a shirt, jacket and tie, a proper Swiss banker. What is the proper attire according to any etiquette book for a widower to kill his wife, she wondered.

"Did you ever love me, *Chérie?* Or was it always your first husband that you loved? Make it the truth. I know when you lie to me."

"It was different."

"You married for money. For power."

"If you believe that, you don't know me at all." She had to speak louder as the rain beat on the tin roof. When she curled up in her sleeping bag feeling not only safe but cozy, she loved that sound. Now she wanted to turn down its volume.

He waved the gun at her. "Your feeble attempts to paint were just an escape. All the time you spent with that lesbian bitch?"

he clicked the hammer.

Leah's throat closed. Her mind raced. Who? "I didn't know any lesbians." Keep him talking, keep him talking. I don't want to die.

"Too bad that bitch didn't die when I had her run off the road. And she wouldn't die when I had that beam cut." He smiled. "But she suffers more not walking. I didn't plan it that way, but it worked out better."

He's crazy, she thought reaching under her pillow for the gun. Thank God she'd put it back that morning. She usually hid it in a cupboard when Jacques stayed over. For three days she'd forgotten to replace it. Where was it? It had to be there. Ping. A bullet shot over Leah's head had penetrated the wall.

"I've a silencer, although who could hear us? Stupid, *ma Chérie,* living in such a deserted area. I've five more bullets, you know. I want to see you grovel and shame yourself as you shamed me."

"How did I shame you?"

"You betrayed me to that stupid reporter. You'll die for it, like him. He's in your grave. Clever?"

Leah held his stare as her hand slowly moved under the pillow. It was a big German pillow, double the size of an American one. Maybe he'd found it. No. Her hand touched cold metal, but it was the barrel, not the handle. She'd need to maneuver it without appearing to move. Buy time. Buy time. "If you're going to kill me, can you at least tell me what the Committee of Ten is? How did you become a part of it?"

"We are ten families. Not families like the Mafia. Real blood families and we go back to the middle ages. Together we control the world, or at least Europe and the Americas. We're still working on Africa and Asia, but for a long time . . . well that's another story."

"I don't understand . . ."

"Of course not. We're too clever. It's easier now with the media. It was hard when we had to wait months to get a message across the ocean. We lost control in the old days. Your American Revolution wasn't planned at all."

"But how . . . ?" she asked.

"Through fear, through religion, through buying politicians. We do what is needed. Fool people into thinking they control something. By the time Yves-Pierre takes over we'll change from government rule to rule by corporations." His eyes saw a future world.

"What?"

"You didn't read that part of the plan in the trunks? Pity. That was my idea. My lifetime work. My father's idea, but I brought it closer to reality. Business will run the world. I pledge allegiance to IBM. I have a BMW passport. And behind the business is me. And my committee." His laugh coincided with another thunder roll.

Leah had the handle of the gun in her palm and began inching it towards her. He's absolutely mad. Why didn't I ever see it? "But didn't things get out of control in the wars, in Bosnia?"

"Wars, *ma Chérie,* are the most profitable of all. Without nationalism and religion we'd never retain power. Those are the easiest strings we pull." For a second he rested the hand holding the gun on the table.

Leah pulled out hers and cocked it. "Drop your gun."

He did. His eyes never left her face.

"How did you find me?" she asked.

"The scarves. In London. I wandered by the store. One in the window reminded me of one of your miniatures. Colors were different, but it was worth checking."

"Do the other committee members know I'm alive?"

"Do you think I'd be stupid enough to admit I couldn't control my own wife? Give me the gun." He held his free hand out, palm up then lunged. As he grabbed it, she squeezed the trigger twice, closing her eyes as she did.

He took both bullets in his stomach. He fell on her as if diving, his arms reaching toward her. Then he slid to the floor, face down on the carpet. The bullets had gone through him, the two holes out the back made red rings in his light beige summer suit coat.

With the gun clutched in her hand, Leah rolled him over using her foot. She kept her eyes on his hands in case he tried to grab her. He was still breathing.

"I didn't think you'd do it. I never . . .." His breath stopped as his head lolled to one side.

Leah backed up, her hand over her mouth. She didn't go near him, afraid that he was faking. When his chest remained motionless for several minutes, she bent down and put two fingers on his pulse. There was none. His eyes stared at the ceiling. She tilted her head. She had never seen a dead person's stare.

Stumbling outside, Leah held onto the door as she vomited, the bile spewing into the dark night. Walking in circles in the meadow, getting wetter and wetter, she kept saying, "What do I do now?" Despite the rain, the full moon shone behind the clouds to light the large hands on her watch. Two in the morning. She didn't want to go back into the caravan. She had no choice.

Jean-Luc's body filled the narrow passage between the cabinet and table. His white shirt was drenched with blood. This man had fathered her two children, had cuddled her in bed. This man had hurt her friend, killed and manipulated . . . no . . . she couldn't put it all together. What now?

After finding an army-green blanket laced with moth holes that she used during the winter to seal off the windows at night, she rolled him into it and dragged him down the three mobile home stairs: bump, bump, bump.

The meadow sloped toward the stream. The angle gave the body momentum as she rolled him over and over letting the gravity do her work. But at the bottom, she had to use all her strength. The sodden blanket was hard to grasp as she pulled and tugged him through the stream and into the pine grove on the other side. The wet needles made a slippery path and she fell several times.

She needed to stop to catch her breath. She was unaware of anything but the need to hide the body where it wouldn't be discovered for weeks or years. There was a pile of rubble from a house that had crumbled one or two centuries before.

She leaned against it, panting. "Jesus, how did I get him this far?" she said. "What do I do next?"

The rain had slowed to a drizzle. She tugged, pulled and pushed the body into the center of the ruin of an old stone house. One by one she picked rocks and pieces of debris from the rubble and piled them over Jean-Luc. No one walking by would see the body. Someone would have to pull apart the crumbled remains of the building. Not that people walked by often. In all the time Leah had lived in her cocoon, she had only seen one hiker. There were better paths.

Her face was scratched and cut from the branches. She was wet to the skin as she went back to the caravan. She picked up Jean-Luc's gun with a pencil and went back to the body and hid the weapon under a rock.

Half way back to the house she stopped and went back to the body. Removing the rubble took almost a half hour. Every muscle in her body hurt. As she patted the body down, she found his wallet. His jacket had a label that said the suit was made for JLP by Paul Fournier of Geneva. Her hands shook so hard it was hard to rip out, but she did. Using the last of her strength, she once again buried her past.

The rain had stopped. The early morning heat had absorbed
the puddles, leaving the street dry. Everything looked fresh
including Leah, who was dressed in clean clothing. She carried
a backpack, stuffed with money she'd squirreled away in the
caravan. She hadn't seen anyone she knew as she passed the
stores that would not open for another two hours. At the train
station, she waited for the ticket seller to arrive. She bought a
ticket to Milan.

"Going on holiday?" he asked, the first time he had spoken
to her pleasantly. Usually he growled.

She nodded. She had no intention of going there, but people
would think that was her destination. In fact, she had no idea of
what she was doing. Her greatest wish was to crawl into a little
ball and sleep for days.

As the train clicked and clacked its way up the coast, the
words, "what to do, what to do," echoed the turning of the
wheels. For the second time in her life she was a fugitive. She
shoved the idea that she had committed murder out of her
head. "I protected myself," she said to the light overhead.

Leah thought of her father talking to her on her childhood
rock so long ago. Thank God he hadn't lived to see his daughter
become a murderer.

Funny. He'd been so upset at the idea she'd be an artist—
that she'd marry an artist. And he'd been so proud of her marriage to a respectable banker. Respectable. Hah! To be fair,
Leah knew nothing in her father's background would have
prepared him for a man like Jean-Luc. Nothing had prepared
her either.

The Pyrenees mountains loomed out the windows. They
weren't green like the Alps and Jura, but sandy with large
boulders and scrub pine. They were solid, surviving through

eons of being blown at by winds. Solid like her grandmother and rooted like her grandmother too, able to withstand wind and storms.

What advice would her grandmother give her if she were here. She could imagine her saying, "Do what you have to—just survive. Make contact with Claire-Lise. Make contact with Chuck. They'll protect you."

Maybe. Maybe not.

Leah watched the sea as the train chugged through Sète. If only Michael had lived, what a different life she'd have had. She could almost hear him whisper, "If wishes were horses than beggars would ride." Then he would have softened it with, "Courage, Indian Girl."

They were gone: all of them—her father, her grandmother, Michael. Her mother was as good as gone or maybe she was dead too . . . no way to know. As they passed through a tunnel she saw her own reflection in the window.

She stood up and walked down the aisle, lurching as the train lurched. She grabbed the back of a seat where a boy, no more than five, sat next to his mother. He was coloring a drawing of Pinocchio.

"Look," he said to Leah.

"Very pretty."

"But I went outside the lines. Mommy says I should stay inside."

"Sometimes it's fine to go outside them," Leah said.

She waited outside the toilet. Finally, the handle turned and an overweight man came out. After entering the small compartment, she locked the door. Tugging on the frosted glass window she needed to use her full weight to pull it down. Outside trees, hills, rocks flashed by. For a few minutes she watched. Then she took the gun with which she'd killed Jean-Luc and threw it as far as she could. She tore his passport, drivers license and identity card into little pieces and threw them out one at a time.

Sitting on the toilet she weighed her options. Her first was starting over with a new identity. Another was to kill each and every member of the Committee of Ten. She saw herself as if in some adventure movie, hunting each member down and dispatching them. It wouldn't work. One of them was probably her son. Even if she knew who the rest were, which she didn't, she wasn't sure she could kill again: yet had anyone asked her twenty-four hours before if she could kill in self-defense, she'd have said no.

Maybe going home, swearing Claire-Lise and her family to secrecy wasn't such a bad idea. After all Jean-Luc had been the only one to know she was alive.

Or she could go back to Argelès. Jean-Luc's body might never be found, and even if were how would it be identified? And there was no way to tie it to Anne-Marie.

She just didn't know. Someone rattled the door handle. "Find another, I'll be a while," she said.

Hiding in a toilet forever was not one of her options, but for a while it was what she felt like doing. Allowing herself a moment of weakness, before starting over from catastrophic events for the third time in her life, she put her head down on the sink and cried.

Claire-Lise slipped out of the Human Rights Conference and took the elevator back to her room where her husband Jason and their six-year-old daughter Leah Abigail, who they called Abbie, waited. The rain was incessant, a record amount, but Abbie wanted to go meet the Queen. They had promised her only to see the Queen's house and the guard.

She would have preferred collapsing with a hot tea on the bed, but Jack was as anxious as their daughter to play tourist. Unlike her childhood, he had grown up along the Maine coast, the son of a lobster fisherman, and a trip abroad was special. For Claire-Lise it brought back too many memories of her childhood before her world fell apart.

She assumed her father was dead. Every now and then an article would appear in her Google alert she had requested for Jean-Luc Perroset. There had been a flurry of such articles two years ago on the tenth year of his disappearance.

The Google alerts for Yves-Pierre Perroset brought stories of his wheelings and dealings. She had not spoken to her brother since her mother's funeral, if you could call nodding at each over a casket talking.

Her aunt and uncle had become loving parents to her, letting her live with them while she went through Boston University then Suffolk Law School. They only smiled when she passed up lucrative offers to work on human rights. Their house was so ordinary, a Cape Cod surrounded by a white picket fence, no national and international politicians for formal dinners. Having other selectmen—Chuck had followed his father into that office—for a barbecue didn't count.

And then she had met Jack, a man who shared her passion for the work.

"Swing me," Abbie demanded as they walked down the London street. They each took one of her little hands and swung her while holding umbrellas over their heads.

"Stop," Claire-Lise said. A store window with hand-painted scarves caught her eye. One was a forest green silk painted with a field of lavender. Another had a teapot and a plate of cookies. A third had a squirrel scampering up a tree.

"You don't wear scarves, honey," Jack said.

"Funny, they remind me of the work my mother did."

"Do you want me to buy you one?"

Claire-Lise paused for a moment. Then she shook her head, grabbed Abbie's hand and with Jack swung her along as they headed towards Buckingham Palace.

ABOUT THE AUTHOR

D-L Nelson is a Swiss-American who divides her time between Geneva, Switzerland and Argelès-sur-mer, France. She is the author of two other Five Star Books: *Chickpea Lover: Not a Cookbook* and *The Card*. Visit her website www.wisewordson writing.com or her blog at http://theexpatwriter.blogspot.com.